Prologue

Max, Six Years Ago

I couldn't tell you the exact moment it happened or even when I first realized it; but somehow, I fell in love with my sister's best friend.

It could have been the long nights we spent in my room, where she would listen to me play my guitar, telling me all about her dreams, fears, and everything in between. I usually just sat back and listened, but sometimes I would share my own thoughts as well. Talking about my dreams and fears wasn't something I was used to doing. In fact, it was something only she could get me to talk about. Sawyer, my sister, was often too busy to hang out, so most of the time it was just Cassie and I. In those quiet moments we spent alone together, she became my person.

Cassie is special, that's always been obvious. But lately, there's been something more between us. Something deeper, more than just a surface-level friendship, and I'd be lying if I said that didn't scare the absolute fuck out of me. We've always connected on a different level, at least for me, and that part I fucking love.

She and I would often commiserate together, usually

about our families, both of which sucked, especially our fathers. I guess that might've helped our connection, being able to bond over some daddy issues and our love of rock music made it feel like we were a match made in heaven.

Honestly though, she's stuck by me through a lot, and I know that's impacted me more than I ever realized. When everything went down between my parents, my father leaving and my mother struggling to hold herself together, it was really just me trying to keep everything together. Sawyer was off at college after her injury, which left me dealing with our mother on my own. She's always been controlling of our lives, but without Sawyer there to share the burden with, it became overwhelming.

After everything happened, I expected Cassie to stop coming by as much, but she surprised me by sticking around, proving she was no longer just my sister's best friend, but mine too. She especially hated the way my mother would treat us. She watched as my mother would call on me anytime she needed anything, no matter how ridiculous or inconvenient it was for me, she didn't care. Cassie hated it because she knew it was just a control thing. She wanted to keep me under her thumb, getting me to drop everything to help her out, basically turning me into her little errand bitch. My mother really hated the way Cassie and I connected, although honestly, I think she hated everyone and everything that took my time away from her.

Well, except for hockey. She's always supported my dreams of playing hockey, often calling it "our success". I'm not sure what she gets out of it, because lord knows that woman doesn't have a maternal bone in her body so it sure as fuck isn't that it just makes me happy.

Cassie may not have the exact same situation at home, but

Puck Princess

Lexi James

Cover Design: @booksnmoods

Editor: Mattingly Churakos

Proofreader: Caroline Palmier

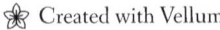 Created with Vellum

*For the girls that feel like they need to change themselves,
and the men who show them they're perfect as they are.*

*May we all find someone who treats us like we're their
princess.*

—

Puck Princess Playlist

1. Figure You Out- VOILA
2. Last Night- Morgan Wallen
3. Fuckboi (feat. Conquer Divide)- Electric Callboy
4. Crash- Mokita, Charlotte Sands
5. Dial Tone- Catch Your Breath
6. Therapy-VOILA
7. Supernova- Nic D and Loveless
8. THE DEATH OF PEACE OF MIND- Bad Omens
9. Granite- Sleep Token
10. Church- Chase Atlantic
11. Say This Sober- Archers
12. Chokehold- Sleep Token

Contents

Prologue   1

CHAPTER 1   15
Max

CHAPTER 2   25
Cassie

CHAPTER 3   35
Max

CHAPTER 4   43
Cassie

CHAPTER 5   55
Max

CHAPTER 6   63
Max

CHAPTER 7   75
Cassie

CHAPTER 8   87
Max

CHAPTER 9   99
Cassie

CHAPTER 10   105
Cassie

CHAPTER 11   125
Cassie

CHAPTER 12   139
Max

CHAPTER 13   161
Cassie

CHAPTER 14   171
Max

CHAPTER 15   191
Cassie

CHAPTER 16   201
Max

CHAPTER 17   211
Max

CHAPTER 18   221
Cassie

CHAPTER 19   231
Max

CHAPTER 20   239
Cassie

CHAPTER 21   251
Max

CHAPTER 22   261
Cassie

CHAPTER 23   273
Max

CHAPTER 24   287
Cassie

CHAPTER 25   299
Max

Epilogue   307
Epilogue   315

Also by Lexi James   319
Acknowledgments   341
About the Author   343

her parents are still the worst. They've been trying to force her down some path they've laid out for her, since probably before she was even born. They don't care at all about her opinion of anything, having no regard for Cassie's emotions or her own dreams, only caring about what they want. I mean hell, it's only our junior year of high school. This is supposed to be the time we're learning who we are, what colleges we want to attend, and thinking about what we want to do for the rest of our lives. It's our time to start laying out our path, but I didn't know until recently that it wasn't the same for her.

I'm distracted from my thoughts when my phone buzzes in my pocket. Sliding it out, I can't keep myself from smiling when I see her name.

PRINCESS

Can I come over?

ME

Get your ass over here, the door is always open for you. I'm on the roof.

PRINCESS

I know, I can hear you playing from here. I uh…I don't want to see your mom right now.

ME

Just come. Climb up, princess. I'll help you.

PRINCESS

See you soon.. <3

I don't expect it to take her long before she gets here. She's lived two doors down from us for as long as I can remember and has been sneaking through our windows for almost as long.

I wait outside on the roof, sitting right outside my bedroom window, mindlessly playing my guitar as I watch for her. It isn't until I see her sprinting across our yard and climbing the trellis that I stop playing to help her up onto the roof. Grabbing her hands, I help her the rest of the way up, until she's standing in front of me. It isn't until now that I finally get a good look at her, she's a mess and I don't mean physically. Her hair is a mess, she has hot pink sweatpants thrown on with a jean jacket covering a tiny crop top underneath, that I'm positive is supposed to be a bra.

But that's not what has caught my eye. No, it's her red and puffy eyes I notice first. She's been crying.

My stomach drops, my chest tightens, and the urge to pull her into my arms and hold her is overwhelming. I hate the thought of someone making my girl cry. Even if she's not my girl, she's still far too fucking special for anyone to make her cry.

I throw my arm around her shoulder, hers immediately wrapping around my waist as I lead her up to my spot on the roof, my back against the window as I pull her down into my lap. Looking at her, I see the sadness in her eyes and it kills me, makes me so fucking angry I want to push her off my lap and go hurt whoever hurt her. But I know that's not what she needs right now. Right now she came to me.

"Max—," she starts but I shush her, pulling her in closer.

"We'll talk soon. But right now, I've got you. Just sit."

A few moments pass by until I finally feel her relax, her body melting into mine as I rub small circles against her back. It isn't until she finally looks at me that I notice her tears have finally dried. Instead of looking happy or calm, she looks defeated.

"You want to talk?"

"No, I've done enough talking today. I want to forget. I want to just exist. I don't want to think about anything, especially my family, or my future," she whispers, her breath tickling my ear as she leans in closer, her arms completely wrapped around me.

"Want to stay tonight? I'm sure Sawyer wouldn't mind you crashing in her room."

Her breathing shallows, her eyes gazing into mine as she bites her lower lip in thought before shaking her head no. "I don't wanna be alone. Can I...can I just stay with you? Just tonight, Max. Please?"

I swallow. All thought processes have flown out the window as I try to slow my roll, take it down a notch. Screaming out "yes!" might scare her off tonight and that's exactly what I *don't* want to do.

I want her here, in my bed. I want to be the one holding her, making her feel safe. Fuck, I've always wanted her.

"Of course, Princess. Anything you need."

That's all I can muster out before I stand up, her legs wrap around me as I carry her through the window, into my room. We don't speak as I make my way over to my bed, sliding the covers back and laying down. Her body stays against mine, her arms clinging onto me.

Taking a deep breath, I realize just how bad of an idea this is as I smell her warm, delicate scent every time I breathe in. Pulling my phone from my pocket I turn on some music, hoping the sound distracts me out of my thoughts before they turn into actions. The last thing we need tonight is me fucking everything up.

"Do you want something to sleep in?" I ask, before remembering what she came over in.

"Do you have a t-shirt I could wear? I normally just

sleep in that. I always get too hot if I wear sweats," she mumbles, gesturing to her clothes.

"You got it." Slipping out from beneath her I make my way over to my closet and grab one of my hockey shirts and hand it to her. Of course, it's a NY Cyclones shirt, the only team I've ever wanted to play for since I was just a little kid learning to skate.

Turning around to let her change, I busy myself with finding something to wear for myself. Not sure she'd appreciate me in a pair of briefs, or naked while she lays next to me. Grabbing a pair of basketball shorts I change out of my sweats before walking back to my bed. Glancing back, the moonlight shines through the window making her already blonde hair, even brighter. She's looking at me with these big, beautiful green eyes so full of trust, staring at me like I just hung the stars for her.

"You know, Max, you don't have to be such a gentleman. I've spent the night here plenty of times with your sister, I've seen you walk around the house in the middle of the night. I'm well aware you don't sleep like that," Cassie says, her voice trying to be brave but her thumb gives her away as she nervously plays with the small hole in the shirt I gave her.

"I know," I smirk. "I didn't think you'd appreciate my normal attire, and tonight's about your comfort, not mine. You came here for a friend, and I want to be that for you. I want you to feel safe and comfortable with me."

She doesn't say anything for a long moment, I just sit and watch her, giving her time to process her thoughts as she stares at her fingers which are still playing with her shirt, obviously refusing to look at me yet.

When she finally does, her eyes no longer look sad, the

defeated look now replaced with something darker, like desire.

I should have known from that look that the next words out of her mouth would change everything.

"What if I don't want just a friend right now."

I'm standing close to her, definitely close enough to hear her words clearly, but my brain is unable to make sense of it, unable to process the words she's saying. I've had dreams like this, imagined every possible way I could get this girl into my bed, in my arms, wanting something with me, *anything*, that was more than just as friends. But hearing her actually say it? It's so much more than I ever could have wanted.

But is that what she's saying? Am I reading too much into it? Maybe it's just wishful thinking. The only thing I know for sure is that I won't do anything, won't make any moves until I know for sure.

Until she knows for sure.

"What are you saying, Cass?"

"I'm saying I don't need a friend right now. I need *my Max*. My person. The one I can always count on. And right now? Right now, I need you to make me forget the bad stuff."

She's finally looking at me, her stare is confident although her words are still timid. Her eyes are filled with so much desire I feel like I can see it sparkle through her the emerald green of her eyes. All of this desire, this lust, it's all for me. She wants this and that's all I need to push me into action. As I lean forward, she reaches her hand towards me, gripping my t-shirt and tugging, pulling me down on top of her as her lips lean up, grazing against my own. I snap, no longer thinking just moving on instinct. No longer giving a fuck that she's my sister's best friend, or that her parents would probably kill me if they found out I touched their precious daughter. I mean hell they've made it very fucking clear they expect her to be a virgin until marriage, and her father has made it *extremely* clear he thinks I'm just some punk kid who will never amount to anything. But I don't care about any of that right now, the only thing I give a fuck about is the girl beneath me practically begging for me to use my body to help her forget.

Our lips slam into each other; our teeth crashing, tongues tangling, in a way I never expected to feel. I've always assumed that a first kiss would be awkward, intimate in an uncomfortable way or even just too...unsure and tentative that it's unbearable. But not this, not with Cassie, she's not fighting me for control nor is she timid with her movements. She's relinquished her control, yet she's moving along like we were dancing, as if we've been doing this for years.

I feel her hands slide down my back, pulling me down until I'm pressed against her, my growing erection no longer hidden. Now it's front and center to where there's no denying her noticing it. Without a word, her hands grip the bottom of my shirt, pulling it up and over my head and tossing it to the floor.

The unease from earlier is gone, replaced with a lust-fueled hunger as she lifts her hips, grinding against my length. All signs point to go, that I could slip my fingers between her legs, just knowing she's probably dripping for me, but I want her words. I want to hear her say it. Which is why I stop her, gripping her wrist when she places her hand against the waistband of my sweats.

"What do you want, Princess?" I ask, the confusion in her eyes melting the more I speak. "I'll give you anything you want. All of it, it's fucking yours, but I need to hear you say it. I need to know what it is you want."

"I want you, Max. I want this."

Pulling her up by the collar of her shirt I slide it off, with a gentleness I'm no longer feeling. But that's always been the type of person I am.

Forceful, commanding, aggressive—yet underneath that, there's a calmness that I'm usually too afraid to show anyone, but not with her.

Maybe it's because hockey is such a physical sport, but I've always been known as the aggressive guy, both on and off the ice.

But here, for our first time, I want her to feel special. I want to take my time instead of just rushing the moment. Standing up, I slide my shorts the rest of the way down, loving the way her eyes widen when I drop my briefs, my full length on display.

We just stare at each other, her eyes drifting down my body, thank fuck this is probably the first time she's seen a naked guy in person. Crawling back in bed, I lean in, my lips finding hers again as I slide my hands down between us, stopping when I reach her core. I graze my knuckles against her, sliding back and forth as I spread her wetness.

"Max," she whimpers, her voice raspy and so sexy that I nearly come before she's even touched me. "I know you're taking it slow, being a gentleman and all, but fuck that. I don't want that, I don't need that. I want you. So please, stop taking your damn time making sure I'm ready and just fucking make me ready for you."

Sitting up, I rest on my heels, for a moment before leaning over to my nightstand and grabbing a box of condoms. This may be my first time, but I've fooled around before, just never let it get this far since they weren't her. But, I'm not an idiot; I'm nothing if not prepared. Opening the box, I grab one, tossing the box back, before tearing it open and rolling it on. Our eyes remained locked together in this moment, almost as if we were both afraid to look away. Afraid that if we do anything but stay right here, we'd pop this quiet, intimate little bubble we've found ourselves lost in.

Gripping my cock, I slide it through her wetness, kissing her ever so gently as I do. Her sounds alone send sparks of arousal straight to my dick and I swallow each and every one that she lets pass those pretty lips. They're mine. They're my sounds, my moans, my trembles. I want them all.

Mine.

Every time my cock grazes against her clit she moans a little louder, her body trembling with every touch, but her eyes are growing impatient, practically begging me to go faster.

"Patience, princess, it's almost time," I mumble against her lips, chuckling as she lets out a dramatic sigh. Lining myself up against her entrance, I slowly press in, surprised when she lifts her hips, pushing me in just a bit further.

She lets out a soft whimper, the only sign that she's uncomfortable with the intrusion.

"Oh, fuck," I groan, my voice raspy as I suck in a deep breath. I feel like I can't breathe, can't talk, can't do anything or I'll lose the battle and come this instant. She feels so fucking good, her tight cunt gripping my cock like she was fucking made for me. "You're practically suffocating my cock, if I move, this is over before we've even really started," I tell her, my voice more of a growl as I try to regain control.

Cassie tenses at my words, her whole body freezing. "Sorry," she mumbles, her body frozen in place as I slide in and out, just barely further each time, my cock, stretching her a little more every inch.

"Don't fucking apologize, never fucking apologize for that. It's perfect, you're so fucking perfect, this pussy is perfect." Each thrust, stretches her tight little pussy a bit more, her moans spurring me on. In one quick movement, I push the rest of the way in until I'm seated inside her. Without a moment of hesitation, she moves circling her hips, begging for more.

"If it's so fucking perfect, Max, take it. Take me, stop holding back," Cassie purrs as she continues coating my cock with her wetness. Without another thought, I start moving, slowly at first, but building up with every thrust. She looks so fucking beautiful right now, lost in her own pleasure. Her breathing is ragged, her tanned skin all pink and rosy as she tries to catch her breath.

She's matching everything move I make, giving just as good as she gets, and I'll be damned if this isn't the best first time I could have ever imagined.

She's everything I've ever dreamed about, but until now I never thought I'd have her. No longer holding back, I continue on, thrusting harder, deeper, gripping her with one hand while my other starts rubbing firm circles against her clit.

"Cassie... baby, I'm getting close," I force out, the tingling at the base of my spine threatening to burst right as her whole body begins to quiver. Her whole body is overcome with pleasure, a rosy blush taking over her skin, and it's so fucking sexy watching her come undone. A quivering, whimpering mess with my cock seated inside her.

"I...I'm co—," Cassie screams, her gentle trembles turning into full on shaking as she wraps her legs around my hips, holding me still as she screams my name. The second her orgasm hits, her pussy tightens even further, practically pulling my orgasm out of me.

If we're being honest, I'm surprised I lasted this fucking long.

Thank fuck I jacked off in the shower earlier or I'm sure it would have been a much less memorable experience, for her at least... Guess it wasn't all that bad seeing Cassie out running this afternoon, her tight little body squeezed into a sports bra and spandex shorts. A fucking crime I tell you. I came all over the shower wall just imagining the things I would've done to her had I gotten the chance.

Even my wildest dreams couldn't be compared to this moment.

The feeling is all-consuming, every point where our bodies touch feels electric, the tingle in my spine now throughout my whole body as I come, thrust after thrust until we're both spent, collapsing on my bed.

She doesn't move though, as we remain tangled up our legs intertwined, our arms wrapped around each other as we both struggle to catch our breaths. Her head shifts moving around, until she's laying on my chest with one hand now drawing circles on my chest.

"Thank you," she whispers.

"For what?"

"For helping me forget the bad."

"Well then, thank you for showing me that there are still good people," I say, gently kissing the top of her head.

She lifts her head up, eyes watching as she thinks about something, her mouth opens and closes like she's unsure how to say it. It's terrifying. I don't want to feel hope that maybe she wants more. I shouldn't even want more than this, more than one night. But I do. Right when I think she's finally about to talk my phone lights up, killing the moment.

"I'm going to go to the bathroom, I, uh, need to clean up," she says as she stands from my bed.

As much as I want to know what she was going to say, I don't want to pressure her. I've had these feelings for so long that I'm used to always being disappointed that she's not mine. Even with that said, I may not want to go too fast, but I'll be damned if I don't at least try to move us forward.

After we've both cleaned up, we're sitting on my bed, Cassie in my t-shirt again while I settled for a pair of shorts. Sliding back in my bed, we both gravitate towards each other, immediately back in each other's arms, the sweet smell of her citrus shampoo invading my senses, the scent locking itself into a core memory of this exact moment.

I don't want this to end, I want to remember this for the rest of my life. I want her, and not just for tonight. I want her in my bed, in my arms. I want to kiss her, make her smile when she's sad and hold her when she needs it.

Leaning down, I run my lips along the shell of her ear, the change in her breathing the only sign I have telling me she's still awake. Taking a deep breath, I decide it's now or never, time to shoot my shot. "Will you meet me at the dance tomorrow?"

I question if maybe she's fallen asleep, the next few seconds feel like they last hours, but the moment she lifts her cheek from my chest and looks up at me her smile immediately takes away my fear.

"Yes," she says almost giddily. "I'll be there."

I can't help the cheesy ass grin that immediately breaks out on my face. "Meet me at the big tree out front, seven p.m. But for now... sleep, Princess."

I'm not sure she's used to having people on her side, hell I don't think either of us are. I've always been told I don't know how to show love, but I'm starting to wonder if it's just that not many people in my life are worthy of receiving it. I just wish Cassie realizes that there's never a time or place that I won't be here for her. She carries a piece of me everywhere she goes. A piece of my heart I didn't even realize I'd given her, until now. Now, I've given her another piece of me, one I can never get back.

Tomorrow, I want to tell her, to prove to her that she has my heart.

I just hope she doesn't break it.

Chapter One

Max

"**G**et the fuck up," I growl as I walk into my room. "The party's over."

The lights are all off, but thankfully, my blinds were left open so the sun is shining in, brightening up the room just enough to be annoying when you're trying to sleep. Good. Leaning against my doorway I stare at the girls who lay sprawled out and naked in my bed, just praying they finally start to move.

This sight used to excite me, but not anymore. At this point, it's just really fucking annoying. Don't get me wrong, I love pussy just as much as any other man, but I want it when I want it, not when it's being shoved down my throat. Or even worse, when it's sprawled out uninvited in my bed. Pussy like that reeks of desperation and isn't something I plan to waste my time with.

I thought moving into this house was a good idea. I figured it was my last year here at university, I might as well enjoy myself a bit and have some fun before adult life smacks me in the face. I wanted to live in the party house, where there would always be something going on, and I could always have my pick of puck bunnies just waiting to play.

Boy was I wrong.

The fun barely lasted two weeks before it became fucking irritating.

I knew this was a party house, but this is next level annoying to the point where I'm just plain over it. There's always people at our house, whether it's a big party or just something casual, the door is constantly opening with new people just showing up.

I live with Danny, another hockey player on our team, as well as two other guys, Fez and Marcus, who are both on our football team. It's no wonder there's always women coming over, ready and willing, it's a house full of D1 athletes so all the jersey chasers come running. But these two? They're the fucking worst, especially the red head, Carina. She's been after me since I arrived at this school, but I've never been interested, not that that stops her from constantly flirting with me.

There's a rumor that Carina's father–who just so happens to be the owner of the NY Cyclones–refuses to offer her a job with his team, also refusing to let her work within the NHL in general. I'm not sure why, or what pull he actually has but it was enough to piss her off. Now, she's apparently trying to pave her own way into the sport, even if it's just as a puck bunny.

Which is where I come in. She knows I'm entering the draft this year, so she's probably hoping I'll let her stick around.

Lately though, she's been practically harassing me, trying to get me to spend time with her and struggling to take no for an answer. When I decline, she likes to conveniently remind me who her father is, like it should matter to me. Don't get me wrong, it does matter to me, especially since it's my dream to play for his team. I'm just not going to date someone just because they want to blackmail me, even if it's just a threat

While I don't believe it'd actually happen, playing with my fate is not something I'm willing to fuck with, so I just try to at least stay somewhat in her good graces.

Thank God my lease is up in December, because I'm not sure how much longer I can handle this shit. I signed midway through the school year when this place became available after some of our seniors left. The other guys are staying though, so Martin, our goalie will be taking my place in December.

Glancing back at the bed I see they have yet to get up, but now Carina is staring at me with a look that I think she means to be sexy but really just makes her look constipated.

"Why don't you come join us?" she purrs from her spot on my bed, while her friend remains fast asleep. I can't, for the life of me, remember her name even though I'm sure they said it at least ten times last night. I'll be honest though, I had no interest in what they were offering so I wasn't exactly paying attention to them. "We missed you here last night. Your bed was lonely."

I glare at her, I can't help it. I know damn well they weren't alone in here for long. "Interesting, I came in here this morning and my bed didn't seem too lonely. In fact, Danny seemed to be taking up most of it while you two were all over him."

You'd think she would at least attempt to look embarrassed, instead she just smirks, probably hoping I'll get jealous or something.

"I mean, we had to make do after you disappeared on us. Your bed gets pretty damn cold," she pouts.

"Then for the love of God, go home. Sleep in your own bed. I, for one, would be fucking thrilled by that. But enough of the bullshit. I need to leave for practice, and you ladies just need to leave. Let's go, up and at em' ladies," I demand, grabbing my comforter and yanking it off the two of them in one quick move.

Carina moves to sit, while her friend moves just enough to snuggle next to her before she's back asleep. "We'll just wait here for you. That way we can help you de-stress after practice."

I don't know how to express to her how over this I am in a way that might matter to her. I don't beat around the bush as it is, I tell her exactly how it is. I'm not interested, I don't want to fuck, I don't want her in my room, I don't even want to talk to her. I want nothing from her except for her to leave me alone.

But I guess you can't fix stupid, so there's not much I can do but continue telling her to fuck off.

This is exactly why I hate women in my bed, they have the opportunity to stay even when you don't want them to. Well that and the fact that the last girl I had in my bed was the little blonde minx who's still always on my mind, especially at night when my hand is fisting my cock.

But in all seriousness, my bed is just for me, it's easier that way. It's not even where the magic happens, that's usually elsewhere. On the couch, against the wall, our kitchen table, anywhere really. It never really mattered to me where we were, or who was watching, as long as we stayed out of my room.

When women start getting comfortable in your bed, they get this idea in their head that you care, and I do everything I can to ensure they know I do not care about them as anything more than a good time. Which is why I make

18

damn sure to never have sleepovers with girls. Ever. It's also why I don't kiss women. My time spent naked with women is a means to an end, a time to get my dick wet, get her off and then go our separate ways.

Kisses are...personal, and that's not what I'm here for.

At least this way, when they get this ridiculous notion in their heads that they can stick around when they're in my bed without sex, I'm able to shut it down easier. I'm known as the no strings attached guy, the playboy of our team, and that's just because it's one and done with me. The funny part of my reputation is I haven't actually hooked up with anyone in at least the last year, but I haven't cared enough to say anything to change it.

"But Max..." she starts, but I cut her off with a dismissive hand as I walk into the room. Stepping over their heels, I grab my toothbrush off of my dresser. "Look, I'm going to go brush my teeth. When I come back, I want you gone. My stance hasn't changed Carina. In fact, now you're just starting to really piss me off. Now get the fuck up and start getting dressed," I snap when I notice she's still laying down. "And wake your friend up, she needs to get out too."

"Why are you being so rude? We just wanted to have some fun. I bet my daddy would hate to—"

"Stop with the talk about your daddy. A. It's fucking weird that you're a grown ass woman calling your actual father "*daddy*". Gross. B. You don't have anything on me, and you won't, so stop threatening to go to your father, I'm over it."

"Max, you don't have to be such a dick, this was supposed to be fun."

"Well, it's not fun that you're not listening. In fact, it's fucking annoying. Do your ears serve any purpose or does your head just hold air?" I snap, frustrated I'm having to

19

find to force someone out of my room. "Go find someone else's cock to ride, I'm not interested."

"You're an asshole." She pouts.

"I'm aware." I shrug as I walk out of my room to find a sink.

By the time I make it to the bathroom and brush my teeth, the girls are finally making their way down the hall. It's pitiful how dramatic they both are, whining about it being too early and how I should have just let them stay. Carina won't look at me, which honestly, doesn't bother me either way. My guess is she's just pissed that I shut down her little threat about going to her dad, that's always been her trump card. She tries to push her limits with me, threaten me, and whenever I get fed up, she's always reminding me of how disappointed her father would be to know how little I respect women. Or at least that's how she says she'd spin my reputation to make her father hate me. He's a girl dad so he hates the thought of men not valuing women.

"Danny, do we really have to go home?" the quiet one asks. Before Danny can even answer, I've pulled up *Semisonic's* "Closing Time" on my phone and started playing it, ignoring their immediate glare.

What? I think it's funny and Danny must too, because he's attempting to cover a laugh with a very obviously fake cough.

"Well, Max and I have practice so staying here isn't an option."

"You know what they say, ladies... *you don't have to go home but you. Can't. Stay. Here.*" I wink.

Carina struts over to him as he's standing in the kitchen waiting for me, keys already in hand. She wants me to be jealous, that would mean I actually care. She likes me because she knows I'm a senior and entering the NHL draft this year. She thinks if she's a good girlfriend, she'll come along for the ride with me. At the end of the day though, she isn't picky. She'll suck anyone's cock if they wear a jersey, two at a time if the situation arises. "We could wait in your bed if you'd like," she says, batting her lashes.

This is why I can't stand most women. Especially these damn puck bunnies. Really though, they aren't just puck bunnies. Girls like these ones are worse, they're like sports bunnies. Athlete stalkers? Ball bunnies? Fuck, I got it. Ball busters!

That's what they are.

These women are fucking ball busters who don't listen to a damn thing and only pay attention to the clout they get from sleeping with one of us, or all of us, They don't really give a shit. Honestly, I'm pretty sure they'd be down for the four of us guys to run a train on em'.

"No, Carina. We've tried to tell you nicely, now stop making this more difficult than it needs to be. We're leaving now so take the cue and get the fuck out. I'm sure you'll be back later, you're unfortunately never gone for long. Maybe then you can find another naive athlete to get naked with you," I grumble as I head into the kitchen where Danny passes me my to go cup of coffee. "Ready to go?"

"Yup. Let's head out."

"Jeez Max, when did you become such a dick? I'm surprised anyone sleeps with you, especially when you won't even kiss any of them."

"Oh, I spend time with women, trust me. But let's get one thing straight, we don't sleep. We fuck. And the women I spend time with know that. They also know to stay the fuck away from my bed. They fuck me for my dick, and

21

interestingly enough, they always leave once they've gotten it. I smile before slamming the door on my way out.

As we walk out to Danny's car, I can hear them whining inside but eventually they follow us out and start their walk of shame back to their dorm. Danny turns his car on, blasting the heat, thank fuck. It's freezing outside and last night, I slept on the couch which was also fucking cold. Now we're heading to an ice rink, and I need to warm my hands up a bit before we get there.

"They're relentless, aren't they?" Danny says, a little shell shocked from this experience.

"Yep. It's why I refuse to sleep with her. I'm pretty sure those ladies are worse than herpes. Once you fuck em', you're stuck for life, so good luck, big boy. They're the gift that keeps on giving."

He groans. He might've thought he was getting a good deal, but really, he's fucked.

Practice is brutal.

It doesn't help that it's still the beginning of the season and everyone is adjusting to having a new coach. We've had a few games so far, but we are still working on getting our rhythm down, learning how to flow together as a team.

Our new coach, Rex Lockwood, is an alumni, but he also played for the NY Cyclones, and I think it's badass that he's back to coach us. He's young, which many of our players have an issue with, but honestly, I think that helps. He's smart and he understands what it's like to play hockey–especially playing so recently–he didn't retire until five years ago. I also get the benefit of being coached by someone who used to play the same position, plus we have very similar styles of play.

The only issue with having a young coach is that they might understand too much, even the things you don't want them to, the things you try to hide.

"Daniels!" Coach Lockwood shouts from his spot on the ice, the rest of the team slowly making their way to the locker room after bag skating at the end of practice. Making my way over to him, I pass Danny who smirks.

"Meet you in the locker room, sucker."

Sighing, I make my way over to our coach, hoping this conversation doesn't take too long. I need a shower and some food before another annoying night of a party at our house.

Chapter Two

Cassie

You know those days where you wake up and everything is an absolute and complete fucking disaster? Yeah, that was today.

I woke up this morning to my phone ringing nonstop, at seven a.m. Who the hell calls someone that early, especially on the damn weekend? If it's seven a.m. there better be an emergency of epic proportions...or a free taco and margarita truck. That's the only way to justify it.

But of course, my father doesn't think the same as I do. Instead, he believes the world revolves around him and the rest of us are here to follow his orders. It's always been like that, but as I've gotten older and more independent, I find myself caring less and less about playing by his rules. Which is why I silenced my phone until nine a.m., I figured that was at least an appropriate time to call someone.

When I finally answered, it quickly went from bad to worse. It only took a minute for me to realize he was blowing my phone up because he wanted to discuss my plans for after college. Like dad... it's nine a.m. on a Saturday. No, I do not want to talk to you about my future plans.

After that, our conversation went terribly. He invited me to go to dinner with my mother and him, as well as one of his partners. I'm sure it's just another way to get me cornered to talk about my *future* with the company. Even though there is no future, he just won't take no for an answer. I've told him I'm not interested so many times that I'm surprised he hasn't gotten the point.

Actually, that's a lie, he probably knows exactly how I feel about it, but he thinks he knows best so he's ignoring it.

So, when I respectfully declined his dinner invitation, he got pissed and threatened to stop paying for everything if I was just going to fuck up my life. I'm very thankful for everything he provides for me, but I shouldn't be his slave. He's had it in his head ever since he found out I was going into Public Relations that I would work for his company. But honestly, the thought of that alone makes me cringe and want to change careers. Don't get me wrong, I love PR, but working for snobby old lawyers day in and day out sounds absolutely terrible, especially with my father as my boss.

My actual dream is to work public relations for athletes, specifically the NHL or NFL. I've always loved both of these sports, moreso hockey, as I grew up watching friends play. I love the behind-the-scenes stuff, all the things that are done to keep the players image consistent and positive, having the ability to spin a negative into a positive by changing the narrative. I get off on that stuff, which is why I'm getting my communications degree.

But unfortunately, that's not the plan my father laid out for me, and like he said, he's currently the one bankrolling my life so I'm sort of stuck between a rock and a hard place.

Which is why I haven't told him that I'm applying for an internship with the hockey team here at Brooklyn University.

Chapter Two

If I get this internship, I'll be working with two NHL teams, the NY Cyclones as well as the NY Ice Hawks. It'd be an amazing opportunity to not only get my foot in the door with different athletes, but also working closely with two different PR teams which could help with future career opportunities. Plus, it's a paid job, so if my father continues throwing a toddler temper tantrum, I'll have something to fall back on.

After dealing with all this shit, all I wanted to do was crawl back into bed with a good romance book and read the day away. But that wasn't in the cards for me as Gwen showed up after lunch with a bottle of champagne, demanding I go with her to a party at some football player's house. It's probably the same party that Fez was trying to get me to go to, but I kept telling him no. Don't get me wrong, he's cute and all, but in a very pretty boy kind of way that doesn't quite do it for me.

He's also very pushy and thinks just because he's attractive and a decent athlete that anyone with a vagina will want him. That might be the case for most, but not for me. He tries to be all big and bad but the second I fight him on anything, he gives up without a fight. If that translates in the bedroom, it's about to be a snooze fest for me and I'm not interested in that.

"Whose house are we going to again?" I ask Gwen while opening a new bottle of champagne. Sawyer's here with Gwen and I, although she's not jumping on the day drinking train as she has work tonight at the club.

"Marcus' house. He's the one that lives with Fez and that hockey player Danny." She smiles, passing me my glass of champagne and Sawyer her glass of orange juice.

"Isn't Marcus our wide receiver?" Sawyer asks with a smile. "He's always been so friendly, plus he's cute!"

"He is, but he's not the kinda guy you call *daddy*." Gwen laughs as she wiggles her eyebrows.

My stomach drops just at the thought of being at a hockey player's house. I've done my best to avoid parties with them because I'm trying to avoid running into Max. The few times I have run into him, he's been a complete nightmare–always so damn rude for no reason. Well either that or he refuses to talk to me, practically ignoring, just glaring at me from a distance.

I don't know why, though. If anyone has a reason to hate the other, it's me. He took advantage of me in a vulnerable moment, only to abandon me the very next day, never saying another word about it. He's an asshole.

"Ugh, are you sure we have to go? You know I hate going to any of those house parties. Let's just stay here and drink more. We can watch reruns of *Criminal Minds*, get drunk, and eat nachos, I know you love my nachos."

"Girl, you are the only one who wants to stay in and watch your serial killer shows. That shit gave me a nightmare the last time I watched with you." Gwen laughs and gives me a little wink. "Sometimes, I feel like you're doing research and I should sleep with one eye open."

"Eh, even if I am, you're not on my list. But don't act like you wouldn't be sitting next to me the whole time. So, hopefully your mama is better than mine and bails us out. Mine would let me rot for disgracing the Wright name, or some bullshit like that. Makes me want to actually do something bad enough to piss them off."

"Then get to drinking, bitch! Let's get fucked up and go cause some shit. One of Danny's friends on the football team has been flirting with me in my bio class, and that's a man I wouldn't mind taking for a ride," Gwen shouts back, a saucy little smirk on her face.

"Fuck my life. Fine, let's really get started, turn the speaker on and play some *Lizzo*. That's about the only way you're getting me pumped up."

Moments later, *Lizzo's* "About Damn Time" started blaring through the speakers as Gwen goes digging in my pantry for another bottle of champagne. I mean, it *is* day drinking so starting our third bottle isn't too bad, but we won't need to drink too much more once we leave here. I guess that's a good thing, that way we won't have to drink that bullshit they serve at these parties. You know—the stuff they keep in the coolers and just stick your cup in to fill your cup? It's always either jungle juice or pink panty droppers, and either way—they all taste like stale beer and regret, and germs.

Lots and lots of germs.

Once the bottles are located and opened, the three of us head into Sawyer's room to hang out while she gets ready. I wish she was coming out tonight, but I also got word from a little birdie that she might have a little surprise at work. Figured I'd help doll her up a bit for work, make her feel spicy and confident.

At least one of us deserves to get some dick tonight.

Gwen made me leave stupidly early to come to this college party, giving some excuse about wanting to come "claim her dick" for the night. Apparently, that means getting here before the jersey chasers sink their fangs in. There's a group of girls here on campus who are constantly trying to bag one of the athletes. Probably hoping it's their ticket into that lifestyle, without having to actually put in the work. Work for the things you want, stop expecting handouts.

I'm well aware that I'm privileged as fuck and my parents raised me with an extremely boujee lifestyle. The issue is, they were really never around while I was growing up, unless financially counts. But that emotional connection you get from your loved one? Yeah, I had my Papa on my mom's side until he passed away, and Sawyer. That's it. I guess for a while there was Max...or at least I thought we had a connection, but that was short lived.

Thankfully when we got here, Gwen found the group of guys she was hoping to link up with, and we started playing drinking games right away. When we got here I did a quick glance around to make sure I didn't see Max, but luckily the coast was clear. Danny is on the hockey team with him so I kind of expected him to be here, but thankfully, that doesn't seem to be the case.

"You ladies want another drink?" one of the guys asks. I think his name is Ben, he's the one Gwen wants to ride like a bull at the rodeo.

"I'm good for now, thanks though."

"Not me!" Gwen giggles, already quite a bit tipsy. "I'll take another."

Throwing his arm around her shoulder, Ben leads Gwen into the kitchen to grab another drink leaving me out here with Danny, Fez, and Marcus. These three are acting like typical idiots trying to make trick shots and bouncing their ping pong balls off of the walls. They're too drunk though and keep tossing them into the girls cups, splashing whatever nasty concoction they made all over the girls.

Like I said, *idiots*.

I don't even realize how long I'm standing there just watching them until Gwen comes back out. I should have known by the look on her face that it isn't good news, but of course, I wasn't paying attention.

"Cass, I'm so sorry. I should have asked them before-hand, but I just figured it was a big enough university that I didn't think I needed to."

"You should have asked them what?" I ask, forcing my voice to remain steady, hoping she can't immediately see my anxiousness start to creep in.

"Max is here. And not only is he here, but apparently he's these idiots' fourth roommate. I'm sorry, you know I wouldn't have brought you here if I'd known. I'm so sorry!" Gwen says quickly.

It kills me that she thinks I'd be mad at her for this, besides with how apologetic she looks there's absolutely no way I could be mad at her. Especially when she's just trying to get me out of the house to have some fun.

"Don't apologize, we're here so it doesn't really change anything. Well—that's a lie. Ben, I'll take that drink now, please."

"What do you ladies say we make this interesting?" Fez pipes in with a smirk.

"What do you have in mind?" Gwen asks cautiously.

"You ladies are a team, Ben and I are a team. Just a little pain-free game of strip beer pong."

"I'm in." Ben fist pumps in the air.

"Uhhh... I'm not sure. I suck at the game, plus I like wearing clothes. It keeps everything nice and tight and right where it's supposed to be." I'm about to tell them all no, but then I glance towards the kitchen and see *him*.

Fuck, he's attractive. He's wearing a crisp white t-shirt that looks like it might've been painted on his body, his muscles filling out the shirt perfectly. I feel like I could prac-tically count his abs from here and that just pisses me off more. No one should be that hot, especially someone who's that much of a prick. What pisses me off even more though, is the little red headed bimbo leaning all over him, trying to press her practically naked tits all over him. I'm well aware me calling her a bimbo is a little judgmental, but *fuck it,* it seems pretty obvious from here.

He doesn't see me, thank God. Because I'm sure I'm not hiding my facial expressions well, and with the green-eyed monster taking over, it's the push I need to say fuck it, let's play.

"I'm in, set it up," I snap, surprising Gwen.

"Alright, alright, alright," Fez says, trying to do his best impression of Matthew McConaughey but falling short. "Let's get this night started."

Half an hour later, Gwen and I are both drunk as fuck only making a combined one cup in the entire game of beer pong. Which also means we're both practically naked just standing in the room wearing our panties. The good thing about being drunk is that you don't give a fuck who sees you naked. The bad part? You don't give a fuck who sees you naked.

Even worse, Fez is driving me absolutely bonkers. He must think we're on some twisted double date with Ben and Gwen, but I'm so beyond uninterested that I can't even entertain the idea. I think he has it in his mind that I'm going upstairs with him later, but even drunk Cassie has standards and Fez is a fuckboy, who is obviously only after one thing. Which is cool and all when you're upfront about it, but he's trying to be sneaky with it. Besides, I doubt the man even knows what to do with his dick, he probably couldn't find the clit even if he played a game of Marco Polo with it.

Looking across the room, I glance in the kitchen,

expecting to find Max and that skank still talking, but they're no longer in the spot I last saw them. Movement across the dance floor catches my attention though and when I finally see him, I realize I'm fucked.

He's on his way over to us, his eyes locked onto me, and boy, he looks pissed.

Fuck me, why is that so hot?

Chapter Three

Max

By ten p.m., our entire house is packed full of people, the party going in full force. Everywhere you look there are people dancing, making out, or just acting like drunk idiots with each other. The music is blaring, and the smell of stale beer has already started permeating the air. Just lovely.

I've been trying to keep to myself as much as possible, doing my best to avoid too many unwanted interactions, mainly from the female variety. So I've just kept my post here in the kitchen to steer clear of the dance floor filled with nearly naked ladies. Besides, by staying in the kitchen the drink refills are close and I get to sit back and have the perfect view of the sexiest, most infuriating woman I've ever had the pleasure of knowing–Cassie Wright.

She's here, in my house, standing half-naked, playing beer pong in my dining room with my roommate and one of his friends.

That alone pisses me off, even though it shouldn't.

From a distance, she's so fucking enticing that I'm tempted to say fuck our past and make my way over to her.

Her long blonde hair is hanging loose, laying down her back, and that–mixed with her dark green eyes–make her a goddamn siren in my eyes. I can't keep my eyes off her as I watch her standing there with one of her friends, both absolutely trash at this beer pong but their laughter at least makes it entertaining to watch.

But then I snap out of it, remembering that she's an evil brat sent from hell just to fuck up my life, or at least that's what I tell myself to soothe the burn. I should get a fucking medal for staying put, because seeing her standing there in my dining room only wearing a matching hot pink bra and lace thong, putting all her assets on full display for every motherfucker in this room makes me stabby. I hate that everyone in this room gets to see her perfect body which has only filled out and become even more perfect as the years have passed.

But that memory is from a different time, hell we were practically different people. We weren't always this way, so full of hate...but life happens, things change and unfortunately, we have to play the hand we're dealt. Even when it sucks. And Cassie and I burned bright for one night before it all went to shit, and that's just something we learn to deal with. But it definitely sucks, because honestly, at the end of the day, the only thing worse than the one that got away is the one you almost had.

Reaching for my fifth of whiskey from the pantry, I pour myself a double before tossing another shot on top for good measure. I don't drink often, but I've been known to throw back if the situation allows, and this is definitely one of them. Cassie is camped out in the dining room dancing to the music in between her god-awful attempts at playing beer pong. But she looks so happy and carefree that I can't help but watch her, almost forgetting I'm supposed to act like I hate her. She's swaying her hips around, laughing as her friend grinds up against her, both just smiling and having a good time.

It's interesting how such a simple thing can invoke so many old memories that I'd hammered down. But it's these memories that seem to stick around. I'll never forget in high school when I came home late one night, and Cassie was in the kitchen dancing in just a long t-shirt and short shorts. She was dancing around to that *Warrant* song, "Cherry Pie" using a whisk as her microphone. It was probably the cutest fucking thing I'd ever seen, and I just stood there watching her, I was lost. But this time? Fuck that?

I'm just about to make my way into the dining room to find this woman some goddamn clothes and demand she fucking cover herself, when I hear my name spoken from the last person I want to talk to right now. Or ever.

Carina. She's fucking relentless.

"Max, baby!" she shrieks in her annoyingly high-pitched voice. Just hearing her say my name is enough to make my eyes start twitching. Forcing myself to look away from Cassie, I face the infuriating woman currently yelling my name.

"What do you want?"

She reels back, my snappy tone must've surprised her, but I find I really don't give a shit.

"Come dance with me," she demands, trying to reach for my hand but I pull it back.

"I'll pass," I deadpan before starting back to the dining room.

"Why?" she snaps, her sugary sweet tone immediately disappearing as her claws come out to play.

"I don't need a reason, I said no. Do you explain yourself when you tell a man no?"

"I mean, no, but—"

"But nothing. Are you saying it's different because I'm a man? Or because in your small mind you think there's no way that I wouldn't jump right in bed with you, accepting your offer of a well-used pussy?"

"Fuck you, Max." She pouts. All she needs is some fucking pig tails and a binkie and she'd look like a toddler throwing a tantrum. "I just don't get it. You fuck anything, so why not me?" she whines.

Unfortunately for her, I've already tuned her out as my eyes search the room looking for Cassie. When I find her, I'm instantly livid. She's now standing in the middle of the room practically naked, wearing only her tiny pink thong. Apparently, the girl really sucks at beer pong.

Fucking Christ.

It's bad enough being in the same room as her when she's fully clothed, but now? When she's basically naked? It's absolute torture. I'm watching her prance around while all these other men are gawking and drooling over her and it's literally killing me. Even worse, the thought of one of these guys making a move and actually taking her home... yeah, that makes me want to punch someone, stirring something inside of me that I'd shut down for years. Since the last time I saw her naked all those years ago

Even just the thought of that night is almost enough to make me walk over to her. I want so badly to grab her, lift her up by her ass, and bring her to the nearest surface and take her, claim her, knowing damn well she's never truly been mine in the first place.

But all thoughts go out the window the moment I notice Fez giving her a hard time, holding her clothes in his hands. Walking towards the dining room, I make a beeline straight for Cassie, who's still standing in front of Fez trying to get her clothes back while he jokingly tries to make her move her hands covering her tit. He's acting like a fucking child who's never seen a naked woman before, not like the wide receiver playboy he's actually known as around campus. Hell, his bedroom is a revolving door usually, so I'm not sure why he's pulling this shit.

Without a second thought, I quickly reach back grabbing my shirt and pulling it off before tossing it at a surprised Cassie. "Put this on. Now."

"Lay off, man," Fez jokes. "We're just having a little fun, right Cassie?" he says, winking at Cassie who returns it with a glare.

Big mistake, buddy.

"She's asking for her things back," I snap, all friendliness thrown out the window, surprising both Cassie and Fez... hell, I'm even surprising myself right now. "Now give them back to her."

"I was just offering to carry her things up to my room for her. Figured I'd be a gentleman and help her get comfortable."

Before I can ever respond, Cassie steps up next to me, thankfully wearing my white t-shirt that looks so much fucking better on her than me. God damn she's sexy, and I immediately feel all the blood rushing to my cock at just the sight of her standing there, her nipples pebbled beneath my shirt. "I already told you, there is not a fucking chance in hell I'm going to your room with you. Now fuck off and give me my damn clothes, you dickbag."

"God, you're such a fucking prude. I've been nice to you for weeks and you won't even show me a tit or anything besides this stupid game? Fuck you, bitch, this has been a waste of my time," Fez mumbles on, only realizing his mistake as my fist makes contact with his face, specifically his nose. The idiot starts bleeding like a stuck pig, and unfortunately for Cassie, he uses her clothes to stop the bleeding.

"What the fuck, Max? I'm gunna kick your ass," Fez starts shouting, his tanned skin splattered with blood in a way that makes him look crazy, but I've seen the guy play football before, I know better. He's an absolute pussy when it comes to taking tackles on the field, even if he catches like a champ. He's all bark, no bite, more like a pest, or a chihuahua. The kind of yappy annoying shits that nip at you, but the second you even look in their direction they run off terrified with their tail tucked.

I don't know if I'm more pissed off that this man was hoping to put his hands on Cassie, or that he was being disrespectful towards her. It's probably a little of both, but the idea of him putting his slimy hands on her hot little body is enough to make me homicidal.

His football buddies try to shush him, telling him to walk it off, but he continues on, goading me like the drunk idiot he is.

"What, Daniels? You think just because you made me bleed for her that she'll suck your dick or something? I've been trying for weeks, and the little slut just kept tea—."

He doesn't even finish his sentence before I've crossed the distance between us, not stopping until we're nose to nose, one hand gripping his throat tight enough that his eyes widen in shock. I can feel his throat fight against my grip each time he swallows but I refuse to back down. I needed his attention and now I have it.

"I'm going to spell this out for you, hopefully in a way that you can understand, because apparently you're just as stupid as you look."

His jaw clenches but this time he's smart enough to keep his mouth shut.

"She's off-fucking-limits." He makes the dumb decision to look in her direction, so I squeeze tighter, forcing his attention back to me. "Don't look at her, don't touch her, don't fucking talk about her. Hell, don't even think about her. Cassie Wright doesn't fucking exist to you. Do you understand me?"

He just stares for a moment like he wants to argue, before nodding.

"Use your words, pretty boy. Want to make sure you understand the expectations perfectly. Wouldn't want you to fuck up, and I don't know, have something accidentally happen to your hand right before the draft. Wouldn't that be a fucking shame?"

He immediately understands that I'm serious, his eyes widening, throat swallowing. On top of the nerves though, he's fucking furious.

"Yep. I understand perfectly," he says with a scowl on his face, voice hoarse from my grip. Loosening up, I look back at Cassie, her eyes glassy from the booze but that's not the only thing I notice. For the first time in years, she doesn't seem angry with me, doesn't seem like she hates me and it's unnerving as hell.

Shoving him away, I walk over to Cassie grabbing her hand and pulling her along with me. Before she can say anything, I yell over my shoulder at Fez who's now standing with his friends, hiding from the rest of the party. "You're a leftie, right?" I wink, and understanding immediately hits him.

He knows I'll fuck his entire career up if he crosses me, and apparently, fucking with Cassie is a surefire way to piss me off. Even if I was unaware of that fun little fact until tonight.

"Nice show, hotshot," Cassie grumbles in my direction.

"It wasn't a show and he knows it. Plus, that fucker had it coming, I hope I broke his nose."

"Fair point," she says, walking a little quicker to keep up with my pace as I lead her out of the main room, unsure of where we're going. Right as we're about to head upstairs, someone from the top of the stairs calls my name, the annoying high pitched voice could only be one person. Telling me that for the second time tonight, my fucking inner zen is ruined by Carina and her stupid, annoying, voice.

Chapter Four

Cassie

I feel like my brain is bleeding.

Or, maybe it's my ears.

But the noise is so painful, it sounds like a dying animal.

Although, it's coming from the top of the stairs where a woman is standing, her voice eliciting the same reaction as nails on a chalkboard. Her voice is so high-pitched and nasally, that every time she talks it almost physically pains me. Even worse, she's determined to get Max's attention which for some reason makes me feel...jealous?

The only positive in this situation is it seems that Max doesn't share the same interest in her. When she first started yelling for Max down the stairs, I could feel his grip tighten on my hand, his shoulders straightening, as he tried to walk on and ignore her voice. It wasn't until she said it again, he finally stopped.

I should have kept walking, should've pulled my hand from his and walked away from him and the drama that often follows him. I don't owe him anything, we don't even fucking like each other. Instead, I curled into his side, leaning into his chest while Max stared at the stairs, holding onto me like I was grounding him and for some reason, I let him.

"Max!" the voice rings out again and I finally look up to meet her eyes and boy, if looks could kill, I'd be dead on the spot.

She's standing at the top of the stairs wearing a lingerie set which leaves nothing to the imagination. She looks like she's been waiting for something, maybe him, which might explain why she looks furious that he's standing here holding me

"Who's this?" I say sweetly, looking up at Max.

"Carina. She's a friend of some of the guys."

I hear her heels walking down the stairs before I see her, my eyes still focused on Max as his features slowly soften when he looks into my eyes

"Max, honey, don't play coy. We're friends, too," Carina practically purrs from the bottom of the stairs where she's popped her hip against the railing. "We could be even better friends if you'd just come upstairs with me."

"I think I've made my stance on this situation very clear, Carina. I wasn't interested in you before, I'm not today and I still won't be interested in you tomorrow."

The look on her face is pure evil, she's pissed that he's turning her down, especially in front of another woman. Her eyes quickly narrow on Max before turning to finally acknowledge me, giving me a very obvious once over like she's taking in the competition.

Which I guess to her that's what this is–a competition.

The issue is, I don't like losing. At all. Regardless of my lack of interest in this game.

By the time she's done with her appraisal of me, her nose is scrunched in obvious distaste as she turns back to Max.

"Max, I don't get it," she whines, her voice slowly getting higher and higher, to the point that I almost want to feel if my ears are bleeding. "Here I am waiting in your bed, dressed like this and you're down here tramping around with this...she's nothing! She's plain and you're down here with her and not me. What the hell, Max?"

I almost start laughing at everything she's saying and the fact that she's practically stomping her foot like a two-year-old throwing a tantrum, but she's serious...like she's actually throwing a fit in the middle of this party over a guy who's obviously not interested in her. I've always hated watching all of the girls throw themselves at him, especially all the times he's enjoyed the attention.

It isn't until Max tenses against me that I realize I'm still standing here just staring at her in disbelief as she whines on.

"There's nothing to get, Carina. Now, for the millionth time, stay the fuck out of my room and out of my way," Max says, his voice quieter, vicious, full of venom. He sounds angrier than I've ever heard from him, and the man hates me, so I'd know.

"You're going to regret this. I'll make sure of it... I wonder what my father would think about you tramping around with yet another little slut."

I laugh, unable to control it. "Well, this little slut sucks dick like it's an Olympic sport, which could be why he's here with me, not you." I lean forward even though her look alone should make me nervous. But I want to be dramatic and whisper-yell the next part. Thanks for that, Tequila.

"Want to know the best part? I fucking love it. I love the feeling of his cock in my throat, seeing just how far I can take it before having to pull back. Kind of like limbo, but with my throat." I hear Max behind me let out a noise that sounds stuck between a laugh and a groan, but I just keep on. "Fuck, it's so much fun when he fucks your mouth, ignoring your struggles, but believing in you, knowing you can take it. I've almost been able to take Max, but as you know, he's huge."

Her face turns bright red, and if looks could kill, I'd be dead already. She hates knowing I've had something she wants, even if, technically, his cock hasn't been in my throat before, but she doesn't need to know that.

"Oh, I forgot, you don't know what his cock looks like," I tell her with a wink, while her entire face has turned bright red from my raunchy words, all hitting their mark expertly, embarrassing her. Looking up at Max I smirk. "I'm bored. Let's go find some more alcohol and cause some trouble," I say as I grab his hand and drag him back down the stairs leaving a completely furious, yet embarrassed, dumb girl standing with her jaw on the ground.

As we weave through the kitchen heading towards the back, Max snags a bottle of whiskey from the pantry before following me outside.

I've always loved the outdoors, especially late fall. It's the perfect weather, a little chillier but perfect for a sweatshirt. Although, I'll be the first to admit that Max's white t-shirt isn't exactly ideal for these temps. Pretty sure they can see my nipples from space, and Max is sitting in just a pair of jeans doing his best to not stare at them.

For an asshole, he's being a good sport.

Taking a long pull from the bottle, he looks at me, something flashing in his eyes, so quickly I can't quite discern it, but in a hot second his usual bad boy smirk is back. "So, you're a gold medalist dick sucker, huh?"

"Given the right dick, definitely," I say as I reach over and grab the bottle from him, surprising myself by continuing on. "I fucking love it. Honestly, I just wish men loved giving head as much as women do. Men are lame, they don't go down on girls enough."

"Princess, you've just been with the wrong men then. Don't let dumbasses like that ruin your outlook of all men. A real man loves to eat pussy, and loves to eat pussy often."

"Yeah, whatever. I'll believe it when I see it."

"Cassie, do you mean to tell me that then men you've been with...they don't go down on you often?"

"No, Max. I'm telling you that no man has, *ever*. I've just assumed men that do are unicorns who should be protected at all costs...once you find them. Maybe it's not fun for you guys like it is for us," I tell him with a shrug, focusing my attention on the fire in front of us.

We're the only people out back, but thankfully, they had a fire going to keep people warm. I can hear the party still going on inside, but right now, I'm stuck in this little bubble with Max and actually enjoying myself.

"Sorry, Princess, any man who doesn't immediately get down on his knees to worship you, isn't worth your time," Max growls, his eyes hungry, whether from the alcohol, this conversation, or...me. I'm not sure, but all I know is that the way he's looking at me right now, I feel like I'm about to become his next meal.

"If you'd been my girl, I would've worshiped you. Your body squirming beneath me as I feasted on your pretty pink pussy until you came down my face."

I feel my face redden from his comment. It hits home too, I feel like he's giving me one more final blow on our history. One last reminder that I was almost his, until he left ghosted me, years of friendship immediately going down the drain.

"I...uh..." I pause, unsure what to say. I can't exactly say, *"Yeah, Max, I would've loved that, your tongue on my pussy until I was coming on your face. But then you decided to go fuck it all up."* But I can't exactly say that, now can I?

Before I can think of anything to say, Max stands up from his chair, takes the two steps over to me and kneels on the ground in front of me. When his eyes meet mine, there's a combination of emotions flowing through, all fighting to be front and center and I'm not quite sure what is even happening at the moment. He seems to be wondering the same thing as he sits there, looking oddly adorable with a boyish grin on his face full of...excitement, which is quite contrary to the hungry look in his eyes.

When he moves his hands towards me, I freeze, unable to move, as he reaches forward and places his hands against the outside of my thighs.

His hands are so warm against the iciness of my skin from being outside wearing just a shirt...which reminds me, we're at a party...out in public.

We may be alone out here but there are people just inside the house, anyone could come out here at any time. I should stop him.

But I don't.

I'm supposed to hate him, but as his hands slowly slide up the sides of my legs, hesitating just long enough to look up at me, his eyes are full of questions.

"What...what are you...doing?" I stutter as his hands slowly begin drawing circles on the inside of my thigh.

"I'm showing you what it's like to be with a real man,"

he says as he begins pressing little kisses and nibbles up my thigh.

I reallllly should stop him. We could get caught at any moment, and just what I need is Sawyer finding out I messed around with her brother.

"Max..." I whisper, my hands in his hair. "Someone could come out here."

"I know," he smirks. "But I think you like the idea of us getting caught just as much as I do. I love the thought of someone walking out here, you squirming as you fuck my mouth until you're coming all over my face. I love the idea of taking this first of yours and with how wet you are now, I think you love this idea oo."

"But we hate each other, you never have anything nice to say to me," I say, my attempt at putting up a fight probably isn't convincing either of us to stop.

"Well, then how about I use my mouth for something better..."

Unable to speak through the nerves, I just nod my approval which is all he needs.

"Okay, Princess. Hold on tight."

When he presses his lips against my clit, his kisses mixed with little nibbles, all thoughts of this being a bad idea go directly out the window. My body is vibrating with pleasure as his tongue expertly works my body like he's studied it. When he flattens his tongue and presses it firmly against my clit, my entire body begins to shake.

The little voice in the back of my mind that's been whispering this is a mistake is now being shut up by the horny bitch between my legs who's salivating at the idea of coming on this man's face.

As his mouth continues the assault on my body, his hand that had been caressing my hip, holding me open for him, slides between my legs as he gently pushes two fingers inside me.

His mouth presses more firm kisses against me until he's pressing gently against my clit, alternating between licking and sucking

"Oh, Jesus," I moan, unable to stop it as Max keeps working my body, his fingers and mouth working in tandem, driving me closer and closer to finishing.

It doesn't take long, until I feel the sensation start building, everything becoming overwhelming as I grip Max's hair, holding him in place. When it gets to be too much, I try to push him away, but he slaps my hand gently.

"Grab your knees and hold them. You're getting in my way," he growls, his fingers continuing to move in and out of my pussy.

Surprisingly, I do as I'm told and am rewarded when he slips a third finger inside of me, my body stretching to accommodate him. All coherent thoughts and words have flown out the window as the only thing I'm able to produce are moans as my body gets slammed with an orgasm so intense, I'm surprised I don't black out.

Holy fuck.

This man knows his way around a woman's body. I've always known he has a nice dick, but I wasn't aware he had other skills to back it up.

Max can get it. All day. Everyday. Twice on Sundays.

Maybe he and I would have gotten along a lot better if he used his mouth like *this* instead of talking and promising me things that he couldn't follow through with. Or if he hadn't ghosted me, but that's a problem for a different day. A day where his tongue hasn't been deep inside my pussy.

Looking down, I see him leaning back on his heels, smirking up at me like the cat that got the canary. He knows *damn well* he just rocked my world and he's very fucking pleased about it. All of this just makes me so much more frustrated that he had to turn out to be an asshole. With the way our relationship was, how good the sex was even with it being our first time, and now this? Fuck, it makes me hate him that it didn't work out.

So instead of being nice, I decide to throw some of his attitude back at him.

"Well, I guess everyone has to be good at something, it makes sense that eating pussy is yours." Is about all I can muster as he stares at me.

"That's it? That's all you're going to say?" he grumbles, a mix of sadness and anger laces his words, which, of course, he tries to cover up. It surprises me though, I wasn't aware Max cared about anyone but himself.

"What were you expecting Max? A gold medal? I can post a review in the school paper or even on Yelp. Would Craigslist be better since you've already gone through the school roster? Let everyone know what they're in for. Five stars," I snap, my emotions suddenly hitting me all at once.

This meant nothing to him, that I'm sure of. He made it clear he enjoys this and the stories I've heard about him, it leaves no doubt in my mind that I am just another girl to play with. Guess nothing's changed.

"I don't know. I guess I was just expecting more. Didn't know this was just a transaction."

"We aren't friends, Max. You've made that very clear," I say, standing and stumbling back all at once, the alcohol from the evening hitting me all at once. Before I can fall though, Max is behind me, steadying me.

The feel of his fingers on my skin now are enough to burn me, even with the rain now falling down from the sky.

I hadn't even realized it had started to rain, it must've

started while Max was making me come all over his face as I'm completely soaked. But I don't care that it's raining, or that I'm not dressed for it. In fact, the rain is helping hide the tears streaming down my face that I'd practically die if Max ever noticed, it'd fuck up years of pretending I am indifferent towards him, no real emotions other than hate inside me when it comes to him. So, I head further outside into the rain. I mean, who wouldn't want to dance in the pouring rain, maybe then the rain can hide my tears. The tears I've been hiding from Max for years.

"What the hell are you doing? It's pouring rain," Max shouts as he runs behind me trying to avoid the puddles from the rain. I ignore him as I stand out in the rain, eyes closed as I look up.

I've always loved the rain and I can't remember the last time I felt free enough to just...*be*. As soon as Max told me not to do this, I knew I had to. I'm tired of everyone telling me what I need to do, I'm tired of everyone making decisions for me, and it may be something as stupid as standing in the rain wearing a white t-shirt, but this is a decision I can make for myself.

I'm not sure if it's the alcohol, or seeing Max, or Carina and her fucking ear-piercing voice, but I'm just over it all right now and honestly? Right now, I don't really give a fuck.

I ignore Max when he tries to talk to me. I ignore his hands burning my skin as he touches my shoulders. It isn't until he's picked me up and thrown me over his shoulder that I'm forced to finally acknowledge him.

"Put me down."

"No. You're acting ridiculous."

"Me?" I shout, hitting his ass with my fist. "I'm not the

one who's carrying someone against their will like a goddamn heathen!"

"Yeah? Well, I'm not the one dancing in the middle of the street in a soaked white t-shirt."

I mean...I guess he's not wrong. For as controlling as my father is, he would be fucking pissed if he ever found out I am out acting like this.

But this was all just for fun, no harm is going to come from this.

Right?

Before I even realize what's happening, without any chance to get down or warn him, I'm throwing up down the back of Max, all over the white shirt I'm wearing. *Fuck my life.*

"Fucking shit, Cassie. You could've warned a guy," Max grumbles, before gently putting me down, his eyes much softer than his voice.

"Sorry," I mumble as I realize we are both covered.

"Let's sneak up the back porch by my room, I left the slider open."

I want to tell him no, that I'll just make my way home, go see if Gwen is still around or something, but the thought of having to do more work is enough to stop that idea, quickly.

Following along, we make our way up the stairs until we are at his door before finally slipping out of our vomit-covered clothes on the porch.

I don't get the luxury of wearing anything under my shirt as dickhead Fez got blood all over my clothes. But even just seeing Max standing there in a pair of black boxer briefs, it's enough to make me question if I want to punch the guy or fuck him. Standing up, I head towards the door, unfortunately moving too fast as another wave of nausea hits me, sending me sprinting through his door to find a bathroom. Which is where I spend most of the night until Max finally picks me up, placing me in his bed.

Where I find myself still cuddled up to him the next morning.

Chapter Five

Max

There's hair in my face.

There's never hair in my face—women do not sleep here, ever.

So, who the fuck is laying in my bed with their tiny body sprawled on top of me? The scent of vanilla and something like oranges hits me as she rolls over, piling more damn hair on my face, the scent causing memories to hit me like a freight train.

Cassie is in my bed, I'd recognize this scent anywhere. The moment I realize who's in my bed, all the events from last night hit me. Between Carina, punching Fez, and going down on Cassie on my back patio, I'd say it was a pretty fucking eventful night. I probably wouldn't have believed any of it actually happened had I not woken up to her in my bed

Not even because I was blackout drunk or anything, I mean I was tipsy, but not that bad. I just honestly never thought that Cassie would ever be in my bed again, let alone sleeping on top of me. Guess I just figured it wasn't in the cards with how much she hates me. Not that I can blame her, I should've fought harder for her. But now, six years later I'm still driving her away, more afraid of what will

"You're breathing on me," Cassie mumbles.

"And you're lying on top of me," I snap back. "In my bed."

She's yet to open her eyes, but the little space between her eyebrows is all scrunched up like she's frowning and sticking her nose up at me. It's cute, and it makes me want to *boop* it.

"How can I not when you're pinning me down with your big, muscular arms," she whines, making absolutely no effort to get up, but her eyes are finally open.

"I'm sorry, what did you say? All I heard was 'big, muscular, sexy arms'."

"Of course you did, Max. You only ever hear what you want...and I didn't call you sexy." she snaps back, immediately pushing back from my chest and standing up like she's repulsed. "Do you ever think about anyone but yourself?"

She's so sensitive, not able to take a joke from me like she used to. Only now, she's gotten up and has made her way into my closet, stealing a pair of sweats and sweatshirts. I'm sure I'll never see those again, not that I mind. I love how fucking adorable she looks drowning in my clothes.

I'm not sure why her comment has gotten under my skin, but it has and it's pissing me off. I don't just think about myself, I never have. I'm always worrying about what other people think, especially when I think I've upset them.

"What's that supposed to mean?" I bite back.

"Nothing, Max. It doesn't matter anymore. I'm gonna go, thanks for...uh...everything." Cassie says, stopping just a moment at my door.

"Aww you're leaving, Princess? I thought we could cuddle," I smirk, reverting back to pushing her buttons, it's the easiest way to keep my emotions and my heart safe. "I'm wounded," I tease, bringing my hand to my heart for dramatic effect.

She just rolls her eyes, before slamming the door on her way out.

Grabbing my phone, I check my messages, shock immediately hitting me with how many I've already received this early in the morning. A few of them are from players on our team, but those aren't the ones that are concerning me. There's a bunch of messages from my mother as well as one from an unknown number.

MOTHER

What's this picture I just received, Max?

It's obviously you but that's all I can see.

I don't know who sent this, but they said they have a video of you that's wildly inappropriate.

Is this some stupid hookup?

Are you really willing to risk your future for a quick hookup? Jesus fuck, Max, I raised you better than that.

You know you can't make these choices when your future is on the line. I've messaged your sister, she's meeting us for dinner next Sunday. We will be discussing all of this then.

ME

Fine. I'll figure it out. Just send me the details.

She doesn't care about inconveniencing anyone, as long as it's convenient for her, and planning a 'family dinner' during one of my practices is nothing surprising.

Max

Opening up the other message, the one from the unknown number, my heart drops. It's a picture that looks like it was indeed taken from a video, but it's different from the one my mother received. It shows me, on my knees, between Cassie's legs, although you can't tell who she is, thank God. Just what I need is to give her another reason to hate me. Fuck my life.

Falling back, I cover my face with my arm, trying to not be blinded by the light shining in, letting everything finally sink in. You'd think I'd be more focused on figuring out everything with my mother, but all I can think about is how even after all this time, Cassie is still the only girl to get under my skin and in my bed.

Fuckkk me.

———

By THE TIME I GOT MYSELF GOING THIS MORNING, I was rushing around trying to eat breakfast, get an easy workout in, and making sure I had all of my gear ready for our game tonight. I've been digging around trying to find my lucky skates, all while trying to keep myself focused on anything other than the messages.

It's been so fucking difficult keeping myself focused today, trying to figure out what the hell to do with this picture. Do I bring it up to Coach? Do I try to track the person down? The only thing I know is they had to have been at our party last night, but besides that, it could've been anyone. All I know is I'm determined to figure out how to clean up this mess before it fucks with Cassie's life.

Finally finding my skates, I breathe a sigh of relief that I don't have to play one of our biggest games without my lucky skates. Well, they aren't exactly lucky skates, more like a lucky coin in my skates. Most hockey players are nothing, if not superstitious, and I of course am no different. I've had this lucky coin for years, had it with me for every game since I was sixteen and I definitely don't plan on ending that streak anytime soon.

I remember when I was sixteen, my best friend's mom was dropping me off at our game. I nearly freaked out when I realized I had grabbed the wrong skates, but thankfully her son Luca played on my team as well so she was used to our crazy antics. She ended up running back to get it, showing up with fifteen minutes to spare before puck drop. I've never been more thankful for her fast driving and her compassion, lord knows my mother would've never done that for me.

But now, I'm stressing about something completely different, standing outside my coach's office less than an hour before the game starts. My mind is running a mile a minute, thinking about everything but the game, all because of some stupid conversation with my mom.

My mom has been losing her edge when it comes to me, and she's starting to realize it. Which only means she's attempting to sink her claws even deeper. Whoever sent her that video probably didn't even realize how big of a shit storm they were creating for me, they were probably just trying to inflict as much damage as they possibly could. My mom's told me for years to avoid women, that they will just bring me down and ruin my reputation before I even get into the NHL. It's part of the reason why I've refused to hook up with anyone recently. With this being the year I'm entering the draft, I don't need my reputation taking a hit.

Only now, with this video or pictures or whatever it is, my mother thinks if we look like a united family, Sawyer included, maybe I'll look like a family guy who got caught up in an innocent mess, but I refuse to expect anything from my sister, especially help.

My mother put my sister and I against each other, always playing devil's advocate between us, making sure we don't lean on each other for anything, or at least that's what it feels like. It's also a lot easier to stomach the fact that Sawyer doesn't talk to me because of what our mother has done, instead of the other option that she truly just doesn't want a relationship with me. I've been trying to figure out a way to actually get some time to talk to Sawyer, see if I'm right, but she's honestly been avoiding me. That's probably the only reason I actually want to go to the dinner my mother demanded I attend, which is why I'm here.

So now, I'm standing outside my coach's office less than an hour before our game starts, stressing the fuck out.

My mind is everywhere except on the ice, and I know I need to get my shit right before the game. Knocking on his door, I wait longer than I expected for him to answer, but he finally does.

"Hey Coach, you got a minute?" I ask, my voice sounding just about as nervous as I feel.

"Of course, Daniels," Coach says, his voice edgy. "You okay?"

"Yeah, of course. Well... I mean, not exactly. Just some family stuff going on, I kinda need your advice," I tell him.

Fuck I hate asking people for favors, especially when it gets in the way of hockey, even worse when it's because of my mother. The older I get, the less and less I trust her, and right now? I don't think I trust a single thing that comes out of her mouth. She's been trying to play this game that Sawyer's off making shitty choices and abandoning her family, but I think there's more to it, than that. Even so...if that's what she's doing, why isn't our mother trying to help her?

Oh right, because she only gives a shit about herself.

Walking in, I sit in the seat in front of his desk, my palms so damn sweaty that I've probably wiped them down my pants a million times already. I'm more nervous right now than in my college hockey game, and I threw up twice before even getting on the ice that day. Looking up, I'm met with Rex's gaze, he looks uncomfortable but also concerned and that combination is unnerving as fuck.

"What's up, Max?" Rex says carefully.

"Honestly, I'm struggling. I'm watching a family member spiral out of control and make a bunch of fucked up decisions while I'm supposed to sit back and watch. It sucks, and I feel like I'm the only one who can fix it, the only one who cares."

"I'm sorry, man that sucks," Rex says in a calm way, patiently waiting for me to continue, like he knows that's not it. "I'm confused on what you need me for, though."

I can't quite put my finger on it, but he's acting weird, or maybe I'm just reading too much into it, fuck if I know anymore. He's just usually so good at maintaining eye contact when talking, all that bullshit about respect and attention, but he's looked down in his lap at least twice like he's avoiding eye contact. It's weird.

"Sorry, Max. I just don't think I'm following. What is it that I can do to help you?" Rex says.

I'm honestly not sure I'm making sense right now, so I get his confusion.

"So, apparently, I'm supposed to have dinner with them this Sunday, and I know we have mandatory practice to go over film, but I was just, uh, wondering if it would be okay for me to miss that practice," I blurt out. "Sir, I don't want you to think that this isn't important to me. It is. So important to me. There's just been a lot going on with my family, and I feel like I need to be there to try and help them see the error in what they're doing."

"Are you asking me if you can miss the practice Sunday evening?" Rex finally asks.

"Yes, sir."

"Not a problem, if there's anything you need to go over, I can meet with you the following week. Take care of your family," Rex says quickly, probably realizing it's about time to meet back with the team.

"Really?" I ask, disbelief shining through my words, I didn't expect it to go this smoothly. "Thanks, sir. I really appreciate it."

"But do me a favor, okay?" Rex adds as he stands up.

"Yeah, anything."

"Go get your head straight. Head back to the locker room, you have thirty minutes till it's show time. Make sure you leave everything off the ice," Rex says with a smile.

"Of course. Thanks again, Coach."

Heading out to meet up with the rest of the team, I'm relieved that the conversation is over but also even more annoyed I had to have it.

With everything I've done for my mom, it drives me fucking crazy that she's getting in the way of hockey, even if it is just one practice. Hockey has always been the one thing I've refused to let people fuck with, but of course she found a fucking way.

This is the last fucking time, though.

Chapter Six

Max

By the time Sunday rolls around, I'm ready for this shit to be over. I've been stressed out about this dinner all damn week, wondering what it is that Sawyer wants from us now, if she even shows up. On top of that, I've been trying to text Cassie to talk to her about the picture, but she's ignored my phone calls and won't respond to any of my messages.

At first it was annoying, now it's just starting to fucking piss me off. At this rate, I'm going to show up to her apartment and force her to talk to me. When I get to the restaurant, I'm surprised to find my mother already sitting at the table, but thankfully Sawyer walks in at the exact same time as me.

To my surprise, Sawyer looks great, happy, and smiling, nothing like the impression my mother has given me.

But of course, our spiteful mother has to ruin the possibility of a civil dinner the moment she locks eyes with her.

"Hello, Sawyer. It's so nice of you to join us. Hope this wasn't too early for your schedule," my mother practically snarls.

"Obviously it wasn't. I'm here early," Sawyer retorts quickly, surprising both my mother and I, but in reality, I'm actually impressed. I know first-hand how difficult it is to stand up to this woman, but Sawyer is doing it.

"Hardly. I said 5:30. The least you could do would be to show up at 5:00 to have our table ready," she snaps, like she's been wronged in some way. Not sure why she is expecting Sawyer to be here even before her when this was her plan.

Sawyer looks dumbfounded. "Do you hear yourself? Or are you just so delusional that you think it's okay to speak to me like this?" she questions, surprising all of us.

Honestly, I'm not sure which way is up right now, I feel like I've entered the twilight zone with the way Sawyer is speaking to our mother, but part of me also knows there's a damn good chance it's justified. I've had this sinking feeling lately that I can't trust my mother...at all, and at this moment, I know I can't just sit back and let them go round and round.

"Enough," I snarl, causing Sawyer to just glare and my mother to gasp. "Stop acting like children. Sawyer, why did you want to meet us?"

"Excuse me? Mom called me and told me to be here for dinner 'or else.' I figured I should show up to find out what it was about."

Looking at our mother, she's staring at me, her big doe eyes filled with a look I can't quite place. We've always kind of just accepted her antics, never truly questioning them, so I think she's shocked that it's all coming to a head right now

"Max, I did this to help you, silly. That whole scandal you've gotten yourself involved in isn't going away on its own. One of the coaches said it would be best for you to have your family by your side. We can't let your dreams die just because you made some poor choices. Sawyer will help us," she claims confidently.

Fuck. This is not how I wanted Sawyer to hear about this situation, especially because I haven't had the chance to talk to Cassie. I'm pretty sure Sawyer would disown me and kick me in the nuts if she found out what happened between Cassie and I.

Besides, I also don't know anything about who sent the message, except that they're obviously a shady asshole if they not only sent it to me, but also to my fucking mother. Lord only knows who else they might have sent it to. Damnit.

My normally passive, non-confrontational sister surprises me when her voice raises, snapping me out of my thoughts. "Excuse me? Max, I'm not really interested in whatever shit you've gotten yourself into, it's not my problem anymore. But, mom, do you really expect me to be a united front with you two? Max has made you believe so much bullshit about me that you were willing to stop paying for my schooling. Mom, you even went as far as trying to get my trust fund dad set up switched to you somehow. How selfish are you two to think I would play happy family with you guys when you can't even support my dreams? No one was there for me when I lost dance, and now you refuse to support me when I let that dream evolve into something I'm still able to do. So, I'm opening a studio regardless of your help, even if I've had to work two jobs to do it," Sawyer snarls at our mother before turning her attention back to me. "And fuck you, Max, for convincing her that I'm a fuck up and that she shouldn't pay for my school. Real fucking manipulative, bro."

I'm shocked. Is this really what she thinks? Why does she think I've told my mother lies?

I look at the woman in question and am unimpressed when I see she's anxious, almost terrified. The more I watch her, the more I question just how much I truly understand about this situation. I'm pissed, I'm hurt, and I want to know what the actual truth is, but I also think Sawyer needs to understand that I'm not out to get her, never have and never will be.

"I've never done that, Sawyer," I tell her, looking between our mother and Sawyer, shocked. "Any of it, I'm not sure what games you're playing, but that's ridiculous."

"Are you joking, Max? You really thought you would get me to come to dinner and all the things you put me through or said about me would just disappear, and I'd help you like the good big sister I am?"

Her words immediately hit me like a ton of bricks, I'm starting to realize just how impacted, how hurt my sister is and all at the hands of this woman I've let control me for years.

"Sawyer, enough. Stop being such a drama queen. We are your family," our mother says before I can jump in.

"Mother, stop saying that. We aren't family because I'm no longer acting like your pawn." When Sawyer stands up, our mother just stares in shock, but it's me Sawyer says her final parting words too. "Max, I'm sorry you've gotten yourself in some shit, but it's your turn to man up and figure it out on your own. I'm not willing to put myself through pretending to be a happy family just to help people who constantly throw me under the bus."

I should respond, I know I should. I should stand up, talk to my sister, and try to figure out what's going on. I'm starting to get the feeling that neither of us really know the truth.

But first things first, I need to figure out what my

mother has done, I want the truth. I'm so over her shit and apparently her lies.

As we watch Sawyer walk away, my mother turns to me. "She's always had a thing for dramatics, what a shame that she couldn't pull off being a dancer, probably would have done wonderfully on the stage."

"Are you fucking kidding me? She isn't a dancer because she got injured."

"She could have worked harder to prevent the injury, instead she's trying to go to school to be a dance teacher. How pathetic, she's nothing like you. You've overcome challenges, with my help of course."

"Good point, mother. She's nothing like me. She's stronger, more capable, more independent than me and that's something you should be proud of. But I don't think she learned that from you," I practically shout, no longer giving a fuck if anyone see's us, although she keeps looking around like she's embarrassed.

"Maxy, it was nothing like this. She just wasn't as strong as you, she didn't have the drive you do. All I wanted was to support you and your dreams, if that meant taking some away from her, then so be it. I did what I had to, to help us."

"Don't lie to me to make yourself feel better, like you aren't a snake. Sawyer got away from you and your toxicity, while I sat around and let you manipulate me into thinking you actually gave a fuck about me. I promise you though, it's over. You pull any shit again, on *either* of us and I promise I will blast it all in every interview I do. Your face will be everywhere, but not in the way you've always dreamed of. I will make sure everyone knows what a toxic horrible human you truly are."

Her face turns white. The only thing my mother has ever cared about is her image, which is why she never told anyone what my father was doing, she left all of that behind closed doors. But that shit catches up to you, and I no longer care if I'm damning her reputation. She doesn't care about us, why should we care about her?

"Maxy, you can't be serious right now. You wouldn't do that to your mother. Besides sweetie, who do you have besides me? No family, no one to love you, support you, or be there for you."

"Fucking watch me," I say, standing up. "I'm done with you. I'd rather be alone, but proud of who I am, then be your son and ashamed of the choices you've encouraged me to make."

"If you walk away, I promise you will regret it," she snarls, her tone immediately changing the second she no longer is control. But fuck it, I don't care. Bring it on, mother.

Ignoring her protests, that thankfully quiet down the further away I get, I leave the restaurant refusing to turn back, refusing to let another parent manipulate me into thinking I'm not worthy.

I'm worthy of more...but what, I'm not sure of yet.

BY THE TIME I COOLED OFF AFTER FINISHING UP MY talk with my mom, I have no idea what I should do. Part of me wants to go to the gym, lift until I'm too exhausted to move or think, another part of me wants to go to the bar and drink until I don't know where I'm at, but I haven't drank in months, minus last weekend...with Cassie, which, *fuck*, reminds me I still have to figure out how to tell her about the picture.

It's still so fucking hard for me to believe that someone

actually took a picture of Cassie and I on the balcony. You can't see who she is, but it's obvious that I'm the one, on my knees between the girl's legs. Figured I should warn her, in case anyone remembers seeing us together.

Before I even realize where I'm at, I'm knocking on the door to Sawyer's apartment. I'm not even sure what I'm going to say to her or why I'm here, all I know is that it felt right to show up here.

When I knock on the door though, it's not Sawyer that answers, Instead Cassie is standing there, and her eyes immediately darken. Sawyer must've talked to her already because she seems extra pissy tonight.

"What do you want?" she demands, barely keeping the door open, but I ignore her, pushing in past her.

"Where is she? Where's Sawyer?" I ask, turning back to face Cassie who looks even angrier.

"Max, you can't just barge in here like you own the place. Besides, she's not here."

"She's not? Well then, I guess it's you and I who need to talk. You've been ignoring me, Princess. I told you we needed to talk."

"I'm not ignoring you, I just don't want to talk to you. End of story," Cassie huffs before pointing to the door. "You need to fucking go, Max. It's not fair for you to show up here. If I wanted to talk, I would've."

"I don't fucking care, Cassie. Don't sit here and tell me what the fuck to do after the week I've had. You don't know the shit that's happened, which is why I've been trying to talk to you."

"Well, I don't want to fucking talk to you. You and your mom treat Sawyer so badly that I can't even stand to look at you right now. You are such a fucking dick, I can't believe I ever..." Cassie says but stops suddenly when something over my shoulder catches her eyes. "Fuck." she mumbles.

Following her gaze, I see Sawyer, who's obviously upset. It kills me seeing my sister so sad and knowing I had a part in it. But my gaze doesn't stay on her, it passes right by her until I see my coach standing directly behind her, looking awfully fucking comfortable.

"Sawyer, what the fuck is this?" I yell, fists clenching

"No, Max. You're in my apartment, you don't get to fucking ask questions first," she snaps, catching me off guard. "What the fuck are you doing at my apartment?"

"We'll get to whatever the fuck this is in a minute," I tell her but continue glaring at Rex. "I came here after I left mom at the restaurant. Well after I made her tell me everything. Apparently, she's not as great of a person as I thought she was."

Cassie doesn't try to hide it one bit as she starts laughing. "I could have told you that, you moron. Your mom's a fucking bitch," she adds, shrugging her shoulders like it's common sense.

She's not wrong.

"That doesn't explain to me why you're in my apartment."

"I came over and knocked on your door, Cassie opened it..."

"Is that really the story you're going with?" Cassie says, turning to me. "No, your brother came over and was banging on our door like a barbarian, refusing to leave till the door was open."

"That's not the point. I wanted to fucking talk to you. But I didn't expect to see you with him. So, care to enlighten me on what the fuck is happening here?" I shout, hurt coating each of my words as things start clicking into place. I had heard she was down by the tunnel before a game which was weird, but I didn't think anything of it.

But no one's talking. Everyone is just staring at me like I'm a ticking time bomb they're waiting to explode. Like once it's all clicked, they know I'm going to lose it.

"Wait. No. This can't be. Are you fucking my sister?" I shout, finally seeing the bigger picture. "That day that you were in the tunnel, Sawyer, I went to talk to Coach. You weren't... you weren't there were you?"

"Max, stop. We aren't having this conversation," Sawyer says, trying to stop me from going off the deep end, but watching Rex's hand touch her, trying to comfort her does the opposite and I'm immediately pissed.

"Answer my fucking question," I shout

"Yes, Daniels. I'm dating your sister," Rex says, his attempt at speaking calmly falls short.

"No."

"You don't really get a say in that, Daniels. She's your sister, not your pet."

"Fuck you. This is so fucked up. How could you do this to me, Sawyer?"

"Do what to you? Date? Sorry that it's cutting into your hockey life, but I didn't do anything on purpose."

"I won't allow this."

"I'm not sure why you think you have any right to choose who I date," she snaps.

I feel like I'm losing everything. First my dad. Then Sawyer. Then my mom. And now, when I'm trying to make amends, I'm just reminded that I don't matter. My feelings don't matter, that as long as I play the perfect part, do everything I'm supposed to, no one actually gives a fuck about me. I'm done feeling unimportant in everyone's lives, I'm done feeling like I don't matter.

"No, but I have control over if I play hockey, and from what I hear, your little boyfriend might have a good shot at an NHL coaching position if we make it all the way through the playoffs. It would really suck for him to lose that opportunity if, say, his lead goal scorer decided not to play," I shrug.

"Are you always this much of a prick, Daniels?" Rex says.

"Maybe not, but it works. So, what'll it be, Coach? My sister or your dream job? From what I heard tonight, you had a good shot at the New York position, which would be perfect for your little girl, not having to move again," I say, my words dripping with manipulation.

The look on Rex's face should be enough to stop me. He looks absolutely gutted. But no, I'm over it, I want to be chosen for once.

"Max, stop," Sawyer cries out, tears falling from my eyes. Looking at me, her eyes are pained, full of torment, and I'm positive I'm making the wrong decision, but when she answers, I don't stop her. "You win," she whispers, barely audible as she grows more and more upset.

"The fuck? What are you saying, Sawyer?" Rex says, turning to face her.

"I'm saying no. I'm not worth it. I'm not worth losing your dream over, so Max wins."

"Sawyer, that's not your fucking choice to make. You don't get to tell me what I think is worth it."

"But it is. I've had my dream taken from me before. You've watched me claw my way out of that mess, helping me along the way. I won't sit here and let my piece of shit brother take that away," she tells him, her eyes welling up with tears. "I'm sorry, Rex. You're better off without me."

I know this is my fault, and that I should stop it, but I

honestly can't bring myself to let them choose each other over me. I want Sawyer to choose her brother. I want my coach to choose me and the team, even though I know it's not fair of me to expect them to. I just want to be chosen, even if it hurts.

"Plus, Rex, Bernard probably wouldn't take too kindly if he found out you were dating my sister, I mean she does go to the university you coach at. Isn't that against policy?"

He still doesn't say anything, just stands and watches me, understanding finally registering on his face that I just don't give a fuck right now and am willing to let this all explode.

"Guess it makes sense. First time I've let myself care about someone and they leave me, again. I should have seen it coming," Rex says quietly before turning back to me. "You may be right that both our dream jobs ride on this decision, but it wasn't my only dream. Here I was, thinking I'd help pull some strings for you, get you on your dream team after that little situation you were in," Rex says, shaking his head in disbelief, hurting me at the same time. "But yeah, you can go fuck yourself," Rex says before turning around and walking out, leaving me stunned and Sawyer a mess.

"Max, what the fuck is your problem!" Cassie shouts as she cradles a crying Sawyer in her lap.

"My problem? Are you kidding me? He's like twenty years older than her and he's my coach! Besides Cassie, I don't think you are really in a position to talk about this little situation I've got myself in," I shout, my tone coated in venom as Cassie just glares at me.

"Don't be so fucking dramatic Max, we're not kids. No this is about you needing to control everyone and everything under this fake impression that you know what's best. Reality check– you don't. And you just fucked up something that actually makes her happy when all you've done lately is make her sad. Now, I'll tell you one more time. Get. The. Fuck. Out. Of. My. Apartment." Cassie growls, her protective instinct kicking it up a notch.

Turning on my heel, I walk out of their apartment in worse shape than I showed up in.

Fuck me.

Chapter Seven

Cassie

I t's been almost a week and I still want to punch Max in his stupid, handsome, perfect face.

That entitled little motherfucker thinks he could just waltz right into our house like he owns the place and make demands, from either of us? Yeah, fuck that. Plus, I've known Max has been an ass to his sister, but I don't think I realized it was this bad until he forced Rex to choose. I wanted to throat punch the dickbag.

Now, to make matters worse, he hasn't stopped texting me every night since the blow up, still wanting to talk.

Every.
Single.
Night.

MAX

Cass, please talk to me.

ME

No.

Cassie

MAX

I need you to talk to me.

I need your help. I can't fix this without you.
Please.

He's nothing if not persistent.

I've been doing my best to avoid any contact with him since then. I haven't gone out with Gwen and Melissa in a couple days, wanting to avoid any chance of seeing Max out and about on campus. I've spent a lot of time with Sawyer, but she's been trying to keep herself busy in an attempt to keep her mind off of Rex.

Walking around my apartment, I can't decide if I'm bored or hungry as I make my way to the kitchen. I've spent today in classes, thankful I got the chance to talk to one of my teachers about the internship I applied for. We're supposed to find out in the next few weeks but it's hard to contain my excitement. I still haven't told my parents about it, I figured I would wait until after I found out if I got it. They've been trying to get me to meet them for dinner still, but I keep pushing them off, telling them how busy I am.

Unfortunately, that only works for so long with my parents before they just decide to pop in, forcing themselves in your life.

Hearing my phone go off, I snatch it off the counter, pleasantly surprised to see it's a group chat with a message from Trevor.

TREVOR

Hudson's tonight?

MILES

Tequila!

ME

Makes her clothes fallll off!

MILES

Harris says he'll be there too, he's currently being a little bitch about deadlifts, so I stole his phone. Told him I'd send all his lady friends a dick pick if he didn't start lifting ;)

TREVOR

Cassie? Gwen? Either of you down for a night of debauchery. Please don't leave me with these fools?

ME

Always. What time?

GWEN

I'm in! :)

CADE

I'll be there.

TREVOR

8pm

ME

See you then!

I set my phone down, leaving Max's message on read knowing it'll drive him even crazier for me to leave him on read. It'll be even easier for me to avoid texting him back now that I'm going out tonight.

I want to know what he wants to talk to me about. Does he regret that night? Does he want to tell me it was just a pity orgasm? But I actually don't want to know the answer to these questions, I don't think I could handle hearing he regrets it, when for some fucked up reason that moment still means a lot. Something about Max taking another one of my firsts...I don't know, it just felt right. But it was so, *so* wrong and it's been so hard for me to look Sawyer in the eyes knowing what I did with her brother.

Which is why I'm excited for a night out with lots of alcohol and very little worrying about Max and all of these problems.

Let's get fucked up.

I WAS WRONG. SO VERY WRONG. TONIGHT GOT FUCKED up all right, and all because Max can't take a hint and has blown my phone up the entire time we've been at this bar. This time though, I haven't even opened them. I don't even want to acknowledge him right now.

"Who keeps texting you?" Gwen whispers in my ear.

We got here after the guys did, but they made sure to grab our usual table in the back by the pool tables and already had drinks ready for us when we arrived. Too bad none of these guys interest me. They're fucking sweet, but not my type.

My type happens to be about 6'2", dark hair, dark eyes with a panty-melting smile.

Oh, and don't forget he has to be a douchebag.

Apparently, I just have this desire to always go for the assholes who don't know how to treat women—both in and out of the bedroom. Well, until Max...but he's only nice in the bedroom, outside of it he's an asshole.

"Earth to Cassie," Gwen sing-songs before reaching for the plate of nachos.

"Shit, I'm sorry. I'm so distracted right now."

Chapter Seven

"Everything okay?"

"I mean, yeah. Everything is fine," I try to sound convincing, but of course my phone starts going off, this time a phone call.

Looking down at the table where my phone sits, I see Max's name lighting up my phone. I quickly try to decline the phone call before Gwen can see it but no luck.

"Why is Sawyer's brother calling you?" Gwen questions but is thankfully cut off when the boys return.

Harris and Cade come back to the table with another round of shots for us. Probably not the best idea for me to take another when we've already had four, but I'm not buying so I'm not complaining.

Although, I'll probably complain tomorrow.

"Hey ladies," Harris says with a smile as Cade just slides in the booth across from us. "We brought refreshments, you look parched."

"Not really sure tequila is the answer, but I'll take it," Gwen says with a laugh. "Where are Trevor and Miles?"

"They're playing another round with some girls. They'll be over, eventually."

"Not fighting the jukebox tonight?" Cade says, his gruff voice void of emotion, but that's kinda just who he is.

Cade is a quiet guy, until you get him to open up a bit. I've seen him with the guys enough to know that he lets loose and has fun when he's comfortable, but he's also happy just sitting back and enjoying everyone's company, not needing to always add to the conversations. I kind of love that about him.

"Not tonight, they've been playing decent songs so I'm letting them have it for the night."

"I guess. Your taste is better, though."

"What were you two ladies talking about?" Harris says as he slides in next to Cade.

"Oh nothing," I quickly stammer, but Gwen ignores me.

"Cassie was just about to tell us who's been blowing up her phone all night," Gwen says, completely ignoring the death glare I'm shooting her.

"It's no one."

"It's obviously not, you're ignoring them. Plus...you're kinda blushing. Wait. IS IT A GUY? You never date! Who is it?!" Gwen practically squeals as she grabs my phone, of course right as Max calls me again.

I try to avoid eye contact but can't help but look up to see her just staring at me, confusion written on her face. Thankfully, she's smart enough to not scream it. Although I'm sure she wanted to.

"Well boys, Cassie and I are gonna take a little walk to the bathroom. Save our shots." She winks before grabbing my hand and pulling me out of the booth towards the bathrooms.

I feel the guys' eyes on us as we walk away, but I just ignore it as I try to figure out what exactly to say to Gwen.

"Start explaining, now," she says as the bathroom door shuts behind us. Popping her butt up on the sink, she just sits and waits with a no-bullshit look on.

"There's nothing to explain!"

"Then why is our best friend's brother blowing up your phone?"

"Umm...it's complicated."

"Well uncomplicate it...spill."

"Uh...I don't even know where to start."

"The beginning."

"I've known them both for years so it's kind of complicated. But when their dad left, it messed them both up.

80

Chapter Seven

Sawyer and Max lost their close relationship when all of that went down. I blame their bitch of a mother. That conniving woman would make the devil seek out religion. I think Sawyer just tried to throw everything into her career with dancing while Max was younger and left to help their mom pick herself up...instead of the other way around. She was never there for them. Anyways...when Sawyer left for college after her injury, Max and I got close. We would hang out, text all the time, but never anything more. There might've been, but he kinda went off the deep end for a while, leaving me behind in the process."

"I always thought there was something between you two, but I never thought you two would have that much history.

"That's not even the worst part. We haven't actually really talked since, unless you count some basic politeness mixed with snide remarks. Until the party you dragged me to a couple of weeks ago.

"Fuck, I knew something was wrong when I couldn't find you. But I'm not going to lie, I was so drunk I only remember bits and pieces. I ended up crashing on the couch in the tv room."

"After he punched Fez in the face for stealing my clothes, I got into a pissing match with this redheaded bitch who kept trying to claim him when he wanted no part of it. After that, we sat by the fire outback drinking. Until, uh...he went down on me and gave me my first orgasm, from someone other than me, since I was seventeen-years-old."

"CASSIE!" Gwen shouts before covering her mouth when she realizes we're still in public.

"What?! I don't think a single woman would turn down a man as fucking hot as Max, especially if they offered that. Not me, for one. Especially not when it came with a mind-blowing orgasm that I'm pretty sure altered my brain chemistry. You know those smut books we read where the orgasms seem too good to be true-- like the guy just pulls it out of her and it completely consumes and overwhelms her? Yeah, those are real, at least it was with Max...he's a fucking tongue master."

"So, then what's happening now? Why aren't you answering the phone if you and him got along well?"

"We did NOT get along well. I still hate him, but that doesn't mean I can't be thankful for his mouth."

"Well why is he calling? Does he want a repeat?!" Gwen asks, a little too cheerfully for my liking.

I doubt that's what he wants, but the idea does sound a little intriguing. I'll blame it on the tequila, no way I'd be thinking like this without it.

"I don't know, I haven't opened the messages," I tell her honestly.

"Do it. Right now. I want to see."

"Fine, but only because I know once you get your mind on something, you refuse to budge. You're a stubborn woman."

"I'm aware, now do it."

Unlocking my phone I open the messages, now up to eight unread messages. But when I click his name, it's not the words that have me confused, it's the picture. It's from that night, out on the balcony, where all I am wearing is Max's t-shirt, and he...he is between my legs giving me that orgasm I just told Gwen about.

MAX

This is what I want to talk to you about. I didn't want to have to show you, but you won't respond to my messages, so this was my last resort.

We need to talk.

"Jesus Christ, Cass," Gwen murmurs.

"Fuck me," I groan. I don't even know what to say or what to think. A tiny part of me wonders if this is some sick game that one of his roommates did that he's using to get back at me? But a bigger part of me wonders if there's something going on...if someone is fucking with us. All I know is I guess I should probably talk to him

"You need to text him back, find out what's going on. Maybe it's something harmless and he's just being a dick, but...maybe there's something going on that you should know about. And you should probably find out before Sawyer finds out...because she might just kill you right now."

"Fine, when we get back to the table I will, I promise. I just want out of this bathroom." Turning around, I push open the bathroom door coming face-to-face with the red headed bitch from Max's. She's obviously drunk, she's got a sway that you only get from too much alcohol.

"Oh, it's *you*," Carina says, her nose scrunching up in disgust, her breath reeking of vodka. "It's Max's little whore. *For now*."

"Oh, it's you. Who's so dense she can't understand the word no," I reply back to her, my saccharine smile pissing her off further.

"Don't try to pretend you have any idea what that man needs. You're nothing," she snaps, getting angrier with every word she spits out. "Plus, I see you're out trolling the bar. I bet Max is already out there finding someone better. Stay the fuck away from him, he's mine."

"Did you hit your head or something? Or are you really just this fucking stupid? He doesn't want you, not here, not there, and definitely not in his bed naked. Take a hint. Besides Carina, he can't be yours when Max is already mine."

"Ugh. You think you're special just because he gave you attention one night?"

With perfect timing my phone rings, and the gods must be on my side, because it's Max, and this time I don't ignore it.

"Hey Max baby, how are you?" I say into the phone, loving the way her face immediately scrunches up in disgust. "I'm still out at Hudson's with Gwen and the guys. Hold on, I'm just trying to get away from your little cling-on," I say as I glare and I push past Carina to get out of the bathroom. The second we're out, Gwen bursts out laughing, and I follow suit, unable to hold mine in either.

That was fun.

Max starts to say something into the phone, but I ignore him until we're further away from her.

"Who were you talking about? Cling-on? Is everything okay?" Max asks, his voice picking up speed with every word.

"Chill out, Max, I'm fine. Your little friend, Carina felt the need to bitch at me tonight at the bar. She said I'm 'just your little whore and that you'll forget about me soon and go be with her'."

As I say it, I'm surprised how much I hate the idea of him doing just that. I know he's been with plenty of women, so why should I care if he does it now? But apparently, I do care because my stomach sinks at the idea.

"Hmm."

"Huh? That's all you have to say?"

"Just had to think about it. I like the sound of you being my little whore. Especially with that mouth you've told me so much about," Max says his voice low and gravely, but with enough humor laced in that I know he's giving me a hard time. Unfortunately, my pussy doesn't realize that as his voice sends heat straight to my core–the idea of being on my knees for him is exciting.

"What do you say, Princess? Be my little whore?" Max chuckles, his sexy laugh making me smile. Turning towards Gwen, I see she's watching me with an even bigger smile, listening to our entire conversation.

"Yeah, I'm ignoring that," I say as I take a seat at our table. "But I'll stop ignoring you. Apparently, you weren't lying and we should talk."

"No Max baby this time?"

"Nope, it was a one-time thing."

"Eh, I'll find a way to make it happen again, trust me. But yes, we do need to talk. Are you free now?"

"Fine, come and get me."

"Thanks, Cassie. I mean it."

Chapter Eight

Max

My life is one ginormous clusterfuck right now and all I can do right now is wade through the shit to try and make it out alive. Between trying to fix everything with Sawyer, while also dealing with whoever sent the pictures to my mother and I, I've barely had time for anything besides hockey.

I'm feeling so many emotions lately, but mainly? Mainly, I'm just disappointed in myself that I've spent years questioning my sister, believing our mother, instead of trusting the one person who's always been there for me.

Now, I've fucked up everything–including her relationship with Rex. Am I thrilled that her and my hockey coach were together? Absolutely not. But at the end of the day, I don't really get a say, it's not like Sawyer really has much trust in me or my opinion right now, so all I can do is be supportive and hope that I can help fix this.

Which is one of the reasons I met with Cassie. I want to be supportive, and I know I need help to fix this situation– even if I hate having to depend on other people, it's just an opportunity for them to let you down. The older I get, the more I realize just how much my parents fucked up how I see the world and how I see myself. Now, don't get me wrong, I'm in no way a saint and I'll take credit for the things I've fucked up. But at the end of the day, those two caused a lot of my damage.

Now I'm left attempting to fix the mess inside my head that *mommy and daddy dearest* left me. What a nice fucking parting gift. It'll probably take years of therapy and actually facing these problems head on instead of constantly having the urge to punch him in the face and telling her to go fuck herself.

My hate for my father is pretty cut and dry. He was an abusive asshole, even when I was too young to realize it. Sawyer was able to avoid it, almost entirely, because her training for ballet took her out of the house more often than not. But I witnessed a lot of it first-hand. He was always super controlling of our mother, refusing to let her do anything unless he okayed it first. She didn't work, was only allowed to spend time with certain people, and only got to spend the money my father allotted her. She was basically the trophy wife he didn't even like.

At first, she became super supportive of us, but eventually she started to resent us for him supporting us. She stopped caring about our dreams and instead of taking us to our games and practices and supporting us like the other parents, she would go out and meet with her friends for bottomless brunch—or sometimes she would go meet friends of the male variety. It was all fun and games until my father found out.

I remember one night he was so angry that I thought he was going to hit her. For the first time in my life, I saw my mother afraid, meek, spineless, just waiting for whatever he was going to do.

Yeah, I felt bad for her, but as a kid, it was her job to protect me, not the other way around. Thankfully, he never really laid his hands on her, at least not that I saw.

Now I see it for what it was, but back then, I just thought my father cared and just had a fucked-up way of showing it. I mean, he always made sure my sister and I were able to chase our dreams, but now I honestly think it was his way of getting us out of the house, giving him the freedom he craved. I later found out their marriage wasn't exactly a marriage. Basically, they got married because they got pregnant with Sawyer and stayed married because their parents would have disowned them if they had divorced.

But now that I'm not talking to either of them, I'm even more determined to fix everything with Sawyer, starting with her and Rex. Cassie agreed to help me, promised she'd make sure Sawyer attended the game tonight, dressed in Rex's old jersey, that Trevor was willing to "borrow" from Rex's office. I think he'll like seeing his girl with his name on her back. There's something about seeing someone you love, someone you care about wearing your name on their back, proudly representing you that just does something to your heart. Even if I hate that it's them together. But if we're being honest, I'd probably hate anyone my sister dated, at least with Rex, I know he's a good guy and a damn good dad so hopefully he treats her well.

So now that the game is over and we've done all of our interviews, we headed to the bar where some of the guys have already started the party, celebrating our win. The champagne is flowing, and the tequila shots are ready, promising a night full of fun and questionable choices. I'm sticking with my bourbon tonight, something I can sip on until I see everything play out between Rex and Sawyer. I was able to check in with him after the game. He congratulated me on my hat trick, which in a championship game was probably the highlight of my career, maybe even my life.

"Want a drink? I'm heading over to the bar," Paul says.

"Sure, will you just grab me a bourbon?"

"You got it." He nods, making his way over towards the bar that's already lined with thirsty puck bunnies. It doesn't take long before one starts talking with him, her hand resting on his bicep like she's holding herself up.

Thankfully I'm distracted from watching them when I notice the rest of the team has shown up, including Rex, who's looking around the bar until he spots me. Walking over, he's smiling, holding something in his hand that he immediately hands to me.

"What's this?" I ask, confused at the envelope he just handed me.

"It's an offer letter. If you're willing to drop out of the draft, there's an offer in that envelope to follow me to the Ice Hawks. I understand it's not the Cyclones, but I made a deal when they recruited me. I told them I'd only be willing if they gave you a competitive offer. I like your style. It reminds me of myself," Rex says smugly.

I'm in shock, just staring down at the letter, the impact of this moment not quite registering yet.

"Take a look at it whenever you want, but I think you'll like what you see inside," he adds.

Holy shit. Did he just really hand me an *NHL OFFER LETTER*?! A cocky smile breaks out of my face when I realize I've done it. If he's telling me the truth, I've made it into the NHL which has been my dream ever since I was a kid.

"You wanna take me with you, huh?"

"Oh, Jesus Christ, don't get all fucking emotional on me.

It's hockey, not a slumber party. Keep your damn clothes on," Rex deadpans, the corner of his lip almost curling into a smile.

I quickly rip open the envelope immediately scanning the offer. Holy shit, it's real. Rex really got me an official offer with the NY Ice Hawks.

"FUCK YEAH!" I shout, my fist pumping the air. "Looks like you're stuck with me for another five years, Coach." I smirk, loving the smile that Rex has stopped hiding. He's obviously stoked about this too.

"Is this official? Like, as long as I sign it?" I ask, wanting to go tell someone the news, but honestly I'm not sure who?

"Yep," he says, laughing as I immediately grab his pen and sign the letter before running off, his laughter following me through the crowd.

Who am I running to? My team? My friends on the team? Sawyer's here somewhere with Cassie, I could always go tell them? Somehow, with my running around the bar, I find myself at the back table where Cassie is actually sitting alone, staring at her phone, my sister nowhere to be found.

"Hey Princess," I say, startling her in the process, making her nearly spill her drink. "Shit, sorry I thought you saw me walk over."

"Well, clearly I didn't." She glares as she wipes up the little bit of her drink that spilled. "Decent game tonight."

"Decent? I'd say scoring a hat trick in our championship game makes it just a little better than just decent, but that's just me. Plus, it may have also earned me this." I smile, waving the envelope in front of her face.

"What's that?" Cassie asks, her curiosity getting the best of her.

"Oh, just an offer letter. From the NHL...specifically

the Ice Hawks," I start to say, and before I even finish, her arms are wrapped around my neck in a huge hug.

"I knew you could do it, I'm so proud of you," she whispers in my ear. I hug her back, enjoying the feeling of her holding me, the feeling of someone being proud of me. I didn't realize how much I needed this.

"Fucking finally. I knew they'd figure it out. I thought I was going to have to make a move and kiss her for Rex to finally pull his head outta your ass."

Turning to Harris, I flip him off. "That's my fucking sister, asshole," I grumble, only partially serious. In the time I'm talking to Harris, Cassie slipped away and made her way to the main table, stealing a tray of drinks.

"Don't act like you don't know what they're about to do, they're going to f—" Harris starts.

"Shut the—" I cut him off, but Sawyer thankfully interrupts.

Right then, Sawyer pulls back, laughing, and turns to face the boys with a smirk. "Hey, Max, wanna see if I can still kick your ass at pool?"

"You're on, sis. Teams?" I ask.

"I'm in," Rex says. "But I'm on her team." He laughs, as he points to Sawyer who's already walking over to the table.

When Cassie returns with drinks in hand, I immediately grab her, catching the tray before she drops it, laughing the entire time. "Deal. But Cassie's on my team."

"Uh, you know I'm fucking awful at this game, right? And why are you touching me?" she growls, but it's all bark, no bite.

"Doesn't matter. I'll do all the legwork, you just reap the benefits, Princess," I tell her with a wink, leaning in so only she can hear me. "Besides, we've got some talking to do, you still haven't told me if you're going to agree to the little plan." Pulling back, I smirk, loving the way the blush creeps up her neck, painting her cheeks with a light pink

"Besides, Princess, we're playing against a man with bright blue nail polish, I'm pretty sure we'll beat them." I laugh, poking fun at Rex.

Rex laughs at me, shaking his head. "Eh, whatever, man, Rory's a persuasive little thing, at this point I just do as I'm told–it's easier that way. You just wait until you have daughters. I'm sure you'll have your hair in pigtails and makeup all over."

I love giving him a hard time about Rory painting his nails, although I'd expect nothing less. I've only met her a handful of times but she's so damn cute, you'd have to be a complete jackass to tell her no.

"Shit, Rex. I'll put makeup on him. I bet he'd look so pretty." Cassie laughs as she pinches my cheek. Her touch isn't anything special, but the moment her fingers brush my cheek, I feel the electricity flowing through my body. God, I crave her fingers on my body. Which is another reason I hope she agrees. After she told me that she told Carina I was hers, I had an idea. If we pretended to date, we could probably make everything go away. I won't have to deal with Carina, plus the pictures wouldn't be as big of a deal because we could just argue that someone took a private moment between a couple and are spreading it around. I still need to figure out who sent it, but at least this way, we'd be getting ahead of everything.

When we get to the table, Sawyer already has everything all set up, and she passes the cue stick to break. I'm about to get into position when Cassie's voice stops me.

"Wait, wait!" she shouts. "If y'all are making me play, let's at least make a bet. Hmm, Max, what should we bet? Drinks?"

"Nah, boring. Losers have to give a lap dance to a song of the winner's choice." Harris smirks

"Fine, but the guys are doing it this time," Sawyer says with a wink.

Looking around at everyone chuckling, I just shake my head. "I don't wanna know." I break to start the game and immediately get three solids right away, and within the first round, I have all but two balls in the holes, one of which is the eight ball.

The rest of the game goes quickly. Sawyer may be fucking killer at this game, but she learned everything she knows from me. Within two rounds, I've finished our game without breaking a sweat, and obviously without any actual help from Cassie, well except for standing there looking fucking hot.

"That was fucking impressive," Rex says with a laugh.

"I told you, he's the one who taught me how to play," Sawyer says, like she's used to it.

"Time to pay up, suckers. Sawyer, sit," Cassie demands, and surprisingly, my sister actually listens. "And you, big boy. Get ready."

Gwen, their other friend, is over at the jukebox changing the song for them. As soon as it starts though, I have to laugh. The idea of my coach giving a lap dance to *Latto's* "Big Dick Energy" is enough to have us all laughing and the rest of the guys joining in to watch.

"Come on, big boy! Dance for us. Show your woman your moves," Trevor jokes.

"Shut it, man. At least let me get used to them before you start making fucking sex jokes," I growl.

"Oh, pull the dildo out of your ass, Max," Cassie says, defending Trevor. "Don't be so fucking uptight. People have sex. We all do. It's fucking fun."

Chapter Eight

I see the moment she regrets her statement. I'm torn between kissing this woman or bending her over my knee—both of which confuse the fuck out of me.

I don't kiss women, at least not on their mouth.

The thought alone has me reaching for one of the tequila shots Cassie brought over and immediately shooting it back, the idea of sipping bourbon only tonight thrown out the window. What is it about her that makes me want to change everything for her? Why does she have this pull over me, making me crave things I've never wanted before?

Shaking my head, I quickly snap myself out of my daydream.

"I'll be back, I'm running to the bathroom," I lean in and whisper to Cassie.

"Why are you telling me? Need me to hold your hand or something?"

"No, but I've got something else you can hold for me," I add, before turning and walking away, ignoring her scoff.

You'd think a bathroom break would be quick, get in and out, just worrying about getting your business done. Not tonight. Everywhere I turn there's someone wanting to congratulate me, buy me a drink, and that's not even half of it. There are women everywhere, some wearing tiny little outfits, in our team colors, of course. Because you can't dress like a skank just because–you have to at least try to make it festive.

Jesus Christ.

I'm never having kids, specifically not daughters. I'm not cut out for that shit. I'd end up in jail. You know the scene in *Bad Boys* 2 where his daughter is going on a date, and they threaten him a bit? Yeah, that's going to be me if I have ever had a daughter. She won't be dating until she's thirty, or I'm dead. But even then, I'd haunt any guy trying to date her.

"Hey handsome, good game tonight," a voice says from behind me, turning around I see that it's Carina's friends... but I still have no idea what her name is.

"Thanks, the team played great."

"They did, but they wouldn't have been anything without you. The goals were incredible, and that cat trick you got was incredible," she says with a smile and her hand comes forward to grip my bicep.

"Cat trick?"

"Yeah, the three goals you scored?"

"I think she means hat trick," a voice I recognize says from behind us. When arms wrap around my waist and she squeezes into my side, I know she must recognize her as Carina's friend.

When I look down at Cassie, she gives me a subtle wink before looking back at the girl whose hand was still on my other arm.

"Ugh, why is she here?"

"She's here with me," I say, bringing my arm around her shoulder, ignoring the daggers now coming our way as she finally moves her hand off of my arm. "Cassie, this is...uh..."

"Ugh, it's Sandra. Carina isn't going to like this, she's been waiting for you to show up."

"That sounds like a personal problem for her," I grumble before looking back down at Cassie. "Ready to go take another shot, Princess? I'm feeling parched."

"Yes, sir. Lead the way." She winks before turning to look at Sandra. "Tell Carina not to wait up for him, he'll be busy celebrating with me tonight."

Walking away from Sandra, I do my best to not laugh although Cassie immediately starts laughing the second we get to the bar. Thankfully, the bartender is already there so we order our tequila shots right away.

"She was so fucking pissed." She laughs as the bartender comes back with our shots. "I thought smoke was going to come out of her ears at one point. Why does she even care if it's Carina that wants you?"

"Uh, that's the thing. They both do. Those two are all about sharing, and sometimes they get in on the action together. I'm never one to judge, don't get me wrong, but that's just not my cup of tea."

"What isn't? Girls together?"

"Ha-ha, no. I'm all for watching two girls enjoying each other. But that's just it, I only like to watch that. I don't like to share, at all. It makes me feel murdery. When I'm with a woman, I want her all to myself, even if it's just for the night, or for an hour. So, their little proposition does nothing for me."

"Good to know."

"So...uh, does this mean you've made up your mind? Because if so, we should probably let Sawyer in on our little charade before she kicks me in the dick or something. Especially because I think that's the only part of me you actually like."

Her swallow is audible, her eyes darkening from the memories of my mouth between her legs, but with a quick shake of her head, she's snapped out of it and is reaching for her shot. "I like your mouth too–when it's doing things other than talking. But yeah...I guess I'm agreeing to your offer. On one condition. *YOU* have to talk to your sister."

With a quick *cheers*, we both shoot our tequila down quickly before turning to go find the rest of the group. Thankfully Sawyer is happy as a clam tonight so maybe she won't castrate me when I talk to her.

Chapter Nine

Cassie

Sawyer is graduating next weekend, which means it's almost the end of the school year. Unfortunately for me, all this means for me is more annoyance from my father about interning at his firm, all while I wait to hear back from the internship I actually applied for.

I know what they say about not putting all your eggs in one basket, but it's my dream internship and honestly, the *only* one I've ever dreamed of doing so I only applied to the one. At least if I don't get it, I can finally take my father up on his offer.

My parents have been constantly texting me after I missed an appointment they scheduled for me with his firm. I guess it was supposed to be my interview for the internship, but I'm refusing to think about working for him unless it's my one and only option.

Which is part of the reason I accepted Max's deal. He told me about the pictures, how one was sent to him and another was sent to his mom. We don't know if they were sent to anyone else, and after he spoke with Rex, he mentioned that teams frown upon this kind of publicity just because it takes away from the actual sport. But if it looks like a violation of our privacy, an intimate moment between a couple, well that's a whole different story.

Which I completely understand with everything I've learned about PR, it's all about how you flip the narrative, make the story work for you. Unfortunately for us, that involves us dating, fake dating, but dating nonetheless. I don't want to piss off the PR people before I even get my foot in the door, so I agreed to the charade.

Besides, now I really get to watch Carina get angry, and that alone is exciting.

Looking back down at my phone, I reread their messages one last time before deciding to close it out without a response. My mother is starting to be more demanding, trying to force my hand and I'm just not in the mood for it. I had to agree to dinner in a couple weeks, thankfully they were going on vacation for three weeks, so it bought me some time to continue avoiding them.

I've spent the last couple of hours perched on our lounge chairs on the patio listening to *Morgan Wallen* serenade me, all while scouring the internet for other possible internships, in case this one falls through. The problem is that nothing sounds interesting enough to make me want to work there every single day, I'm pretty sure I would die of boredom. I have no desire to do PR for a law firm or politicians, the idea of working in a stuffy building with misogynistic men who want to tell everyone what to do, makes me want to quit when I don't even work there.

My cell phone in my lap buzzes again, hopefully this time, it's just Sawyer letting me know she's on her way back with lunch and not another stupid text from my mom.

SAWYER

Hey, I'm grabbing us tacos then I'll be on my way. Don't worry, I won't forget to grab your extra chips and Salsa.

ME

Thank God. I'm about to perish. I'm so hungry. But wait, why tacos? Are you bribing me? Is something going on? WHO'S DYING?

SAWYER

You're dramatic.

ME

Don't act surprised. You've known me since I was 7. I'm withering away, so please hurry home. Also, if you're bringing me tacos for a reason, make sure to lead with the tacos.

SAWYER

Noted.

I'm about to put my phone down when I realize I have another text. Opening it, I see it's Max again. He's nothing, if not persistent.

MAX

I spoke with my sister, she completely understands and is all for me dating her best friend.

ME

FAKE dating.

MAX

Semantics.

ME

You're incorrigible.

I hate that I get a little bit excited when I see a text from him. There's a little voice in the back of my head telling me that maybe, *just maybe*, he's changed. Maybe this can actually matter between us this time, even if it starts as something fake.

But the last time I listened to that voice I got my heart broken. Now, I'm left with pieces of tape holding up my cracked and broken heart and I'm doing everything I can just to keep it all together. The thought of helping Max out, letting him in, letting him get close enough to hurt me is enough to nearly send me back in time, back to being devastated and broken.

I don't know how long I stay on the patio staring off into space, but the next thing I know, Sawyer is walking out with a bag full of the best carnitas tacos here in the city, a little place called Crazy Tacos that I'd literally die for.

"Hey. Here's your tacos, don't worry, I didn't forget your extra salsa."

Snatching them from her, I immediately open the bag of chips and salsa and dive in, the warm crunchy tortilla chips melting on my tongue with the hot salsa. Fuck, this is food porn at its finest.

"Thank you, I needed this," I groan as I bite into the first taco, looking up to see Sawyer just staring at me. "Oh fuck, did you bring me tacos actually because you need to talk?"

"I mean, kind of," Sawyer says nervously.

"Did something happen? Is someone dying? Are you okay? Are you mad about Max and I?" I stammer out, my nerves immediately getting the best of me.

"I mean, yeah, we need to talk, but I promise, I don't care about you and Max. I understand what you are doing... I understand you're helping him out," Sawyer says, her hand rubbing down her legs, a nervous tick she does when she's really anxious. "I'm just going to say it. That's the only way I'll tell you."

"You're freaking me out." Did she find out it was me in the picture?

"Rex asked me to move in with him and I said yes," Sawyer says, her eyes focused on her lap, refusing to look at me. "I know we still have our lease through October, and I know this isn't ideal, but I told Rex that I would move in with him as long as you are able to find someone for this summer...I know Max hates where he's living right now, maybe you could help each other out? If he moved in here, I mean, that might help with appearances...right?."

Am I sad? Of course, Sawyer is my best friend and the only roommate I've ever had, so thinking about living with someone new makes me sad. On the other hand though, I'm happy for them. They're so in love it's disgusting so the thought of them moving in together is enough to make me giddy.

"We'll figure it out, girl! I'm so happy for you! When did he ask you? Tell me everything."

"Wait...really? You're sure? You're not mad at me?"

"No? Why would I be mad? You're so happy and I love seeing you this happy, Sawyer. Seriously, you've been through enough, and now you've found happiness with Rex and girl, that's enough to make me happy, too. Even if it means I'll have to live with your dickhead of a brother."

"I love you, Cassie. Thank you. You're the best bad bitch anyone could ever want on their team."

"Love you too. Now spill, I want all the details."

"Okay. But uh, we don't have much time."

"Why not?"

"We're going back to Rex's with everyone for dinner

tonight. He wanted to have a big "family" dinner to tell everyone about us moving in together."

"Isn't it not happening until summer?"

"Yeah. But honestly, I think he's just so excited about it that he wants to tell everyone so they can be excited for him too. It's actually cute if you think about it."

"Aw, Daddy Rex is excited. That is pretty cute...is Max going to be there?" I smirk.

"Yep, Rex is talking to him while I am here, giving him a heads up so he doesn't go postal when finding out his sister is going to be shacking up with him."

"Fair point."

We spent the next hour just chatting, sitting out on the patio, and finishing our lunch. Sawyer told me all about her conversation with Rex, what plans they have and then worked on convincing me that maybe living with Max might not be all that bad, if one of us doesn't kill each other first.

Fingers crossed I don't end up in jail or on the news.

Chapter Ten

Cassie

Rex's place is nice. It's big enough that there's enough room for our big group of friends, but not too big that it's ridiculous for him and Rory, well soon to be Sawyer too.

After Sawyer and I got ready this afternoon, the two of us headed over to his place to help him get everything ready for dinner. Thankfully, Rex is barbecuing so we were just helping him with the sides. When Gwen came over, she brought her famous macaroni and cheese, and Stella came carrying freshly baked rolls as well as enough baked desserts for all of us to get diabetes but fuck it. Sugar is life and that's a hill I'll gladly die on.

The guys, of course, only brought drinks–mainly beer and whiskey but Trevor and Max were smart enough to bring enough Tequila that the girls and I will be just fine.

"Uncle Trevor! Uncle Maxy! You're here!" Rory shouts from the living room, immediately running to the door as they come in. She latches herself to Max's leg and sits down on his foot, making him carry her the rest of the way in.

If he wasn't such an annoying pain in my ass, I would

probably think it's adorable. Okay, that's a lie. It's still cute as fuck, I just refuse to ever let him know I think that.

Max carries her all the way into the kitchen before finally stopping to peel her off his leg. Kneeling down, he waits until they are at eye level before he starts talking to her, her entire face lighting up. Another thing that if he wasn't such a prick, I would probably think is cute. "Hey, little Ro. How's my favorite girl doing?" Max asks, a boyish grin on his face when he talks to her.

I'm not sure why this surprises me, Max has always been good with kids. Back in high school, one of my favorite things to do was watch Max coach the little kids in hockey. The patience he had with them, and just the way he would interact with them, I could've watched it all day. It was that adorable.

"I'm good, Uncle Maxy! Did you bring me anything?"

"Rory, you can't just start hounding people to bring you something every time they come over."

"No daddy, I know that that would be rude. But Uncle Maxy is different, he always brings me something special."

Rex just rolls his eyes, knowing we are all lost with this girl. She's so damn cute, she has each of these big, bad hockey men wrapped around her tiny little finger.

"Well, you're in luck. Today, I brought you two things. The first is your favorite juice, I figured since we were in charge of refreshments, I should make sure that you were covered too."

"Thank you!" Rory squeals as she wraps her arms around his neck. "What's the second thing?"

"Sawyer told me you loved painting your nails, so I figured I would get you a new color. But don't worry, I made sure it has sparkles."

Rory's eyes light up like it's Christmas morning, and I'll

be damned if it's not the cutest thing I've ever seen. Watching Rory and Max talk together and the patience and love he already has for her, it amazes me how strong their bond is already, but I love it.

"See, Daddy! I told you Uncle Maxy is different! He's going to let me paint his nails BLUE!" she shouts with excitement while Max just laughs.

"That one fucking backfired on you, didn't it?" Rex whispers to Max with a laugh.

"Eh, fuck it. Guess I get to be like you, Coach. Get a manicure and have pretty fingernails." Max shrugs, giving Rory a little wink that makes her giggle before running off.

He attempts to come talk to me, but I do a good job of avoiding him, grabbing Sawyer to pull her back in the kitchen to finish setting up dinner.

By the time everyone has eaten and put themselves into a food coma, Rory is ready to paint Max's nails and it's the best thing I've ever seen. Not only is it adorable that Rory is so excited about painting someone's nails, but it makes my ovaries hurt watching her with Max. He's so good with her, even if he tries to be all big and bad.

"Ro, are you sure we can't do clear? I mean, hell, even a blue color without all that glittery shit?" Max groans from the floor, earning a laugh from the rest of us.

"That's a daddy word, you're not supposed to say that," Rory tells him, not even looking up as she sits across from him on the floor painting his nails. "And no, Uncle Maxy. The glittery sparkles make the color, besides it's sooo you, don't you think?"

"Rory, I agree. I think the sparkles are just a perfect fit for Max," I chuckle, earning me an adorably boyish smile from Max.

Harris and Cade start laughing, obviously enjoying the

"torture" Max is enduring at the hands of a cute five year old. After Rory's birthday last month when she picked out a hot pink nail color for Rex, Max hasn't let him live it down, so I think this is some version of poetic justice. Rex is getting his payback in the form of his cute little five year old. Rory has taken to calling Max her uncle which is probably the cutest damn thing I've ever heard. Watching them bond and get close makes my heart happy and my ovaries want to burst, even if he is still a huge pain in my ass.

"I think he meant a grown up word, I think it'll be okay, Ro," Max tells her, patiently watching as Rory does her best to paint his nails.

"Stop moving, Uncle Maxy. I'm getting the color everywhere."

"Sorry, little Ro," Max says, chuckling as he gets scolded by a little girl. I watch him look up and scan the room, his eyes finding us girls as we sit on the couch talking. He offers me a soft smile before turning back to Rory.

We've been sitting here in Rex's living room since we finished dinner, just laughing, and watching some random movie they put on TV.

I'm so happy for Sawyer that she's going to be moving in here with Rex, but it's also sad. Her and I have lived together all through college and it just feels like an era is ending, and it sucks.

I watch as Rex walks up behind Sawyer, wrapping her arms around her waist and pulling her in close. These two are perfect for each other. Rex looks over Sawyer's shoulder with a smirk at Max. "Your nails look beautiful, Max. You should always have sparkles, maybe do the Ice Hawks colors next, I'm sure the guys would dig it."

Max just laughs, shaking his head with a subtle eye roll,

all while Rory smiles proudly. As soon as Rory looks back down, Max flips him off with a laugh.

"All done!" Rory exclaims proudly, her smile wide and her cute little face beaming. "Uncle Maxy, go show everyone your pretty nails. They'll love them so much."

Standing up, Max looks down at his nails which are bright blue. She did paint his nails, but she also painted around the nails and the tips of his fingers in the process. He does a good job of telling her how much he loves them though, which only makes her happier.

When he walks over to the guys, I love that they all make a big show of oohing and aahing at his nails. Whether to give him a hard time or to make Rory smile, I have no idea. Either way, I love the way she beams, and he blushes.

Just then, Sawyer and Rex make their way back into the kitchen, leaving me alone on the couch, drinking my wine. My peace and quiet ends though as soon as Max notices though, as he immediately makes a beeline for me on the couch, a smug grin plastered on his face that immediately tells me he's up to no good.

Fuck me.

"Hey, Princess," he smirks, as he sits next to me on the couch. I hate that I love the way he's always called me Princess, even when we hate each other.

"Why do you call me that?" I ask, never truly under-standing why it started, just always loving how special it's made me feel.

"It just suits you, you've always been Princess to me," he answers, almost looking bashful. "You've been ignoring me today. Did Sawyer talk to you?"

"She did. She also told me that Rex was talking to you."

"Well... have you thought about it? I know living

together isn't necessarily ideal...but it could help solve a lot of problems," Max says nervously.

"Problems that you got yourself into."

"I seem to remember you being there that night too, Princess," he snaps back, catching me off guard. "Besides, weren't you saying that your father keeps threatening to cut you off if you don't go and work for him? This way, that threat wouldn't be hanging over your head. If I moved in, it wouldn't be a concern, with or without the internship."

I mean, he's not wrong. If I don't get the internship, I'd have no choice but to go work for my father unless I'm okay being a bum on the streets with no money. But if he moved in with me, he'd be able to help out until I found a different option for work. Rookies don't make millions, but they make plenty to afford an apartment in the city.

"What are you two talking about?" Sawyer asks as she plops down on the couch, practically on top of Cassie as she squeezes herself in between the two of us.

"Me moving in with Cassie," Max says before I can change the subject.

"Of course, I think that's a great idea. Although, please let's not talk about the picture or video again. I *definitely* don't want to think about my baby brother getting handsy with someone."

I shift uncomfortably at the mention of the picture. Although she knows it's Max in it, we avoided telling her that I was the girl in it. I know Max and Rex had to have a conversation about it, but he said that'd be something we'd need to tell her when the time is right.

"Yep, thanks for reminding me of exactly what happened, sis, Definitely couldn't have remembered that night without that little reminder," Max says with a laugh as Sawyer just moves the conversation along.

"So are you going to do it?" Sawyer finally asks, I wonder if she would be so unbothered by this topic if she knew it was me, her best friend, in the video with her brother. He played it off that it was his playboy reputation he was worried about, and this would help him clean that up. Honestly, I'm thankful for that–he's protecting me by not telling her, so I guess we truly are both helping each other out.

"Well, I guess. But doesn't it seem like a bad idea?" I ask honestly, truthfully wanting her opinion.

"I think it's a good idea," Sawyer says. "It'll help you both out, plus you guys are comfortable with each other, you've known each other for years. It's a win-win, if you ask me."

"Why did I think you'd hate the idea?" Max asks, clearly unbothered by anything knowing that he has his sister on his side.

"You can't be serious, Sawyer. How is this a good idea?" I ask.

"Well, Cassie, you need a roommate, this would be perfect for you. You wouldn't have to post a creepy *Craigslist* ad and pray to God that you don't get that guy like Chandler had in that *Friends* episode. You know the one I'm talking about? Where Chandler would wake up in the middle of the night and the dude was just in his room watching him sleep? Yeah, fuck that shit. Besides, if you really want to play the fake dating card, it'd make the most sense that he moves in with you. It's not forever, it can be short lived, but it is the best option you have."

"Well. Yeah...I'm still not convinced. Serial killer guy still sounds like the better choice, who knows, maybe he'd have a nice dick," I say, before turning to Max and glaring. "If we're doing this, we're doing it my way."

Cassie

"Yes, ma'am. You can take charge, in or outside the bedroom." He winks before standing up from the couch. "Let's meet for coffee on Monday. It can be our first date, we'll figure out everything there.

"Fine, but you're buying me breakfast, too. I want all of it."

"Anything you want, Princess."

"Gross. I did not need to hear that," Sawyer says a disgusted look on her face. "Cassie, are you ready to go drink some tequila now?"

By seven a.m. Monday morning, I'm up and ready to go to the cafe. Trust me, I'm in no way a morning person, but I was so stressed about meeting Max at the coffee shop that I could barely sleep. Instead, I spent a stupid amount of time figuring out what to wear and perfecting my hair and makeup. It may not be an actual date, but I still want to look hot if people think we're together.

I'm not sure what's making me so nervous, but I'm fucking stressed. It's not like Max and I have never been alone together; it's just that it's been such a long time since we've sat down and talked about anything real.

I don't count the night of the party, we may have been alone, but we were doing a whole lot more than just talking.

I still can't quite believe this is happening, that both Max and Sawyer think this is a good idea and somehow convinced me to let him move in with me as my fake boyfriend. Although, I guess we wouldn't be in this situation in the first place, if I hadn't gotten drunk at the party and thought him eating me out where anyone could see was a good idea.

But I mean, if it weren't me, it probably would've been another girl, and I think I hate that idea even more.

My brain keeps telling me that I can't trust him, that we haven't been friends for a long, long time. But my heart? My heart still remembers how, at one point, he was everything to me. Even if I never got the chance to tell him.

The easiest part is that we've always had chemistry, an intense relationship that no one could deny. We were best friends, and even after everything happened, you still couldn't deny the remaining chemistry. I think the only person who didn't see it was Sawyer. Thank God for that.

When I get to the café, I still have time until he's supposed to be here, so I get in line to grab a coffee before I go find a table to sit down at.

"Hi," I hear a voice say quietly behind me.

Spinning around, I smile, not expecting him to be here so early, let alone at a table full of every breakfast option this place has, plus two coffees. God, he looks so handsome this morning, decked out in a black Ice Hawks sweatshirt with messy hair, and his panty-melting smile on full display. I can't help but stare for a moment before snapping out of it and heading toward him.

"Hi," I muster, unable to think of anything more intelligent at the Moment.

God, I hate how attractive he is.

"Caffeine before we talk," I grumble as I sit down across from him.

"Good to know nothing's changed. Here's your Americano with one sugar and cream," he says, passing me one of the cups.

"You remember?"

"Of course, Princess. I remember everything about you."

Cassie

I remember everything about him too. I just never expected that something so mundane would've made an impression on him. Especially considering how easily he threw it all away.

I sit back and stare at the food, taking little pieces of everything and trying them. The cinnamon roll is the most delicious thing I've ever eaten.

"So...are we going to talk, or are you just going to sit here and moan over baked goods?"

"Um, if you have that attitude, I'm definitely going to sit here and moan over baked goods. I'm pretty sure this cinnamon roll could bring me to orgasm, don't make me test it."

His brow raises, and I quickly get embarrassed and look down at my coffee.

Raising his hands, he chuckles. "I don't think this café could handle your screams. Let's save that for behind closed doors."

"Had we done that the first time we wouldn't be in this predicament," I murmur, and I'm surprised when he chuckles.

Without thinking, I blurt out the question playing in my mind. "Why me?" I ask, one hand still on my coffee cup while the other mindlessly spins my plate around and around, keeping my focus.

"You're gonna have to be a bit more specific if you want me to know what you're talking about," he responds.

"Why do you want to fake date me?" I whisper, my voice so quiet I'm surprised he can hear me.

"Why not? It's you. I know you, you know me. It'll be easy."

"Will it, though? It shouldn't be this easy."

"But it is. What do you think the problem is, Cass?"

"The problem is that we hate each other. Why would we willingly choose to act like we're in love or whatever?" I say, fumbling my words, doing everything I can to avoid eye contact with him. It sucks because I'm afraid if I do, I'm going to fall deeper and deeper into this trap and fuck up by catching feelings.

"Look, it's just a couple of months, and it'll help us both out. Once you finish your internship and get your job, it'll be easy for you to get your own place. It'll give you stability if your parents decide to be dicks and take the apartment you're in now, and it'll make sure both of our reputations remain clean in case the video goes out to more than just myself and my Mom. I doubt she'd do anything with it, but I don't trust her as far as I can throw her anymore."

"Why would you help me? Especially after everything between us?" I ask, honestly confused why he's being so . . . sweet.

"Because everyone deserves to choose their own path. Even brats like you," Max says, adding a little wink at the end.

"Well, we need ground rules," I stress. "That's the only way this will work."

"Okay. Whatcha thinking?"

"No kissing, no touching, and absolutely without a doubt, no sex."

"How the fuck can we expect someone to believe we're dating if we don't touch? Don't be ridiculous. We can hold hands, touch, hug, all that fun stuff," he throws out.

"Fine. But no kissing and no sex."

"I'm fine with no kissing. I don't kiss anyway. But when you beg me to fuck you, don't blame me when I turn you down."

"Fat chance, dickhead. That's what Kyle is for."

"Who the fuck is Kyle?" Max asks, jaw clenched as his hands ball into fists.

"Slow your roll, turbo. Kyle is my handy dandy vibrator. He's the perfect man. Doesn't talk, doesn't mess up, and he makes sure I cross that line. Every. Single. Time.

"We both know that's a bald-faced lie. Don't pretend my mouth isn't better. And, Princess, it may have been years, but we both know my cock is better too."

"The only time I like your mouth is when it's quiet," I snap, but realize my mistake immediately when he smirks at me.

"Why don't you sit on my face then, Princess. You can keep me quiet, and I can prove just how much better my mouth is than 'Kyle'."

"Ugh, you're such a pig," I groan. "But look, I've gotta get to class. I'm not sure why I thought summer school was a good idea, but here we are. Do we have a deal?"

"We have a deal," Max says, standing up and pulling me into a hug. With a quick kiss on the top of my head, he waves me off. I'm left wondering what the fuck I just got myself into. "Oh, I meant to ask you. Rex was trying to surprise Sawyer with a date night this weekend. He asked if you and I would mind hanging out with Rory until his Mom can grab her. Rory asked for us both." He grins.

"Of course, let him know it's no problem. We can take her out for something fun."

"Sounds good. Have a good day, Princess," he says with a smirk.

Max is infuriating, sexy, and the biggest pain in the ass I've ever met.

But by the beginning of August, he'll be my new roommate.

Oh, and my boyfriend.

Chapter Ten

"Uncle Maxy, where are you taking us?" Rory asks from her brand-new car seat in the back of his truck.

"It's a surprise, little Ro, but I promise you'll like it."

When we went to pick Rory up from her house, Max had surprised all of us by already having the car seat in his truck. This man actually went out and bought a car seat, then took it to the fire station and had them help him install it.

He's so damn sweet it's infuriating.

"Ugh! Waiting is no fun." Rory adorably pouts from the backseat, but I can't focus on anything except how Max looks as he drives us to get ice cream.

He's in his typical outfit of faded black jeans that are molded perfectly to his body, showing off his strong, powerful leg muscles. His crisp white t-shirt is so white it looks brand new, which is surprising since his shirt is already putting in work, stretching to accommodate his massive biceps.

It's even worse watching his muscles flex as he grabs his baseball hat off the dash of his truck and puts it on. Backwards. It's like the man is purposely torturing me, trying to make himself as irresistibly annoying as possible, which is confirmed when we make eye contact, and he sneaks a wink before looking back at the road. That move alone has turned me into a pile of mush, electricity flowing through me, my body reacting to every little thing this man does. His devilish grin shoots shocks directly to my core.

God, I bet he could pick me up, slam me into the wall and fuck me without even blinking an eye. I clench my thighs, hoping to alleviate at least some of the ache, my clit throbbing just from the thought of it. Him and his stupid body. But tonight isn't about us. I mean, yeah, we're using this little outing as a "date" on social media, but besides that, it's just a fun time with Rory and her Uncle Maxy until Mrs. Lockwood meets us to take Rory for the night.

When he pulls up to the curb right outside of Sprinkles —the best make-your-own ice cream sundae place in the city—Rory squeals.

"Guess you made the right call, big boy," I chuckle, looking at him as a big, toothy smile breaks out on his face.

It's not his usual boyish grin or the devilish smirk he loves to shoot in my direction when he's feeling naughty and wants to give me a hard time. No, this is just pure joy that he can't contain. Shouldn't contain. It's so pure, so happy, that it feels like an electric shock to my heart. It's stirring up feelings and emotions and memories that I locked away all those years ago. The part of my heart that has always been his that is slowing thawing.

I'm fucked.

"Did I make the right call, little Ro?" Max asks with a smile, but I know he still wants to hear her say it.

"Yes! Uncle Maxy! This is my favorite place, like, ever! THEY HAVE RAINBOW SPRINKLES."

"That they do. We'll make sure you get as many sprinkles as your little heart can handle," Max says proudly.

Hopping out of the car, he runs around to my side, before I can even unbuckle my seat belt, opening my door with a smile. Helping me down from his truck, he walks me over to the sidewalk before helping Rory out too, where she promptly leads him directly to the door, practically running inside. Watching him interact with Rory is adorable. He's so sweet, so attentive, and just so perfect with her that all I can think about is one day, this man will be a great daddy. The best daddy. And fuck, the thought of some girl, someone who doesn't know him like I do, giving him that, makes me want to scream. It makes me want to tell him that this may be fake for him, but I'm starting to think I may not want it to be.

The second it crosses my mind, I feel like I'm at a circus. My brain starts waving red flags, and all the alarms go off, telling me it's not a risk I should take. At least not yet. For now, I'm just going to see what happens.

By the time I make it inside Sprinkles, Max and Rory have already filled up their bowls and are adding a generous helping of sprinkles to hers. I go to grab a bowl, but Rory's sweet voice stops me.

"Cassie! We already got you one," Rory says, a cute chocolate-covered smile on her face already.

"What'd you get me?" I ask, heading over to them, unable to stop the smile slowly creeping out.

"Uncle Maxy said you loved the peanut butter chocolate chip ice cream, so we got you that. He said it was your favorite, like, ever."

It is. It always has been.

"Well, your Uncle Maxy is pretty smart. It is my favorite. But I love it with—"

"Extra fudge and whipped cream, then two cherries on top to make it pretty," Max finishes for me, practically word for word of what I was about to say.

"You remembered."

"Of course, I remember, Princess. I already told you, I remember everything about you."

By the time we've paid and found a booth to sit at, I feel like my brain is spinning. Max is being kind, attentive, and so sweet. And not just to Rory either. He's making this fake relationship feel a whole lot more real.

"Cassie! Look!" Rory snaps me out of my daydream, yet

again, to watch her eat a bite of her ice cream covered in a million sprinkles. She's adorable. She got cotton candy ice cream with chocolate sauce and sprinkles. It may not be my cup of tea, but she's five, so who can blame her for wanting her ice cream to be pretty?

I laugh when she looks back up, and her whole face is covered in chocolate.

"We need some napkins, little Ro," Max says with a smile.

"I can get them," I say, standing up and heading to the register. Grabbing a bunch, I turn back around and am met face-to-face with Satan herself.

"You're in my way," she seethes, spewing her venomous words directly at me, as she stands hand in hand with a smirking Fez.

"My apologies, Your Grace." I smile, finishing with a dramatic bow which only seems to piss her off even further, especially when Fez laughs.

"I see you've still got him tricked into thinking you're worth his time."

"And I see you're still just a bitter bitch who wants to blame anyone other than herself for Max seeing right through your little charade." Smiling sweetly, I walk right past her back to our table, where Max watches me with concerned eyes.

"What was that?" he demands as I kneel by Rory to clean her up a bit.

Looking back, I smile, and see her still glaring in our direction, only now she's making her way over to our table, leaving Fez behind typing on his phone.

"Oh, just Carina being Carina, like always. Thinking the whole world revolves around her."

Max rolls his eyes, pulling Rory's chair closer to him as Carina stops at our table.

"You really should keep your bitch on a leash. You'll never believe the things she just said to me," Carina spits out, obviously not caring enough about the kid here to watch her language.

"I've tried, but she's just so feisty and protective that it's more fun for me to watch her attack," Max says, his eyes twinkling with laughter as he leans back in his chair, ignoring the bite still on his spoon.

Leaning back, I open my mouth, and without a word, he feeds me his bite of ice cream. Holding back a moan at the creation he made, I laugh when Rory breaks the silence.

"What's wrong with her face?" Rory asks Max honestly. He's quick to cover up his laugh with a fake cough, which Carina chooses to ignore.

"What do you mean?" Carina snaps back.

"Your nose . . . it's so scrunched up like you smell something stinky. It makes you look angry cause your eyebrows crunch in too. Is that why you're so grumpy?"

"Ugh! Kids!" Carina shrieks as she turns around and leaves the store. We watch her leave and practically howl with laughter.

It's funny—what could have ruined the night actually turned into one of the best parts of it, at Carina's expense, of course. Who knew that sometimes a kid's honesty can turn into the perfect insult?

We spend the next twenty minutes finishing our ice cream, sharing bites, and laughing until Mrs. Lockwood arrives. Rory is such a funny, sweet kid. She started Kindergarten this year, and it's been so cute watching her learn new things, especially the ones we know will drive Rex and Sawyer crazy.

Cassie

I start clearing the table and throwing everything away to make sure we aren't leaving a mess while Max and Rory have a joke contest.

I'm pretty sure she's winning. Something about a flying skunk and a helicopter? Smellicopter? I don't know, but she has Max practically in stitches with her jokes.

"What's so funny over here?" a voice asks from behind us.

"Grandma!" Rory screams as she jumps off her chair and into her grandma's arms. "We got ice cream! Uncle Maxy let me have sprinkles! Lots and lots of sprinkles! And then! Some grumpy lady came over to talk to us, but she wasn't very nice." Mrs. Lockwood looks over at us in question, but she lets Rory continue. "And! Uncle Maxy and I were telling jokes. But he's not really that funny."

"Hey! Be nice, little Ro, I am too funny," Max grumbles, pouting.

"Sweetie, that sounds like such a fun time! Are you ready to come stay at Grandma's tonight?"

"Yes! Can we make pancakes tomorrow? With sprinkles? And chocolate chips?"

"I think we can make that happen." Turning to us, she smiles. "Thanks for bringing her out. It sounds like she had a lot of fun. The grumpy lady?" she asks, eyeing me and Max.

"Just some confused college girl. She's harmless, just dumb," Max says with a smile.

"Well, speaking of grumpy ladies, Max. Your mother reached out to the Foundation. She's, uh, I don't exactly know how to say this . . . well, I don't know how to say it kindly," she says with a grimace.

"Don't then. Just say it," Max says. "I'm sure Cassie has heard me say worse. Hell, she's probably said worse about my mother. I'm pretty sure she's the president of the 'I hate Max and Sawyer's Mom' fan club."

He's not wrong. I founded that shit. I think she's a bitch, and he agrees. Now, I would never bad-mouth someone's parents to their face unless we had some sort of understanding. Not my place. But their mom? She hasn't earned that title in my eyes, so fuck it. Plus, Max and Sawyer agree with everything I've said.

With a chuckle, Mrs. Lockwood smiles. "She, uh, requested an invitation to the fundraiser. Said she was supposed to be your plus one but that you've elected to bring someone else."

Rolling my eyes, I lean back and listen. This is no surprise at all. She tries to manipulate her way into these events whenever she can't use Max as her ticket in. Honestly, it's pathetic how she tries to play the victim card. I can't believe she said that he was supposed to bring her. Like that's his job, like he shouldn't be able to bring anyone he wants. Like somehow, she's earned the right to attend everything.

"What'd you say?"

"I told her the event was by invitation only, and unfortunately, I didn't have one with her name. She didn't like that and informed me she was going to speak to my boss. I think she meant my husband, which is laughable. We all know Mr. Lockwood can't boss me around. But, yeah, I just wanted to tell you since I probably pissed her off by telling her no."

"She's always pissed, that's nothing new. But thanks for telling me," Max says with a laugh. "I'd love to hear that conversation with Mr. Lockwood, it'd be pretty entertaining. If she even has the balls to make the call."

Her eyes twinkle with joy at the mention of her

husband, her whole face brightening. I love when someone is so in love that you can see it in their eyes. It's magical. It's something I've only ever dreamed of. But when I look at Max, I find that he's watching me as we listen to Mrs. Lockwood.

It's only for a moment, but for that brief moment, I see a twinkle in his eyes, the same look Mrs. Lockwood has. In that brief moment, I feel a tiny bit of hope start to take hold.

Maybe, just maybe, he still wants me.

Chapter Eleven

Cassie

MAX

Knock, knock.

ME

Who's there...?

MAX

Boo.

ME

Boo, who?

MAX

It's only a joke, don't cry about it.

Have a good day, princess.

ME

You, too.

S ix weeks of being someone's girlfriend, and I'm surprised by how fast the time has gone. On top of that, it's been six weeks of squeezing in as many brunch dates and wine nights as possible with Sawyer before she's a big girl and moves in with her boyfriend. At least she's taken pity on me these last few weeks and has watched as many *Criminal Minds* episodes as possible with me.

We've kept busy and tried not to think about it, but now it's moving day. Fuck my life.

"Don't go," I whine from my spot on Sawyer's bed, or what used to be her bed. Now it's just a mattress thrown on a frame, waiting for Max to take over the room.

I've done everything I can these last few weeks, trying not to think about everything that's going on, but we've had to make a few appearances. We've gone out to the bar with friends and have had a couple coffee dates here and there. The worst part though, is that it's actually been kind of nice spending time with him. Well, when I'm not thinking about our stupid history.

Don't get me wrong, since we're supposed to be "fake dating," it makes perfect sense that we would be seen out and about before moving in together, but it would've been nice to have some distance before living together. Now we're just going to be shoved down each other's throats and just have to make the best of it.

"And you say I'm dramatic. You act like I'm moving to another country, not barely a fifteen-minute walk away." Sawyer laughs as she carries another box out to the living room for the guys to bring down to the truck.

"Ugh, it feels that way. Now I can't just yell your name

from my bed and have you appear at my door. How inconvenient! And you're leaving me with the lesser Daniels."

"I take it things haven't been going well?"

"I mean, I don't know. I guess they've been fine."

"So, then what's the issue?" Sawyer questions.

"It's just been weird, Sawyer. He's honestly been...dare I say, pleasant? It's just . . . bizarre." I choke out a laugh, a little unsure how to explain it. I feel like it's so hard to talk to Sawyer about this because she has no idea about the history her brother and I have. If she did, I don't think we'd still be friends. We've never discussed any of it, although I'm sure Sawyer's always had her suspicions since when she left for college, we were friends, and when she came back, we could hardly stand being in the same room together.

"It's just weird as fuck. Your brother and I don't get along and haven't for years, and now we're just supposed to forget all of that and be roommates pretending to be dating. It all sounds like it's going to end in a disaster."

"I'm going to give you some advice, even though you didn't ask for it. Just ride it out. Who knows what could happen? Maybe you two will end up being friends, or maybe this apartment will go up in flames. No one knows, so there's no reason to stress until you have a reason to."

As I'm about to speak, the guys come walking up the stairs, ready for the next round of boxes, but surprisingly there's no more. Sawyer and I have done a great job supervising the move while the guys have done all the footwork. We also ensured everyone had refreshments and that our mimosas were always full.

"Where's the next load, ladies?" Miles asks. "I need to earn my beer and pizza," he finishes as he walks into the room, plopping down on the bed beside us.

"I think that's everything." Sawyer smiles as she looks at Rex. "I think I'm officially all moved out."

Max walks in and drops a couple of boxes onto the floor before jumping on the bed, squishing Sawyer and me in the middle.

"And now, I'm all moved in," Max chuckles.

"Greatttt," I deadpan.

"Oh, stop it, roomie. We're going to have a blast." Max elbows me as he says it. "Or should I say, girlfriend?"

"God, you're a pain in the ass, little brother," Sawyer says with a smile. I'm pretty sure nothing could bring down her and Rex's good moods. They've both been so excited about moving in together that hanging out with them has been disgusting, they're all mushy and lovey. Barf!

"Sawyer, before we leave for the bar, double check the mail, make sure you have everything you need," Rex says as he walks around the apartment, making sure all her stuff is packed.

"Oh! Good idea," she says, jumping up to go into the kitchen. She isn't gone for long before she comes back into the room holding a pile of mail. "Cass, you have a letter from the NHL."

The second I hear that, my heart immediately drops into my stomach, racing a million miles an hour. I'm not sure if I'm going to pass out or puke or do both all at once. I'm both terrified and excited.

My fate lies in that letter and I'm almost too fucking nervous to read it.

Almost.

"What's the NHL doing writing you a letter?" Trevor asks.

I don't answer—hell, I don't say anything—I just stand up, my hands still shaking as I grab the letter. Fuck. This is it. This is the moment I've been waiting for, for weeks, years even. Fingers crossed all of my hard work comes to fruition right here, and I don't get my heart broken.

I still feel their eyes on me as I open the envelope. I hear Sawyer say something. I'm unsure if she was talking to me or one of the guys, because I can't focus on anything but the letter in my hands. Everything around me feels warped, like I'm heading inside a tunnel and can only focus on the light at the end.

Ripping it open, I immediately pull the letter out, nearly passing out when I read the first sentence. "Congratulations, Cassie Wright, on your acceptance into the Empire State Hockey Internship. You will be placed with two teams: The NY Cyclones and the NY Ice Hawks."

I scream—shriek is probably a more accurate description. I'm filled with so much pure joy that I can't control myself. Everyone is watching me, and I don't care. I'm practically dancing through the bedroom as I finish reading the letter, elation running through my veins.

I did it. I fucking did it.

Without my parent's influence. Without their help. This is a culmination of my hard work.

It isn't until I feel arms around my waist that I realize Sawyer has been reading over my shoulder. She's squeezing me so tight in a bear hug and squealing along with me. I'm not sure how long we stay like this, but when I pull back, the guys are all staring at us and smiling, obviously having figured out what was in the letter.

I can't believe this is my reality, that I'm actually going to get to work with the NHL. And not just any team in the NHL, but I'll be working with my two favorite teams right here in New York. This is an absolute dream come true, and I'm so damn excited.

"Good job, Princess. I'm so proud of you. You earned this," Max says, surprising everyone in the room with his rare but authentic compliment. "Let's all get ready to go. Now we have two things to celebrate!"

By the time we make it to Hudson's, it's after eight, and the bar is packed with college students. Since Sawyer just graduated, we haven't been back to the college hangouts as much. Usually, we just hang out together at the apartment or spend time with Rex, Max, and the rest of the guys. But tonight, we thought we'd come out and do some celebrating at our favorite bar.

Sawyer and I head to the table that Gwen and Cade snagged for us earlier since they weren't able to help with the move. And the rest of the guys went up to the bar to grab some pitchers for our table.

"I hear celebrations are in order!" Gwen smiles. "I'll buy you a shot tonight! I think if we're at a bar full of fuck-boys, we'll all need a shot. Or two," she says, smirking as she looks around the bar at the ridiculousness already taking place.

"Fuck, at this rate, I'll need the whole damn bottle, especially if these little twats keep eyeing you ladies like you're their dessert," Cade says, grimacing at the crowd before looking back to Gwen and me. "Wanna take a shot, Cass?"

"I'm okay right now. I'll wait for the pitchers."

"Then let's go, trouble. I'm buying this round," Cade grumbles as he leads Gwen back to the bar, his hand resting on her back, directing her through the crowd.

Their interaction isn't overly flirtatious but more like

they're comfortable with each other. I hadn't realized they had become such good friends, but I love it. I guess I didn't expect Cade to be the one she got close to. He can be a little intimidating at times, although so can she. I mean, she may be tiny–and that's saying something because I'm 5'2'–but her presence is intimidating as fuck. It took forever for me to work up the nerve to talk to her in class one day. She's like Tinker Bell in a more badass font.

We're regulars here, so it doesn't take long for everyone to grab their drinks. By the time the first pitcher of beer is gone, we're all dancing around and acting like idiots, just having a good time. For the first time in ages, I feel happy. I sit back, sipping my beer, watching Sawyer and Rex grind on the dance floor like a bunch of drunk teenagers in love, and although I'm so happy for them, it makes me kinda sad. I'm jealous of what they have and that they've found their person, their partner, their lobster, all while I'm still alone and, apparently, a little bitter.

The more I watch them and think about my love life, the more I realize this might be why I agreed to Max's arrangement. With everything going on, sometimes it's nice to not feel alone, even if it's just for pretend.. The only challenge is that he is so much better at the little nuances of dating and flirting than I am. He's made me blush more times than I can count from the crooked grin he gives me. And he's so attentive, always giving me little touches here and there, and the way he brushes my hand or grazes my arm, it's maddening just how hot and bothered it makes me.

Draining my beer, I go to set down my glass when a hand comes from behind me, snatching it before I can.

"I've got it," Max says from behind me, filling up my glass from a brand new pitcher.

Taking a seat next to me, his arm reaches around me

and pulls me close until I'm standing between his legs. His touch feels electric. Goosebumps cover my skin, and my whole body feels like it's on fire. It's short-lived, though, just long enough for him to plant a gentle kiss on the side of my head before he's gone.

I didn't expect his touch to still have such an impact on my body. Even worse, though? I didn't think it would still impact my heart this much. As he walks away to join our friends, I can't help but feel like our little moment didn't affect him the way it's affecting me. It's hard to watch him fake this when it feels so real to me.

He's now joined in on a debate between Cade and Gwen about who the best rock artist is. I tune them out when one of them brings up *A Day To Remember* and someone else mentions *Volbeat*. I get up to go with Sawyer to grab a drink at the bar.

"How are you feeling?" Sawyer asks with a smile. "Has it sunk in yet?"

"Which part? Your brother and I moving in together or the internship? Or that I have to talk to my father and tell him the news, even though he'll probably disown me?" I say, word vomiting all over her, my nerves taking over. The hardest part about everything that's been happening is that I'm not sure which emotion to focus on since they're all over the place, each fighting to be front and center. "Sorry. I'm just overwhelmed." I shrug.

"Well, that's to be expected. It's a lot of change and big things happening all at once. It's scary. Change is terrifying. If you think I wasn't scared to death about moving in with Rex, you're high. But, I know that the reward is worth the fight."

"Well, my father is pretty good at the fighting part, so it

makes it seem terrifying, and your brother and I have so much history."

"I know for a fact that Max—"

"Is going to drop you the second he finds someone better," Carina pipes in as she slips next to us at the bar. "Once he gets what he wants from you, he'll realize he's worth so much more."

"And what? You think you think he's just going to dump me and run to you?"

"Isn't it obvious? He's just playing the long game with me. I mean, look at me. I'm everything he needs. Plus, everyone can see he's just not that into you. Once he's done slumming it with you, I plan to be the first girl he finally kisses. Just you wait."

"Too late."

"Too late for what?" Carina asks, confused.

"For his first kiss. I already claimed that years ago. Now, if you don't mind, I'm going to leave you here with your delusions and go back to celebrating with my boyfriend."

Turning around, I don't even check to see if Sawyer is following me, I just head straight to Max. It must be obvious I'm upset because he immediately looks concerned as I walk up to him, but I don't care. I only care about shutting Carina up once and for all, even if it means throwing all my rules out the window only a couple weeks into our little charade.

Looking up at him, I take a step closer as he leans forward, whispering in my ear, "Everything okay? Did something happen?"

"Nothing happened, but I . . . I just need you to kiss me."

"But that's against your rules," he responds, brushing a piece of my hair back as he stares down at my mouth.

"Can you just do it, please?"

"No," he finally says, shaking his head like he's snapping himself out of a daydream, one hand gripping my hip, keeping me in place. I can't move any closer to him and make a move myself, but I also can't retreat. It's unfair, especially because his rejection makes me want to cry, but I refuse to let him see that.

"Cassie, you were the one that was so adamant about these rules. I agreed, and just because you've changed your mind, it doesn't mean I'm just going to follow along like a lost little puppy."

I feel myself losing the battle with my tears, my eyes welling up more. His refusal hurts worse than I expect, bringing me back to that night years ago when I stood outside of the dance waiting for over an hour for him to show up.

Motherfucker! How have I let this man get under my skin like this, *again*? Haven't I learned my lesson? I'll never be the one he wants. Nodding quietly, I go to take a step back, but his other hand continues to grip my body, pulling me into him. He lets one hip go, but only long enough to lift my chin, forcing me to meet his eyes. They're darker than usual, his normal bright, emerald green eyes now a deep forest green, filled with indecision, frustration, and desire. His gaze switches back and forth between my eyes and my mouth.

"Tell me what's going on. Did somebody say something to you?"

I shake my head, teasing my bottom lip between my teeth as I lean back, trying to pull out of his hold. Without letting me move away, Max looks around the bar, gazing at the crowd until suddenly he stops, his jaw clenching, and fury immediately takes over his face.

Bingo. He found her.

It's not difficult to do. She's loud, obnoxious, and thinks she's the life of the party when in reality, the guys just hang out with her because she's an easy fuck. At this point in their lives, they're more interested in quantity than quality.

When he looks back at me, his eyes fall to my mouth once again as he grips me tighter. A silent battle is happening inside of him as indecision weighs on us both.

"Fuck it," is the last thing I hear before his lips slam down on mine.

Everything around me stops the second our lips touch. It's like it's happening in slow motion. It's not forceful or aggressive like I expect. Instead, it's slow, passionate, and so intense I'm seeing fireworks.

It's everything I've dreamed about since I was seventeen, and it's filled with enough emotion and silent promises that I'm feeling things I swore I'd pushed down. All the feelings from before, during, and even after he broke my heart come rushing back like a tidal wave, just ready to swallow me whole–but I don't pull back, I don't stop him. Instead, I bring my arms up around his neck and bring us closer together. His hands move to my ass, pulling me flush with his body as our tongues tangle together.

It isn't until he pulls back that I remember we have an audience, all of which are whistling and hollering at us like a bunch of teenagers. It isn't them I'm interested in, though. It's the redhead whose evil glare feels like she's stealing a part of my soul as she stares at us both with disgust.

If looks could kill, I'd be six feet under.

But with Max's help, I just ignore her, looking back up at him with a smile as he quickly spins me around, pressing my back up against the wall as he presses his hips into mine, his hard cock pushing against me, proving just how much he enjoyed our kiss. "Now, Princess, all you had to do was tell me Satan was here with us, and I would've given you anything you wanted. Want to fuck on the pool table she's playing at? That'd really piss her off."

Leaning in, he kisses me again, but this time it's different. This kiss is hungry, passionate, more aggressive than the first. His mouth attacks mine, biting and sucking, obviously not giving a fuck that his sister is watching us. It's like we're in our own little bubble inside this crowded bar, and the only thing we care about is getting closer to each other.

His teeth nip at my lip, a metallic taste coating my tongue, spurring me on. One of my hands grips the back of his neck while the other grips his hair, tugging him closer to me.

We stay like this, lost in our own little world for longer than I care to admit until we're both breathless from our kiss.

"What . . . was that?" I ask, my fingers brushing against my swollen lips.

"The kiss you deserved. Albeit, I wish it had been behind closed doors so I could finish what we started," Max whispers as he pushes his hips toward me, pressing his impressive length against my clit. Even through our clothes, it's enough to have my body vibrating with pleasure. "Besides, it was also the kiss that bitch deserved to watch. Whatever she said to you to make you upset, I promise you, it was a lie."

With a cocky smirk, he reaches down to adjust his erection before looking at our friends. "Let's grab another shot before I end up fucking you against this wall. If you're still feeling frisky, I'll let you take some body shots off me. I know you like my abs," he adds with a wink.

"Don't push your luck, big boy. We just had to prove a point."

"Whatever you say, Princess."

Turning around to head to the bar, he grabs my hand, tugging me along with him. I'm grumpy, confused, bewildered, and completely fucking turned on.

This man is such a complete and total pain in my ass, but for some reason, my traitorous body has amnesia because my pussy is aching, practically begging for more.

We're supposed to hate him, but she doesn't care.

Traitorous bitch.

Chapter Twelve

Max

ME

Random fact incoming

Did you know that hummingbirds are the only birds that can fly backwards?

PRINCESS

It's six a.m. Why are you texting me so early?

From down the hall.

ME

I was catching up on animal facts.

PRINCESS

At six a.m.?

Go back to bed, Max.

Max

Nothing about this has been easy, and absolutely *nothing* has gone as planned. This situation was supposed to solve our problems, not create more.

After the night out with our friends at the bar, Rex received a picture the following day from an unknown number.

Surprise surprise, it was another snapshot of the video, only this one left nothing to the imagination. Thankfully he checked his messages while Sawyer was still sleeping because I'm pretty sure we both would have had to bleach our brains if she had been awake. Plus, I'm not sure we could have hidden Cassie's identity any longer had she seen it.

The worst part? Everything between Cassie and I feels natural. Like it's something we've always done. It doesn't feel fake, and I don't know how to wrap my brain around the fact that it's supposed to be. All I can think about is the night of the party, with me on my knees, finally tasting her. Or even the night at the bar, the look on her face when she begged me to kiss her. At that Moment, I fought it, but truth be told? I would've given her anything she asked for. When I caved and our lips finally touched, I forgot everything around me and just wanted to live in that moment forever.

I haven't kissed anyone in six years since the first time my lips touched hers. I forgot what it feels like to lose yourself in someone so completely—not just giving them your body—and now I'd do anything to feel it again. Six fucking years later, all it took was one brush of her lips, one simple reminder of what it's like to be drowning in her, and it's like I've forgotten everything we've gone through. I want to claim her as mine. And not just to clean up a mess. I want her to be all mine, in public, in private, in real life, in every version of reality. I want Cassie to be *mine*.

Hell, she already is mine, her body still responds so perfectly to my touch, her eyes prove just how much she still cares. It's just her mind that needs to catch up.

Even now when I'm in my room listening to her throw shit around the kitchen like a toddler having a temper tantrum, I'm tempted to go out there and drop to my knees in the middle of the kitchen just to steal another taste.

Fucking Cassie.

Why is it still her? After all this time, after everything that happened, it's still only her. It's only ever been her. I only spent years pretending to hate her because it was easier than facing that I was just a sad and depressed mess, unable to face the fact that she didn't choose me. But now, I can't deny the butterflies I get every time she looks my way or how my cock only hardens for her, whether she's in a tiny pair of shorts and a crop top or baggy sweats and a messy bun. She does it for me every single time.

It would have been so much easier to move on, to find a new girl and let that piece of my life go, but no. Six years later, I'm still in my bed fantasizing about the grumpy girl currently throwing shit around in our kitchen.

"Damnit!" she yells as something crashes down in the kitchen.

Rolling out of bed, I throw on my sweats that I left on the floor last night and pull them back on before making my way into the kitchen. There's a broken mug on the floor, a mess of coffee and glass absolutely everywhere, and a barefoot Cassie in the middle of it all, cursing up a storm.

If I knew it wouldn't piss her off even more, I'd probably laugh at the sight. But that woman has a vicious mouth on her that I don't need aimed in my direction.

And now I'm thinking about her mouth. Thinking about her pretty pink lips wrapped around my cock. Son of a bitch.

"Uh, morning, Princess. Everything okay?"

When she looks up at me, I can tell she's on the verge of tears as she hops around on one foot, trying to avoid the mess she's created. "Does it fucking look like everything is okay?" She looks murderous and defeated all at the same time.

Walking over, I grip her by her hips, effortlessly lifting her onto the counter. I lean forward and grab a new mug and a spoonful of sugar before filling it to the top and handing it back to the pissed-off little gremlin who is still sending a glare my way.

I hear if you see an uncaffeinated gremlin in the wild, you're supposed to throw caffeine at them and run. Kind of like a Molotov cocktail but in a good way.

She takes the cup from me slowly, a look of confusion on her face as she stares at me. Like I'm a complete and total contradiction to everything she expected.

"Drink it, Princess. The world isn't ready to experience you without coffee. Hell, I don't think *you're* ready to experience you without coffee. Do us all a solid and drink up."

"Fine, but only because I have a meeting this afternoon," Cassie says, glaring over the cup.

Shaking my head, I take a deep breath, immediately realizing my mistake when her scent smacks me directly in the face. It's a faint citrus smell mixed with coffee. My cock stirs from it. Her voice interrupts my thoughts before I can take them further. "I have to meet with the PR team for the Cyclones today. I've met Amanda but haven't met with this team yet, so I probably shouldn't give off the bat shit crazy vibe. At least not this early in the game."

She's rambling. It's cute as fuck. I can tell she's nervous because she's always been a nervous rambler. While she keeps talking, I grab the broom from the pantry and start sweeping.

"You don—" Cassie starts to say, but I just glare at her, her voice immediately stopping. "Alrighty then, uh, thank you, Max. I've had a pretty shitty morning, so I appreciate your help."

I finish sweeping up the rest of the glass before grabbing the mop, quickly cleaning up the rest of the mess before finally grabbing myself a cup of coffee. Sitting on a barstool, I look at Cassie, who finally seems to be feeling human again, although there's a look in her eyes I don't like. She's not sad. She just looks . . . defeated.

"What happened?" I question after taking my first sip.

"It's nothing," she says, waving me off, but it's obvious she's lying. She just smiles at me as I stare at her with one brow raised, waiting for her to elaborate.

"Ugh, fine. It's my parents. They're still bugging me about this job they think I'm taking at my father's law firm. They have a hard time understanding the word no. Except now, they're threatening to stop paying for my apartment if I don't 'make the right choice.'"

"So, basically, they're blackmailing you into doing what they want?"

With a defeated look Cassie nods. "Yup, pretty much."

"I forgot how much your parents suck."

"I wish I could argue with you," she says with a sad smile.

"Look, mine aren't much better. We all know my Dad's an asshole, and, well, my Mom, she's just a bitch. Even if it's in a fucked up way, I, at least, feel like your parents actually care about you. But I'm just a pawn in my mom's fucked up game of chess."

"Eh, I guess you're right. Your mom is a bitch. Pretty sure I told her that the last time I saw her."

My eyes widen, and I can barely contain the laugh wanting to burst from my chest. "You said that to her?"

"Yep, she was trying to convince Sawyer to start dancing again or something equally stupid. She said that was the only thing Sawyer was good at and the only way she was going to make something of herself that was deemed 'worthwhile.' I told her Sawyer wasn't her doll and that she needed to stop being such a crazy bitch before both of her kids realized what a nightmare she is."

"You're my fucking hero," I tell her, unable to stop the cheesy-ass grin from taking over my face. Just the thought of her saying that to my mother is enough to make me cackle in delight. I can imagine my mother clutching her pearls and pretending to be so offended that someone would have the audacity to say that to her, even though it's the damn truth. Looking over at Cassie, I'm surprised to see her smiling back at me.

"Yeah, it's funny now. But at the moment, I was pissed. Thinking about it now though, I was probably just projecting my own issues with parents controlling life decisions, so I snapped at your mom instead of my own. I guess it was easier to tell your mom off than my own parents. Not sure what that says about me, but fuck it, at least it got your sister a little freedom."

I've always known that Cassie and her parents had a strained relationship, but I didn't realize it had continued past high school, and the sounds of it, it's only gotten worse.

"Do they know you applied for an internship?"

"Uh, no. I know I need to tell them They're just so fucking intimidating. Besides, now they're not taking no for an answer about meeting them for dinner to discuss everything . . ." she trails off and looks down at her hands.

"Is there more?" I ask.

"Uh, well. They found out we're dating . . . so I kind of need you to come with me," she rushes out, not meeting my gaze.

"Not a problem, Princess. As long as I don't have a game, I'm there. But no promises I'll keep my mouth shut if they act up," I tell her. Do I want to go to dinner with her parents? Hell no. Do I want her getting ambushed by them, especially since they know she's dating me? Absolutely not. Besides, it might be the best time for her to tell them about the internship, so I want to be there to back her up.

"Okay, uh. Thanks, Max. But I've still gotta figure out what to do if he follows through with his threat. What the hell am I going to do come December if he really stops paying for my apartment? I'm going to be homeless, Max!"

"Cass, you're not going to be homeless. We both know there's zero chance I'd let that happen."

"What are you going to do, pay my rent for me? Yeah, right. It's not like you can talk to him and change his mind."

"Why do I need to talk to him? You're your own person. You can make your own decisions. You got a fucking badass internship with the NHL. I'm pretty sure you're gonna be just fine with the job search."

"But he's going to cut off my money in January. That means I might not be able to afford to live here. What if I have to resort to selling my body, Max? I'm not cut out for that life. I mean, I could always sell pics of my feet. I'd need to get a pedicure,but my toes are kinda cute, don't you think?" she whines, trailing off from the conversation.

"You're not selling your body. Fuck that. Besides, if they stop paying, I'll cover it. We are dating after all."

"That's expensive, Max! I can't allow you to do that."

"You're not, Princess. I'm offering. Besides, it's not like I can't afford it. It's not a problem. I'm not letting my girlfriend sell her body. That wouldn't look good for my nice guy image."

"You know we're not actually dating, right?"

"Poh-tae-toe, pah-tah-toe. Same difference. No way am I going to let you sell your body when I have enough money for the both of us."

"Max, why would you do that?"

"You're helping me out, it's the least I can do. Honestly, keeping my reputation clear helps me keep my job. It may just be a rookie contract, but it's still plenty of money. I gotchu."

"I...I don't know what to say," Cassie says, her eyes downturned, staring at her cup in embarrassment.

"Just say thank you and that I'm the best fake boyfriend ever. And if your parents are rude during dinner, we can leave." I wink, hoping to calm her a bit. "Besides, I'm going to need a good PR person if that video or picture—or whatever the bitch-ass actually has—gets out."

"Thank you, Max. I really appreciate it."

Downing the last of my coffee, I rinse my cup out before putting it in the dishwasher. When I look back at Cassie, she has this incredulous look on her face as if she's just now seeing me for the first time and isn't sure what to make of it. "Like I said, it's no problem. Let's just move on and figure it out as we go. Let me know when the dinner is, and I'll be there."

"Thank you, Max," Cassie says, her smile forced, but her eyes relieved.

"Good girl," I say. The slight twinkle in her eyes goes straight to my cock, and now is not the time to question it. "I'm meeting Sawyer for lunch, but I'll be back later. If I bring home a pizza, will you be here?"

"Yeah, I'm going on a run, but that's it. Would you get—"

"Pepperoni with extra pineapple? Of course," I say with a smile as I turn around and head to my room to get ready, leaving her with the cutest shocked face ever.

I guess she didn't expect me to remember that. But I remember everything about her.

Everything.

———

WALKING INTO THE GREASY SPOON, I'M IMMEDIATELY hit with the smell of French fries and bacon. Fuck, I love bacon. I chose this place as soon as Sawyer and I planned to meet for lunch because the food here is absolutely delicious. Don't get me wrong, the location is convenient for both of us, but Sawyer and I both share a love of cheeseburgers and French fries, so this was an easy choice.

The older couple that runs this diner has sort of taken me under their wing since I started coming here my first year at Brooklyn U. The husband does most of the grill work while his wife makes some of the best pies I've ever had. Her huckleberry pie belongs in heaven. I'd sell my left testicle if it meant I could eat her pie every day for the rest of my life.

Slipping into my usual booth, I order some fries while I wait. Things between my sister and I have finally started to feel good again. Feel normal. Thank fuck, I've missed her more than I can put into words. Besides, she's the only family I have left. I know it will take time to really rebuild our relationship and get it back to what it used to be—if that's even possible. But I'm willing to put in the effort if it means I can be a part of her life. The thought of her living her life, and starting a family without me, kills me. Watching her and Rory bond fills me with so much pride, and I can only imagine I'll feel just as excited if and when she and Rex decide to expand their family and build a life together. As cheesy as that shit sounds, I can't wait to be the cool-ass uncle.

I pop a fry in my mouth right as Sawyer sits down across from me, a bright-ass smile on her face as she reaches for my fries. "Sup, little bro."

"Hey, big sis."

"Sorry I'm late. I, uh, got a little tied up back at the apartment," she says, her face flushed and her hair haphazardly thrown up in a bun like she had to get ready in a hurry. Gross.

"Ew, I don't need or want to know about any situation where you're being tied up. I feel like I need a lobotomy," I groan, covering my face with my hands.

"Oh, stop being dramatic. You're playing house with my bestie. Don't act like you don't have stories of your own."

My eyes immediately snap up and meet hers from across the table. She's smirking at me like the cat that got the canary. What does she know? Did Cassie talk to her? Is she just waiting for me to fess up? Cassie would've for sure given me a heads up if she told Sawyer anything . . . right? I've never told Sawyer about the feelings I've always had for her best friend, solely because of how fucking weird that conversation would be. I also didn't want to strain my relationship with Sawyer any more than it already was, let alone make things weird between her and Cassie. So, what the fuck is happening now?

She starts laughing, the kind of full-belly laugh that confuses me even further. She reaches for a menu with a shit-eating grin on her face as she continues to chuckle to herself. "Shut your mouth or a bird will poop in it," Sawyer says, her eyes never leaving the menu.

"What's that look for?" I question, my voice quieter than I anticipated.

"Oh, nothing. Just waiting to see how long it takes."

"How long *what* takes? What the hell are you talking about, Sawyer? Why do you girls speak in code? Just use your damn words and tell me what you mean."

Setting the menu down, she looks at me with bright eyes and a big smile.

"Max, I've known you your whole life. And Cassie has been in our lives for what? Almost fifteen years?"

"Yeah . . ."

"I'm not an idiot. I've known you've been in love with her since we were teenagers. I just figured you'd always be too big of a pussy to do anything about it."

My jaw drops, and my brain feels like it's misfiring—or short-circuiting. I'm not able to process what she's saying.

She's known.

For years, I have been trying to hide my feelings about Cassie from everyone, mainly my sister, but she's known the entire time? I feel like the world's biggest dumbass right now.

"I . . . I'm not exactly sure what to say," I say honestly, still unsure how much to tell her. Usually, I would love to talk to her about something like this, get her advice, and even just have her listen to me, but I don't want to say something and have Cassie get upset she didn't have the opportunity to tell her instead. "Has it really been that obvious? That I've been in—that I've had feelings for her? This whole time?" I ask, shocking myself with how easily the word love almost fell out of my mouth.

"Max, anyone could've figured out that you are in love with her. Or that you 'have feelings for her' if that's what you want to go with. I just figured you weren't ready to admit it to yourself and I didn't feel like it was my place to point it out. You had enough shit going on back then with our parents that I didn't want to add to it. I knew you'd realize it at some point. Either that or you'd eventually move on."

I want to tell her. I want to tell her everything. That I did realize it. That I've known the whole time just how strongly I felt about Cassie, but was too scared to get my heart broken. Again.

"Truthfully? I've always known. Well, at least since I was about fifteen," I tell her, her excitement palpable as she leans in, not wanting to miss a word. I can't promise her the entire story, but I'll give her my side, well, at least about my feelings. I'm not sure I need to go too far into details about how I fucked her best friend when we were teens. How we took each other's virginity. If she wants all that, she'll have to get it from Cassie.

"Look, I don't know exactly what you want to hear. Did you know she was my first kiss?"

"What?! I thought you didn't kiss anyone, Max. Or at least that's the gossip I've heard, especially from that twatwaffle, Carina. She tried to tell Cassie she was going to be your first kiss. I'm glad you helped prove that wrong at the bar," Sawyer says with a wink. "I'd have hated for that bitch to be right. I'm still grumpy that neither of you assholes thought to tell me about this. Start talking. Now."

I spend the next fifteen minutes telling her about Cassie and I. How we'd gotten closer while Sawyer was busy with dance and off at college. I tell her how when our parents split up, Cassie was there for me, and when her parents came down hard on her, I was there for her. We became each other's person, although, at the time, it was platonic. We were just two unlikely people who ended up becoming best friends. But after that kiss? After having sex with her? I knew there was no chance I was okay with just being her friend. I wanted more. I wanted her.

I tell her about the night after our kiss—because, of course, for the sake of this conversation, I leave it at just a kiss. As I think back to that night, I feel all the emotions come back like a tidal wave, threatening to drown me all over again.

I'VE GOT TO GET GOING. I'M ALREADY LATE. I ASKED *Cassie to go to the dance with me tonight because I want— no, I need to show her that maybe we can be more than friends. Actually, we've always been more than friends. I've just been too damn scared to admit that I've always wanted more with her. There's never been a moment that I felt was appropriate to bring it up, to tell her how I feel.*

Until last night.

But right now, I'm stuck inside my house while my parents argue back and forth. My father's getting angrier with every passing moment. I know the second I leave my room, the second he sees me, I'm going to become another target for his frustration, and that's something I'm usually good at avoiding.

But I'm not going to make her wait. It would kill me to know that even for a moment, she questioned where I was. Shutting my door quietly, I sneak down the hallway, hoping to make it past my father's office without him seeing me. Grabbing my phone, I start to type a message to Cassie, letting her know I'm on my way when suddenly, my phone is snatched from my hands.

"Where the fuck do you think you're going?" my father sneers down at me, my phone held tightly in his grip.

"Heading out. Tonight's the school dance," I say, glancing between him and my mother, noticing the bruises on her arms. She quickly hides them behind her back while my father seethes. He knows I won't do anything, I tried once, but when she took his side, I knew there was nothing I could do.

Motherfucker. I can ignore a lot of the bullshit between my parents, but allowing my mother to get physically assaulted? That's not something I can ignore.

"The fuck you are. Get your ass back up to your room."

"Let him go. There's no reason he should be home," my mother chimes in.

Before I can respond—before I can even think—my father has turned around and slammed my phone against the brick of his office fireplace. One moment he's shattering my phone and the next, he's walking toward my mother, his arm cocking back, but I move between them, not caring what happens next.

I'm not thinking. I'm not worrying. I'm just protecting. It's one thing to see her bruises, it's a whole different situa-

tion for me to watch it happen. But he doesn't stop. My father sees me and shoves me back before cocking his arm and bringing his fist down right on my nose.

With a crack, I feel it break, immediately tasting the coppery taste of blood in my mouth as my nose starts oozing blood everywhere.

But it doesn't end there. Before I can defend myself or even block his next move, he's punched me again, this time in my mouth.

I can't think. I can't move. All I can hear are his vile words as my mother screams about all the blood. She's not crying about me getting injured. She's worried about the fucking cream-colored rug that I'm apparently getting blood all over.

Grabbing her jacket off the back of the chair, I cover my nose, hoping to control the bleeding, all while in a staring contest with my father. No words are said, but his eyes show his understanding. He just fucked up. This may have been the first time he's laid hands on me, but it will certainly be the last.

Turning on my heel, I ignore my broken phone as I make my way outside to my car. My mother yells at me to stop—to not be stupid—probably worrying about me telling someone. Little do they know, I couldn't give a fuck about what just happened. All it did was solidify how shitty my parents are. But I'm not an idiot. My mother chooses him every time, so there's really no point in going to the police. They'd probably turn it around on me since I'm almost eighteen.

No, I'm driving straight to the dance. Straight to where I asked Cassie to meet me. I may be bruised and bloody, but it'll all be okay once I'm hers.

By the time I make it to the school, it's almost eight p.m. I throw my car in park and rush up the stairs to the tree I asked *her to wait for me at. I know it's a long shot since I'm almost an hour late, but I still have to try. Looking around, I don't see her anywhere. I'm about to give up and search inside when I catch a glimpse of long blonde hair flowing over a dark blue dress.*

It's her.

Only she's not alone. She's walking hand in hand with another man. I start to walk over to her to ask what's going on. But when he leans down and places a chaste kiss on her lips, and she wraps her arms around him in a hug, I realize what just happened.

She used me.

She used my emotions. She used my body. And once she was whole, she threw me to the side, moving on to someone better.

I can handle my parents not caring about me, not wanting me. But I can't handle that the girl I've fallen in love with is choosing someone else without a second thought.

So, I walk away, knowing her happiness matters more to me than my own.

"Okay, I'm going to need to process all of this information in parts. First, I cannot believe you went through all that alone. And I can't believe our fucking father actually put his hands on you, and I never knew. I never knew that my baby brother had to go through abuse while I was running away from my injury. Running away from feeling like a failure," she chokes out. "I'm not saying I didn't need the time away because lord only knows, I did. Badly. But I never would've left you to deal with that alone.

I could fucking kill him right now," Sawyer growls, her hands shaking with anger, her eyes welling with tears.

I tried to gloss over the bad stuff, but it's kind of hard to tell her what happened without going into some detail about why I was late to the dance.

Plus, how else do I explain a broken nose and a broken cell phone? So, I told her everything about that night. How I felt like I was failed by my mother, yet I was more upset that I didn't protect myself. It hurt knowing that even though I protected her, she still blamed me for getting in the way. Said I had those punches coming, all because it kept her from getting into a bigger fight with him.

Could I have taken him back then? Yeah. I was 6'2" and 195 lbs, and I was used to getting in fights, but they were usually on the ice. Besides, they'd probably press charges If I laid a hand on him since I was almost eighteen, and I knew that would ruin any chance I had of playing hockey professionally, so I just bit my tongue and dealt with it.

"I'm sorry, Max. I'm so, so sorry. I should have been there. I should have taken more responsibility with mom instead of just leaving you to deal with the fallout. I've always regretted that, but I would do anything to shoulder some of that for you, even though I know it's too late. I still should have protected you. Did you tell anyone? The police? A coach? Anyone at all?"

"You don't need to be sorry, Sawyer. It's not your fault, and honestly, I'm glad you weren't there when it happened. At least that way, you were protected. Mom just didn't know how to hold him accountable, and as I got older, I realized she was just so manipulated and broken down by him that she was willing to do anything and everything she could to keep the pretty little lifestyle she'd grown so fond of. I thought when he left that she would see it and realize her mistakes, but I don't think she ever will."

Looking up, I meet Sawyer's gaze and feel my heart breaking at the look on her face. Had she known, I know she would've been there in a heartbeat, but I love her too much to ever want her to go through what I did. I'll gladly carry the burden so that she doesn't have to. Honestly, I wish I'd never told her any of this. She's so upset it kills me, but keeping secrets and not talking about all of this is what broke our relationship in the first place, and I'll be damned if I let it happen again.

"Max, I'm so sorry. I think–no, I know–I've blamed you for so much—too much. I always thought you were trying to control me and using mom to do it. I never realized what was happening. I always assumed the worst of you. That's on me, and I don't know if I'll ever forgive myself, but I hope one day you can forgive me. I would give anything to go back in time, back to the way things used to be between us, but I understand if you aren't ready. I understand if you never get there."

She's wrong, though. I've already forgiven her. In my mind, this was never her burden to carry because I kept it all to myself. How can I blame her for something she didn't know was happening? If I'm being honest, I still think it's the other way around. I still feel like the immature prick who ruined our relationship because I was hurt instead of understanding that she was dealing with everything the only way she could manage, and that started with her mental health. All of this makes me out to be the villain of the story, not her.

"You don't need to apologize. For anything. You were taking care of yourself. You had no idea what was going on, and I didn't want you to. That's not your fault. At this point,

I'm good with never talking to either of our parents again as long as I have you."

"Of course, you do, Max. Always," Sawyer says, reaching across the table and grabbing my hand. "Plus, now we have Mama and Papa Lockwood, and I promise you, they're so much better than our parents. They rock! I can't wait for you to meet them."

"I met Mrs. Lockwood when we took Rory out for ice cream. I still haven't met Rex's dad, though."

"You will meet him at the charity gala in a couple of months. Rex told you about that, right?"

"He mentioned it briefly. That's in November?"

"Yup. Should I help Cassie pick out a dress? I mean, you are bringing your "girlfriend", right?" Sawyer says, putting girlfriend in dramatic air quotes and giving me a sly wink that tells me the wheels are turning inside her brain, and she's probably up to no good. But fuck it. It can't hurt to have Cassie's best friend on my side if I want to somehow pull this shit off and convince her to give us a shot.

"Yeah, she definitely needs a dress."

That's all my sister needs to hear before letting out a huge squeal of excitement. "Can I give you one little nugget of information? I promise it will come in handy when you least expect it," Sawyer adds.

"Hit me with it."

"Graham crackers and *Jif* creamy peanut butter. Keep them on hand at all times. Make sure it's hidden, though. The peanut butter must be Jif, and it must be the creamy kind. She hates that crunchy shit, and she despises *Skippy* peanut butter. She always buys the healthy, no sugar bullshit to try and limit her sugar because of her mom's toxic attitude surrounding food growing up, but that's a topic for another day."

"So, the secret information is to keep graham crackers and *Skippy* peanut butter on hand at all times?"

Sawyer swats my shoulder and pins me with a glare. "*Jif*! Don't fuck it up, or it'll just make her more upset. When she's stressed or overwhelmed—hell, even just over-stimulated—she likes to snack on graham crackers and peanut butter. But she refuses to have them in the house because she knows she has no self-control and will eat them all the second she opens them. I've kept a stash in my closet for years, even at our parents' house, just to make sure she has it. If you bring this out when she needs it the most, you'll be in her good graces forever."

"Just how good of graces are we talking?" I joke, earning me a slap on the back of my hand.

"Ew. I don't want to know, and I definitely don't need those images running through my brain. Keep it PG, little bro," Sawyer says with a fake gag.

"But yeah, I know," I tell her with a smile.

I remember everything about this girl.

"How?" Sawyer asks, incredulously.

"I just do."

"Who woulda thought, my brother the romantic," Sawyer says with a smile before she starts laughing.

I can't help but join in, a genuine smile taking over my face for the first time in a while. Everything has been so tense between Sawyer and I that I'm just so happy we're at this point again. It's nice being able to talk to her, and joke around a bit, but it's even better being on the same team again. Even if that means I had to tell her about Cassie and me. We spend the next hour ordering food and chatting about the studio Rex's mom helped her get and all the plans she has for it. Luckily, she didn't bring up Cassie and I again, but I have a feeling she's plotting something and waiting for the perfect time to weasel her way back into that conversation.

By the time I make it back to the apartment–with the pizza I promised in hand–I'm feeling optimistic about everything for the first time in a long time.

Chapter Thirteen

Cassie

MAX

When does a kitty want to be pet?

ME

Is this going to be dirty?

MAX

No, it's not dirty.

Just answer.

ME

I don't know?

MAX

Right meow. ;)

ME

face palms

"**W**hat are you doing?" I ask when Max walks into the living room. His stupid basketball shorts are hung so low on his hips that his V muscles are perfectly on display. It doesn't help that the man never wears a shirt, so his rude-ass is showing off his eight-pack. His abs practically scream at me, just begging me to touch them. They speak straight to my pussy that's drenched just from the view.

Doesn't he realize what his body does to me? That every time I see him shirtless, my vagina gets a mind of her own and practically begs me to get naked with him, to touch him, run my tongue over every inch of his skin until I've engrained it in my brain.

"Scoot over. You're hogging the couch," he says, snapping me out of my fantasy as he slides in, stealing my blanket before covering us both.

He's been around more these last couple of weeks, making more of an effort to be present and spend time with me when we're both home. He's even watched *Criminal Minds* with me without complaint. Except now, he's decided that he gets to join me for all my binge-watching parties, despite never receiving an official invite. In his defense, though, he's definitely made it more fun. After he brought me pizza that first night, he's made sure to always have snacks we both love, proving yet again that he remembers more about me than I realized. Although I love him being nice and attentive, it makes this feel way more real than it should be.

"You know there's another couch over there, right? With more blankets. Why do I have to share?"

It's becoming more and more challenging to fake hate Max, even to fake indifference is becoming challenging, because honestly, he's been a dream to live with. He's been kind and attentive and has given me space when I need it. But he's also really been there for me when I need him. That alone has made a bigger impact on me than I anticipated.

"I'm not sitting over there. You're making me watch a show about fucking murders! It's way too far away. No, thank you. I'll sit right here under your blanket where you can protect me."

"Ha-ha. Very funny. I didn't peg you as the guy who'd be afraid of a little crime show."

"I'm more terrified of what it's teaching you."

"Smart man," I deadpan before turning back to the screen. "What snacks did you bring me this time?"

"I brought *Milk Duds* for the popcorn and jalapeno chips if you're feeling spicy."

"I guess that'll do."

"Why are you so grumpy?" he jokes, but I can tell deep down he's being serious.

I hate how intuitive he is. He can read me better than anyone—Sawyer included. I'm not sure what it is, but he's always been able to figure out my emotions, sometimes even before I can. It's frustrating and sweet all at once.

"I'm not. Just sit still and watch. It's been a long day, and I want to relax and watch my show."

"Your murder show," he whispers under his breath before shutting up.

Thank god.

It isn't until the first episode is over that the panic starts to hit.

As stupid as it sounds, I watch these shows because they help me take my mind off my own life. I don't have to think about everything that's stressing me out or making me anxious because I'm watching someone else's problems, even if their problem is getting murdered. Other times, it's like a compound effect. It sends me into a tailspin of stress and anxiety, my own coupled with whatever stress the episode brings me. Today, that's how I'm feeling.

My internship starts Monday, which is only two days away. I have two days to get my head on straight before I, hopefully, make a good impression. Two days until the most important thing I've ever done for my career begins, and I'm terrified of fucking it up. I'm terrified of having to tell my parents that I failed. If I fail, I know I can't go back to them with my tail between my legs and beg for the opportunity again. They aren't like that. Once you've turned them down, they won't offer again.

Without even thinking about it, I jump up, flinging the blanket off before heading into the kitchen. I'm a stress eater. Well, more of a stress snacker because I like variety and finger foods. Digging through the pantry, I search for graham crackers. I never keep them in the apartment, but Sawyer was an angel and kept a hidden stash for me when she lived here for occasions like this.

I look on every shelf, behind everything, but can't find graham crackers or peanut butter anywhere. I turn around, accepting defeat and deciding to walk to the store for them, but I bump headfirst into a brick wall. At least, that's what it feels like. When I look up, I see I bumped into Max, who's looking down at me with a smile, his hands neatly tucked behind his back.

"Looking for something, Princess?" he asks before bringing his arms into view. The sight before me is enough to make me swoon. He has a brand-new pack of graham crackers and a tub of *Jif* peanut butter in his hands. Creamy.

Is this man for real?

"Is that . . ."

"For you? Of course." He smiles as I take them out of his hands, immediately wrapping him up in a hug. "Thank you, Max," I whisper, earning me a tight squeeze in return.

"Of course, Princess. Let's go. I've gotta try this snack. Besides, you stopped midway through the episode, and I'll die if I don't find out what happens to Spencer."

Rolling my eyes, I jump back on the couch, squishing in next to Max as we watch *Criminal Minds* while snacking on Graham Crackers smothered in peanut butter. It isn't until this moment that I realize how content I feel with him. Not like the kind of contentment where you've settled, and you have to deal with where you're at. No, this is serenity. This is happiness. And this is me being so at peace with my life, especially the man sitting next to me.

How can this be? Things between us have felt so different lately, almost like how it was when we were younger. I promised myself I would never go down that road again, that I couldn't trust him, that I shouldn't want to trust him again. It ruined me. So, what do I do now that all these feelings and thoughts keep coming up that make me question if it's not all in the past?

It isn't until I'm waking up in Max's arms as he lays me down in my bed that I realize I'd fallen asleep in the living room. He doesn't know I've woken up as he covers me up, placing a kiss on my forehead. A kiss so soft I can barely feel the touch, but my heart swells at the brief contact.

"Good night, Princess. I love you. Always," he whispers before standing up, leaving me alone in my bedroom, wishing he'd stayed.

Cassie

WALKING INTO MADISON SQUARE GARDEN FOR MY first day as an intern is equally terrifying and exciting. I feel like a kid on Christmas morning. I barely slept last night. I was so anxious to get here. Between today being my first day and what Max said to me last night, I had a hard time getting back to sleep.

To fuck up my mind even more, he was already sweet enough to leave me coffee and breakfast from my favorite spot down the street, and now he's texting me good luck? Gwen and Sawyer did too, but something about receiving a message from Max, knowing he's thinking about me, makes me feel warm and fuzzy inside.

But I shouldn't be thinking about Max right now. Instead, I should be thinking about the New York Cyclones and the job I have to do. To say I feel like a fish out of water is an understatement, but thankfully I am paired up with Amanda, one of the PR team leads, and she's been a huge help. I think she expected me to be nervous because she explained everything about the job in intense detail, and I'm so damn thankful for her.

When I first received my assignment, I was low key bummed that I didn't get to be with the Ice Hawks first. As much as Max and I have had our issues, I've known him for years, so I know what to expect with him. At least his kind

166

of crazy I know I can handle. This right now? It's a whole new ball game...or a guess, hockey game?

At least Cade threatened the rest of the guys, told 'em he'd kick all their asses if they gave me a hard time, and honestly, I believe him. He's not one to fuck around with, he's the typical grumpy goalie, and he's known to get his hands dirty if necessary.

Harris is the only one I worry about. That man has trouble written all over his devious face, but he keeps it hidden behind a boyish smile. I just know it means extra work for me and the team.

I got paired with another intern, Spencer, so the three of us spent the morning going through the logistics of the job. After getting our schedules all figured out, we met with the PR team and went over each of the athletes on the team. Basically, we were all given a binder, filled to the brim with information about each of the athletes so we could study them and learn about everyone on the team. This way, when shit goes awry, we have some background information to go off of. Today, we just got the cliff notes version and even that felt like a lot.

It's been a fucking busy day, but I've loved every second of it, even if it's almost one p.m. and we're just now sitting down for lunch.

We aren't expected to do too much PR work during Training Camp as interns, it's just a lot of information, sort of like an orientation time for us where we get to meet everyone and really learn what our job will be. We get to meet everyone, figure out where everything is, and we get the opportunity to watch the PR team do their job. We'll be getting a behind-the-scenes look at all the things the public doesn't see.

It's been fast-paced and a little overwhelming but so

much fun. Okay, maybe it was a lot overwhelming, but it was still fun.

"So, what made you two decide to come intern for the NHL?" Amanda asks in between bites of her sandwich.

"My brother plays in the NHL, so it's just something I've always been around," Spencer responds. "But PR is the only part of sports that really interests me. Oh, and their butts. I'm definitely interested in their butts."

"Oh, dear lord. You're going to be a PR nightmare, aren't you?" Amanda says. Half serious, half joking.

"No, no. All jokes, Miss," Spencer says with a laugh, shooting an overly obvious wink my way and thankfully earning a laugh from Amanda.

"How about you, Cassie?"

"Kinda the same. I grew up around the sport. My best friend's brother plays. He actually plays for the NY Ice Hawks now."

"Oh, who?" Spencer asks, and Amanda perks up. She works with both teams through the internship program, so she's well-versed in the players for both teams.

"Max Daniels. He's their new—"

"Left wing!" Amanda cuts me off excitedly. "Girl, anyone who's anyone knows Max Daniels! I didn't know you knew him. Can you introduce me?"

This is the moment I knew I needed to prepare for, but no matter how much I hyped myself up, calling him my boyfriend still feels so foreign.

"Uh, yeah, I could introduce you. Max is, uh...he's my boyfriend," I say, hopefully exuding more confidence than I actually feel because currently, I feel like a fifteen-year-old talking about their crush.

"How does it feel to be God's favorite? That man is fucking sin in skin, which, as I say that out loud, I realize just how inappropriate that is. Sorry, Amanda. Sorry, Cassie," Spencer says in embarrassment.

"No apologies needed here. I've known the man since I was a kid. I'm well aware of just how hot he is," I tell them with a laugh.

After we've finished lunch and dispersed back to our stations, I go in search of Amanda, and hope she's alone. I figure now is the perfect time to talk to her since the topic has basically been brought up already.

Wiping my palms, I see Amanda outside of her office and walk up to her, willing myself to not be so nervous. "Hey, do you have a second? I wanted to talk to you about something," I say, my voice unsteady.

"Of course, is everything okay?" Amanda asks curiously as she waves me into her office, closing the door.

"Yeah, I hope so. It's about Max."

"Oh, Cassie, don't worry about everything with Max," Amanda starts.

Does she know already? I knew Max was going to tell them, but I figured he'd do it after practice today.

"We have no rules in place saying that a player and an intern on the PR team can't be together," she says with a smile, assuming what this conversation would be about if only it were that easy.

Damn. I really hoped she already knew.

"Yeah, about that. It is about Max, but it's more than that. He's already given his coach a heads up and they were going to talk to you guys today, and figure out what to do and all." I stumble my words out, Amanda's eyebrows raising in confusion.

"What are you talking about?"

"I...we were... we were videotaped, without our consent...in a compromising position. And now, it's been sent to us. Max and Coach Lockwood were going to talk to you guys today, I just...I needed to tell you."

Finally stopping to breathe, I realize I'm staring down at my hands, fumbling with my bracelet. Forcing myself to look at Amanda, I see she's lost in thought as she chews on her lower lip. I wait for what feels like ages before she finally says anything.

"Do we know who sent it?" she questions.

"No."

"Well, hopefully, it's just a stupid ploy for attention. Whether it's media attention or attention from you guys, I don't know. I wouldn't worry about it though. You two are together. We'll just play it off as revenge porn if anything comes from it. He's got the boy next door look down, I'm sure we can spin it our way, and make everyone see that a nice couple had been violated."

Oh, if she only knew just how *literally* he was the boy next door.

"Are you sure? Shouldn't this be a big deal?" I ask, but Amanda just carries on with a smile, her carefree attitude making me feel just a smidge better.

"Cassie, this type of thing happens all the time, and honestly, usually nothing else comes of it after the threat. But even if it does, we just spin it–like I said. It'll blow over in no time. Don't even worry about it. Go grab a coffee before our next meeting in ten. Relax your mind."

Not a chance that's happening, but I'll gladly take more caffeine.

Chapter Fourteen

Max

Why shouldn't you play poker at the zoo?

PRINCESS

They don't have hands?

ME

Too many cheetahs.

PRINCESS

I like the zoo. and poker.

ME

We can play poker ;)

PRINCESS

We are not playing strip poker.

ME

Aw, man. You're no fun :)

PRINCESS

By the way Max...your messages do make me smile.

L ongest. Week. Ever.

Training Camp started this week, and to say that I wasn't expecting to have my ass handed to me like this, would be the understatement of the century. It's the kind of tiredness where you feel like you need help keeping your eyelids up. I almost needed help lacing my skates up this morning. I kept dosing every time I bent over. Rex watched with a smirk the entire time.

Such an asshole.

It's not like I haven't been preparing for this, I may be a rookie, but I'm not a complete fucking idiot. I spent months preparing, ensuring I was in the best shape of my life, knowing damn well I'd be fighting for my spot the whole season. I've worked my ass off these last few months, skating, working on drills, and kicking my own ass in the gym. I had to make sure I came into camp ready to prove myself. Prove that I'm exactly where I'm meant to be.

With everything else that's been going on in my life, between the video, the gnawing fear of never knowing when another message could pop up, and trying to figure out what's going on with Cassie and me, working out and skating has been the most effective way for me to destress. It keeps my anxiety at a more manageable level.

I'm not saying I'm perfect, I've been known to go out with guys and have some drinks and shitty food, but I try to do it in moderation. Thankfully, I know my limits and what my body can handle, which will hopefully help me land my spot on a line. Left wing is a difficult spot to achieve on this team–they've always had incredible players. Truthfully, though, and at the risk of sounding conceited, I know how I play. My ability to handle the puck and score like few can make me worth the risk of taking on a rookie.

Even with all the grumbling I've done, this week has still been incredible. I thought I would be a little disappointed for not being with the Cyclones, but I'm so fucking happy I ended up with the Ice Hawks, especially having Rex as my coach. He was an incredible hockey player—one I've always loved to watch—but I think he might be an even better coach. He's able to use his skills on the ice to help us be our best. He has this innate ability to see each player differently, in a different light than others can. It allows him to switch things up and make different moves that you'd think would end up being a fucking disaster, but somehow it works, and it works really fucking well. It's an incredible feat for such a young coach to make such an impact in only his second year coaching.

The challenge is that it's taking some players, and hell, even some of the coaching staff, time to trust him. At the start of Training Camp, I could tell that some of the more seasoned players were apprehensive and didn't like change. They didn't like having a new coach or being moved from where they were comfortable, and they truly believed it would be the team's downfall.

But as they slowly see the glimpses of success made by Rex's coaching, their stony demeanors have softened. It's nice to see them accepting him, however slow that acceptance may be.

By the time practice is over and we're all heading off the ice to the locker room, we're struggling to skate forward. Our captains, Alex Mitchell and Knox Wendell, split us into two groups and had us play against each other. You'd think it would have been fun, but it was brutal.

Physical.

Exhausting.

A battle.

Every player knew just how vital this scrimmage was. You could cut the tension in the room with a knife. We all knew this could easily decide what position we would play and with which players we shared the ice. As brutal and rough as it was, it was exciting as fuck. I enjoyed playing against people who are at the top of their game, people that challenged me to be my best.

"Great job out there today," Knox says as he skates to a stop, chuckling as he sprays me with ice. "You're fucking killing it with those shots."

"Thanks, man. It feels great being out there," I say, slipping off my helmet, my soaked hair falling in front of my eyes. Running a hand through it and pushing it back, I look back at Knox, who's watching some of the new guys who are still out on the ice fucking around.

"You've got something not all rookies have," Knox says. The statement is directed at me, but it's almost like he's talking to himself, his eyes never leaving the group still out there.

"What do you mean?" I ask, patiently waiting as he's lost in thought. With a shake of his head, he snaps out of it, looking at me with a devilish smirk. "The fire, the badass skills on the ice, but even better, your drive and ability to put the two together. You're a fucking unstoppable force out on the ice, and we've needed it. Alex is a killer right wing, but he can't do it alone."

"Thanks, boo," Alex says with a wink, eavesdropping on our conversation while talking with Coach and a few of the other rookies. I hadn't even noticed how close he was until now.

So far, this week has mostly been the rookies and

newbies out on the ice. But for some reason—whether it be to scope out their competition or to meet their new coach—more of the seasoned players joined us today. It was nice to meet everyone and see how we jell together as a team.

"No, but seriously, Max," Knox starts before turning to face me, "You're the shit. You've got what it takes to make it and be an absolute menace on the ice. You've got what we've been looking for, so keep it up, keep it going, and keep making those badass shots. I still can't believe you scored on Davis! Twice!"

"Oh, fuck off, man," Davis grunts from the bench behind us. Looking back, he winks at me. He knows he's one of the best goalies in the league, so he's not holding a grudge over a couple of missed saves. "But he's right, Daniels. Your snapshot is wicked, and those one-timers," he says, shaking his head in disbelief. "Yeah, you're definitely gonna be in the running for Rookie of the Year if you keep that shit up."

I feel like I'm in a dream world. *The* Jon Davis is complimenting me? This man has been a goalie in the NHL for over ten years! He's a walking legend. I can't believe he's telling me how great my shots were, even after I scored on him twice. Yeah, I feel like a badass Motherfucker right now. I feel like a kid going to Disneyland for the first time.

But, like, what the fuck am I supposed to say to that? I suck at taking compliments. I never know how to respond. I always feel like I sound like an arrogant prick.

"Thanks, dude. I'll do my best to keep it going. It's a great experience going up against you," I tell him with a casual nod, hoping I don't sound too much like a twelve-year-old getting a compliment from their idol, even if that's exactly how I feel right now.

For the next fifteen minutes, we sit around bullshitting

about Training Camp, our pre-season schedule, and the charity event that Rex's Mom is putting on this year. Apparently, this event is a big deal, and before Rex and his parents moved to Texas when he got injured, it had been the event of the city. Everyone wanted to be there, and it's invitation only.

No surprise. I guess that's why my mother tried to wiggle her way in by talking to Mrs. Lockwood. Thankfully, she put a stop to that. Just what I need is to be at a big event my rookie year and have her drama and bullshit follow me. By the time Alex and Rex finally join us, the rest of the players have already cleared up and headed to the locker room.

"Sup, Daniels," Alex says as he sits up on the boards by Knox. "You ready to make magic happen together?" he adds, kicking his legs like a child while wiggling his eyebrows up and down. He looks like a goof, but he's sure got skill. "The two of us on a line . . . we'd be fucking unstoppable."

"Don't get ahead of yourself. We haven't even officially decided anything. Plus, this is the NHL, not college. You never know what the other teams have hiding away. It's like poker—we don't show our cards until it's time," Rex says, ever the diplomat. "Besides, maybe another rookie is gonna join Max."

Rex is just giving Alex shit, and we all damn well know it. He's one of the best right wingers in the league, if not the best. There's not a chance in hell he's being replaced. Watching them, I don't miss Alex smirking at Rex like he knows something the rest of us don't. Based on what I've been overhearing, it sounds like Alex and I might already be a done deal.

Which is exciting as fuck.

Doing my best to play it cool, I laugh before looking out at the rest of the guys. "Yeah, man, ya never know. Anything could happen. Although, I think it's safe to say that you and I were able to cause some damage today. I'd be stoked to see what we could do in an actual game."

"Fuck, yeah!" Alex fist pumps, earning a laugh from Davis and Rex, while I smirk at him.

"Yeah, y'all are gonna be pretty badass together," Davis pipes in. "As a goalie, I'm fucking thrilled that I don't have to go up against the two of you in a regulation game. It's one thing when you have one player taking most of the shots, but it's another when you have two players you've gotta keep your eye on."

"Thanks, man. We'll see how it all plays out. Still got a couple days left till we'll know for sure, right Coach?" I ask, trying to deflect the conversation back toward Rex. We have a good repertoire, even here on the ice. The guys know he's dating my sister, and they make sure to give me a hard time anytime she's brought up. I'm glad we decided not to keep it under wraps. I don't want anyone assuming anything. It wouldn't have looked good if we tried to hide it.

Even so, we still have the championship win from last season to show my worth, so there's no reason to add any drama about special treatment.

There's really only been one player who's had a problem with how I was brought on, but if we're being honest, I'm sure it's because he feels threatened. Alex and Dylan have played together for the last couple of seasons. Dylan has basically rode Alex's success the entire way. He had a ton of assists but wasn't scoring as many goals as they would've liked to see. The hope is that if Alex and I can work well together, we'll be able to score as many goals as fucking possible.

Max

"Alright, guys, it's about that time. Go hit the showers. We have a quick team meeting tomorrow morning. Besides that, I want you all to go home, refuel your body, take ice baths, rest, and all that bullshit to get your body ready for the season. The rest of the returning players come back next week, so prepare yourself, it's going to be brutal."

"Deal, Coach," Knox says as he and Davis skate off, leaving just Alex and I with Rex.

"You both had a killer practice today. If you keep it up, you might not be wrong about getting to play together. Now get moving, I've got my lady waiting in my office ready to go have dinner."

"Ew," I say as Alex starts to skate off.

"If you didn't want to hear it, you'd have been in the showers already," Rex says with a laugh. "But, hey, in all seriousness, great practice."

He's not smiling, at least not visibly, but I can see in his eyes that he's impressed with what he saw today.

Looking around, it's surreal being here, skating in the Empire State Arena. I've dreamed of this day for years. But now that it's finally here, I'm terrified of fucking it up. So, without a second thought, I head off to the locker room for a quick shower before going home to rest as much as possible.

If Rex has faith in me, I'll do everything I can to make sure I don't let him down.

When I finally drag myself into the apartment, I know it will be empty. Cassie mentioned having plans tonight and that she'd be home pretty late. As much as I would love to see her, a long, hot shower before refueling my body with food sounds perfect this evening.

Chapter Fourteen

I think I've used up all of the hot water for the entire building, if not the entire block before I finally make it out of the shower. My whole body feels tight and in pain, but I know if I sit down now, it'll be lights out until tomorrow. And as tempting as that is, I know if I don't take the time to eat something and stretch before bed, I'll pay for it tomorrow, and I can't afford to fuck up.

My body is my responsibility. It's part of my job, and refueling it so I can perform at my best is my number one priority. After I dry off, I don't bother doing anything with my hair, I don't have the energy to care. I throw on a pair of sweats and a baseball hat and head out to the kitchen. The first thing I do is turn on music because as much as I love food, I hate cooking, music makes it at least tolerable.

Don't get me wrong, I'm thankful that I know how to cook and am halfway decent at it, but damn, sometimes I wish I could stomach those meal preps people buy. I'm so jealous of some of my teammates who just order those and can pop them in the microwave when they need to eat, but I can't eat the same thing over and over again. I tried back in college, but I never found any meal prep that I could actually eat.

Standing at the stove, I continue stirring my sauce until, out of the corner of my eye, I see Cassie standing in the doorway. I almost laugh at the look on her face because she's just staring at me, slack-jawed, and her eyes trailing down my body.

I'm a confident man. I mean, I know I look good. I work hard for this body. But, fuck, I'd be lying if I said it didn't make my cock hard watching her check me out. She's trying to be sneaky, thinking I haven't noticed her, but I fucking love the way she bites her lips as her eyes continue down my body. I wonder what she's thinking. Is she imagining something? That thought makes me want to say fuck it, pick her up, and feast on her pussy until she's screaming for more. Until she's begging to be mine.

"You just gonna stand there and check me out, or are you actually going to come into the kitchen?" I question without even turning around, and thankfully, she can't see the shit-eating grin on my face.

"I was not!" she grumbles, walking the rest of the way into the kitchen. "I was just lost in thought, thinking about work and everything. I've got a lot of shit on my mind."

"Lost in thought about my body? That explains why you were drooling, and your neck is all flushed." Turning to her, I smirk. "What were you thinking about? I can always help bring some fantasies to life."

Her cheeks immediately redden, and before she can turn away, I see a flash of hunger in her eyes. She's thinking about me. My cock immediately hardens, but I don't move to hide it from her. At this point, I want her to notice the effect she has on me. I want her to see just how hard she makes me without even touching me.

I know I'm pissing her off, but I also know that's the only way I have any chance of breaking through to her, so push I must.

"I . . . uh . . ." she trails off, embarrassment on her face, but the fire remains in her eyes. "I brought beer. It's the hazy IPA I know you like. I–I went there on my way home after my plans got changed to next week. I just assumed we both could probably use a little break tonight after work and training camp and everything. But...if you're not in the mood, I'll just put these in the fridge and go jump in the shower."

She goes to turn around, and I almost laugh. "Stop fucking rambling, Princess. Just sit your cute ass down and tell me about your day while I finish dinner. Are you hungry?"

Cassie stands in the same spot, jaw dropped, indecision written all over her face.

Oh, Princess, I get it. Trust me.

I know I should keep my distance, that she's not ready for me to push this further, to see if there's a chance that she might still want me. But another part of me says fuck it, go for it, and deal with the repercussions later.

But that would only work if it were a one-time thing. If she was someone I wouldn't see tomorrow. Someone I hadn't thought about every single day since that first kiss. She's the girl I've compared all other girls to and the reason I haven't been able to date anyone since. Cassie and I are far away from being just a one-night stand, and we both fucking know it. But neither of us is quite ready to face it.

I watch as she slowly makes her way into the kitchen, grabbing us each a beer before lifting onto the counter next to me. With a smile, she passes me a beer. "What're you making me?"

"A slightly healthier chicken parmesan. Thanks for the beer," I say, taking a swig.

Should I be drinking tonight? Nope. But I'm fairly certain that she could get me to do just about anything. Hell, I'd go swimming with sharks or skydive without a parachute if she so much as asked me to, because the thought of her stopping by Two Sails Brewery to pick up my favorite beer makes me giddy. It took me forever to get her to try it, so this is cool as fuck, especially considering it's one of the only times she's gone out of her way to do something for me in years.

That thought excites me and makes me optimistic about the future. But it also terrifies the absolute fuck out of me.

There's always the chance that I'm reading into things too much. Like the way she smiles when we both find something funny on TV, the smile she doesn't know I notice. Or how she smirks when she catches me staring at her ass, obviously liking it. Or the way she's been proudly introducing me as her boyfriend to her coworkers on the PR team. Okay, it may have only been twice, but it still counts. Fuck, I'm just not ready to take that chance. It's terrifying. More terrifying than playing in my first NHL game. Hell, it's scarier than waiting to find out if I'm even starting. She may not truly like me yet, but she's been different. Different enough that I'm too afraid to fuck it up. Because if I lost her again, if she went back to hating me, I don't think I could survive it. It killed me the first time. And at least now, we're friends.

"I thought you weren't going to be home tonight?" I finally ask, plating our pasta and chicken before walking to the patio. She follows, grabbing our beers as she passes.

"I wasn't. But Gwen couldn't make it out, and, honestly, I'm glad. After the week I've had, I wasn't really in the mood for a lot of socializing."

"I get it. Sometimes at the end of a busy week, I want to do nothing other than lay in the dark and stare."

"Weirdo." Cassie smirks.

"Nope. Just need a break from stimulation. Too much happening, too much to think about. It's kind of nice not to see or hear anything except my breathing. It sounds corny as fuck now that I'm hearing it aloud, but fuck it. It is what it is, and this is relaxing as fuck."

"I get that. Today has been stressful as fuck. I heard from my father again."

"What'd he want from you this time?" I grumble.

"Just for us to meet him for dinner. He sort of already made a reservation for later this week, and he apparently expects us both to be there . . . but I completely understand if you can't make it, you have a life. I can just come up with an excuse," she says sheepishly, obviously uncomfortable.

But I could never do that to her. I can't bail and leave her to fend for herself with her parents, who are both sharks. If she showed up alone, they'd smell blood in the water, and I guarantee they'd go into attack mode.

Fuck that. Nothing but a game could keep me from that dinner and being by Cassie's side.

"I'll be there. Let me know the details. We'll ride together."

She doesn't go on, instead, she just nods and smiles, the first genuine smile I've seen from her in a while, and it fills me with happiness. This is everything I've ever wanted in a relaxing evening, being able to spend time with someone where the conversations are easy and not forced.

The sky is clear tonight, and since it's been getting darker earlier, we already have a good view of the stars. Of course, there's the regular hustle and bustle of the city, but somehow the noise of New York is relaxing from up here. It's the people and all the talking that gets to be over-whelming.

This would probably be the perfect time to tell her that I received another message from an unknown number after our team meeting and have yet to open it, but I don't want to ruin the night, especially when she seems content for the first time in ages.

We eat quietly, minus the noises she makes every time she takes a bite. Apparently, she likes my cooking, too.

"This is so good. I demand you make this, like, all the time," Cassie moans over her last bite. "I didn't know you knew how to cook."

"Well, my mom sucked at it. Her idea of a good meal

was whatever could be delivered to our house, so it was up to me to learn when I got serious about hockey. I spent a lot of nights and weekends watching the cooking channel. Rachel Ray taught me a lot," I say, adding a wink at the end, hoping she can't see the sadness in my eyes. As much as I hate my mom, every kid wishes for an attentive, loving mother, so telling this story eats me up a little inside.

"I'm sorry about your mom," she says, her shoulder gently bumping into mine.

"It's all good. She made her choice, and, unfortunately, it wasn't her kids. At this point, we have to live with it."

"I know, but it still sucks."

"It does. But I've learned that it's the people you were born into that matter. It's the people who choose you day in and day out. The people who fight for you, fight with you, and just let you be your true self. Those are the people that matter, and sadly, my mom didn't fit into any of those categories."

"I get it. I'm proud of you, Max. For making the tough choices so that you can be happy. I'm even prouder that you fixed shit with Sawyer. I hated seeing you two fight."

"Thanks, Princess. That means a lot. I couldn't have figured it out with Sawyer without your help, so thank you for that too."

We finally head inside and turn on one of the newer *Marvel* movies, but I couldn't tell you the name of it, if my life depended on it. I can't stop thinking about how she thanked me for fixing things with Sawyer. I know she was being honest when she said that and that she wasn't trying to bring up our history, but it upset me that even through everything that's been happening, I still haven't fixed things between me and her.

That's on me.

Sitting up from the couch, I spin until I'm facing her, startling her while she watches the movie. "Look, I...uh...I wanted to ask you something."

"Okay?" she questions nervously. "This isn't when you kill me, right? Did you poison me during dinner? This is like all those *Criminal Minds* episodes. Were you playing the long game, Max?" Cassie questions. I know she's not being serious. She rambles when she's nervous.

Normally, it's cute and distracting, but right now, I don't want to be distracted. I need to talk to her, and if she keeps on, I'll chicken out.

"Umm. I guess I'll just ask. What happened? Why do you hate me so much when it was you that moved on? I've never understood, and it's made me so angry, so frustrated all these years. But mostly, I'm tired. I'm tired of pretending to hate you. It's fucking exhausting."

When I stop, I take a deep breath, feeling my chest expand as I watch her purse her lips, staring at me with a look of confusion on her face. But that's not the only emotion I see. Underneath is anger.

"Excuse me? How can you even ask me that?"

"What do you mean? We kissed, we slept together, then the next day you were with Tommy fucking Shepherd at the dance I asked you to!"

"Are you fucking serious, Max? The only reason I was with Tommy was because I waited outside for you for so long that I was crying. He came to console me and then offered to drive me home. Wait." She looks at me quizzically. "How do you know I was with Tommy that night?"

"Because I saw him kiss you right outside his car!" I yell, standing up from the couch. What does she mean? I get that I was late, but I didn't think that was all it would take for her to move on and choose someone else.

"You saw him kiss my cheek. That's it. Why were you even at the dance? I waited all night. I texted and I called, but it went straight to voicemail. I felt used, like you'd manipulated me, and once you got what you wanted, you were done with me. For you to just ghost me afterward, I knew I couldn't trust you. You obviously didn't care since you took advantage of me in a vulnerable state."

"It doesn't matter why I was late or why I couldn't respond. Besides, you and Tommy started dating the very next week, so obviously, I didn't matter that much to you."

"It does too fucking matter! Why, Max? Why did you take everything from me and then just leave and forget about me like I meant nothing?" Cassie shouts through the tears that are now steadily streaming down her cheeks.

I have spent years covering my feelings, pushing them down instead of actually facing them, but seeing her like this, it kills me. It brings all those memories, all those feelings rushing back.

I've spent years broken. Thinking I wasn't good enough for anyone. That I wasn't good enough for my parents. I mean, fuck, I wasn't close with my sister, and the only girl I'd ever loved left me. But now . . . now that she's telling me she waited, that she called, reached out, and was broken over me not showing up? I'm shattered.

"Cassie, I have no idea what you're fucking talking about! I thought about you every single day since that kiss. EVERY. SINGLE. DAY. I had to watch you date Tommy, who made damn sure that anytime I tried to talk to you, he was there to intervene. Every time I went to your house, no one answered the door. Eventually, I realized that you'd just used me, probably too nervous to lose your virginity to Tommy, so you took comfort in me," I scream, fists clenching as I remember it all too clearly.

"Then why did you leave me waiting? Why did you stand me up at the dance? You didn't even have the decency to text or call me, and I tried! I tried over and over to call you, but you kept sending me to voicemail!" Cassie continues to cry, the floodgates now open for both of us. A mix of tears and words just tumbling out, all jumbled, mixed up, and raw from years of pushing them down and hiding them.

"He shattered my phone! I tried to text you, but the second he saw me with it, he threw my phone, shattering glass everywhere. I couldn't do anything about it either! When I tried to protect her, he took it out on me. There was blood, and then I just left," I'm shouting now, fighting back tears as the memories of that night hit me like a freight train.

"Who? What are you even talking about Max?" Cassie says, unease fluttering through her eyes.

"My father."

"He . . . hurt you?" she asks, her voice softer, less abrasive than before.

Besides Sawyer, I've never told anyone this in the six years since it happened. It's not something I'm proud of, but I also don't want someone's pity, so it's been easier to keep it to myself. But Cassie doesn't pity people. She feels for them, she truly empathizes, which has always made it so easy for me to talk to her.

"Yes."

"How? What happened that night?"

"I, uh, I don't even know where to begin, Cass," I murmur, running my hands through my hair before sitting back down on the couch. "I heard my parents arguing, but I was getting ready. Them arguing wasn't anything new. Only this time, when I tried to walk by, he stopped me and grabbed my phone. He started to direct his anger at me, which only escalated when I told him I was leaving for the dance. Apparently, he didn't know anything about it, and it pissed him off."

I stop briefly. Long enough to catch my breath and take a drink. Staring down at my beer bottle, I peel off the label, looking anywhere but at her. Because right now—this conversation—is proof that the years of us not being together, the years of us hating each other, were all for nothing. All because of a stupid fucking miscommunication. When I finally look up, I'm met with kind, patient, and loving eyes, giving me the time I need to keep talking.

"My mom said it wasn't a big deal, that I should go, but I'd seen the bruises on her arms, and I knew what he was capable of. But as she spoke, he got pissed, broke my phone, then turned to head toward her. I got in the way, so he took it out on me instead. After that, I took off, cleaned myself up, and headed to the school to find you."

"And when you got there, I was with him," Cassie mumbles, finishing it so I don't have to. "Is that why you fought him the next day? I figured you'd heard something and got mad."

"I mean, kind of. I didn't want anyone to question what happened to my face. I figured if everyone knew I'd been in a fight, they'd leave me alone. Besides, I did want to fucking punch him, so there's that too," I smirk, unable to help it.

"Why didn't you say something?" she asks. "You could've come to me after."

"Because I couldn't do that to you," I growl, remembering how happy she looked when she was with him. I remember wanting to punch him every time I heard about them together. I hated it, but I knew that I wouldn't do anything to jeopardize her happiness.

"Do what?" she questions hesitantly.

"Ruin your happiness just to save my own. If I had gone after you and tried to ruin what you two had, it would have only been to make myself happy. Besides, you made your choice, and it wasn't me. I'd lost you before I'd even truly had you," I tell her, unable to hold back anymore, but instead of understanding on her face, her jaw clenches and her fists ball.

"I bet you were so sad. Is that why you slept with Tanya? Or Vanessa? Or maybe that was why you slept with Kim? Because you were so heartbroken over me."

"You mean, did I do everything I could to forget about you and Tommy? To forget about what you two were probably doing? How he was going to touch you in places I'd only ever touched, and how I could do it so much better? Yeah, Cassie. That's why I lost myself in those girls for a while. I tried to move on, I tried to get past you, but I couldn't. I never could. You have invaded my mind, my body, my whole entire world. You've buried yourself so deep inside my heart I knew I would never get you out, but yeah, you're right. It didn't stop me from trying."

"Look, I'm sorry I wasn't there for you, but I still can't get over that night. I trusted you, and it all went to shit. You should have found me after."

"And you should have known that the only thing that would've kept me from you would be something outside of my control. You didn't give me the benefit of the doubt, which makes me believe you didn't feel the way I felt about you."

"I want to trust you. I do. I just can't get out of my mind the way it felt hearing about you with those girls. The way it felt when I watched you flirt at parties. It felt like you just didn't want me, that you were too much of a chicken to tell me that I just wasn't enough for you."

Max

"Think what you want, Cass, but the truth is, you're so beyond wrong it's not even funny." Standing up, I shake my head, no longer able to have this conversation without losing it. Turning to head to my room, I look back at Cassie, who's sitting on the couch staring up at me with sad eyes that I can no longer face. "Do what you want, but I'm done being your punching bag."

"Max, I—"

I ignore her, shutting the door on this conversation.

Chapter Fifteen

Cassie

MAX

Did you know that dolphins use pufferfish to get high?

ME

What do you mean 'use' the pufferfish?

MAX

It's some natural defense mechanism or whatever, but pufferfish release toxins that apparently make dolphins hallucinate. And they like it.

ME

Ok. That one was interesting.

MAX

Had to do better after you told me my slug fact was dumb.

ME

That's only because it was.

MAX

I'm wounded.

"**E**arth to Cassie," Spencer sing-songs, waving an espresso in front of my face.

I don't acknowledge him.

I barely slept last night. I stayed up tossing and turning, my mind reeling over our conversation. All I could think about was that a stupid conversation could have prevented years of misery. We've spent years at each other's throats and worse–ignoring each other because we thought the other person betrayed our trust.

"Anyone in there?"

"Kind of," I mumble, finally grabbing the coffee.

"She speaks! She's alive!" Spencer mocks. "Girl, what's going on with you? Is it your parents again? Or are you and your man fighting? I see him over there with the team. He's kept his eyes on you the entire time. I can't decide if he looks like he wants to devour you or strangle you. Maybe both? I'm not sure what you two are into."

I look up. I want to tell him everything. I want his advice. But what if I don't like what he has to say? What if he tells me to walk away? Am I really ready to hear that? Hell, would I even be able to? After last night, I'm so confused. I stayed up all night thinking about everything he said, and it still just hurts that he never talked to me...about any of it. I understand it looked bad at the dance when I left with Tommy, but in my defense, I thought Max had stood me up. I just wish he had come back for me.

"I don't know what's going on, Spencer. I wouldn't even know where to begin. My whole life is a freaking mess right now. Max probably does want to strangle me right now. He's pretty mad at me. And . . . he's not exactly my real boyfriend."

Chapter Fifteen

"The fuck you mean he's not your real boyfriend? I haven't even seen you interact, and I can already feel the tension between you two. Girl, you better start explaining this mess you're in. I want the whole story. Especially considering he's practically fuming over there watching us together. I'd be scared if grumpy men didn't turn me on so much."

I laugh but still refuse to look over in Max's direction. Instead, I spill my life story to Spencer over coffee. I tell him everything, starting with when we were teenagers sneaking over to each other's house to hang out with each other. I tell him about the heartbreak, the betrayal, and the video that got us into this mess. By the end of the conversation, Spencer's staring at me with a shocked expression, and I'm doing my best to hide my tears.

"I could tell there was something intense between you two, even just from the looks he gives you any time you're in the room. I noticed it the first time we were here. He acted like the entire room froze, and you were the only person he could see. But this . . . damn."

"I know," I mumble. Feeling my phone vibrate, I check my messages, surprised when I see one from Max, who's sitting on the other side of the room. It's the meet-and-greet portion of the day, so everyone is mingling and getting to know each other.

MAX

Why are you upset?

ME

I'm fine.

MAX

Don't fucking lie to me, princess. Did he make you cry?

I chuckle and set my phone back down on the table. No Max, my friend didn't make me cry. You did. I feel the intensity of his gaze on me as I look back at Spencer and continue talking, ignoring Max.

"So, what are you going to do? Have you told Amanda about the video?"

"She knows about the video. My best friend, Sawyer, is Rex's girlfriend, so he gave us some advice. We figured letting them know before anything happened would eliminate the drama of it being a surprise if it does get released. She talked to the team lawyer, and since we're together, it would be revenge porn. So as long as we can find out who it is, we can press charges."

"Well, that's good. I fucking hate people who think it's okay to treat others like this. Who cares that you were outside? People should respect other people's private moments. It's not theirs to share. But here's my unsolicited advice about your little boyfriend, you can take it or leave it. He seems like a good guy, and obviously thinks you've hung the moon. Just hear him out. Maybe your trust wasn't actually broken, just skewed by perception."

"I—"

Before I can respond, a deep, raspy voice from behind me speaks.

"Hey, Cass. You got a minute?"

Max.

He's staring at me with a fire burning in his bright green eyes. His jaw clenched. He's obviously pissed about something. But I can't talk to him right now. Not after Spencer told me to hear him out. Not after Spencer told me he can see how Max looks at me. All of that makes me want to give him a chance. I want to figure out if we can trust each other again. If the feelings from years ago never went away and just laid dormant inside our hearts, waiting to be revived. But I can't do that here, not right now. But I know if he tries to talk to me that's what will happen.

"I can't right now. We're kind of busy," I say, sounding much braver than I feel.

When his gaze flicks between Spencer and me, I know I've fucked up. Taking a step closer to me, he grabs my hand and pulls me up to stand.

"Okay, Princess," he says calmly, pulling me in for a hug. At least, I thought it was just a hug. I'm shocked when his lips press against mine. It's not a quick peck, it's claiming. Right here in the middle of the crowded room. If Max wasn't holding me up, I'd have collapsed already as my legs turned to Jell-O the second his lips took control of mine. When he pulls back, he quickly nips my bottom lip between his teeth before spinning me back to the table.

"I'll see you after the meeting, Princess," he rasps before turning around and walking away.

When I look up at Spencer, he has a shit-eating grin on his face.

"You're so fucked."

I know. Don't I fucking know. And, of course, out of all the fucking nights, I have to have dinner with him and my parents.

Fuck. My. Life.

———

"Hello, Cassie. You look nice," my mother says, her words coated in disdain as I take my seat across from her.

I thought I looked nice, I actually dressed up for this dinner, a nice skirt and heels, but considering her tone, it's still not good enough for her. She sits across from me, dressed like she just left a courtroom in a business dress, pearls on full display, and not a single hair out of place, while my father just scowls at Max and me.

"Thanks, Mother," I muster before turning my attention to my father. "Hello, Father. This is my boyfriend, Max. You probably remember him."

"Hi, Cassie. Yes, I remember Max. He was one of the boys always out in the streets playing some stick and puck game," he states. He won't even acknowledge Max's presence.

His lack of effort and attention to both Max and I is already getting on my nerves, and we haven't even been here for five minutes. If the only reason they wanted to meet was to be rude and nasty to me, they could have done that on their own.

"It's called hockey, Father and he plays professionally. He's on the New York Ice Hawks." Turning to Max, I smile, one that I'm sure only he can tell is fake. "Max, you remember my parents, right?"

"Of course, it's a pleasure to see you, Mr. and Mrs. Wright," Max says, his hand finding mine beneath the table and offering a gentle squeeze.

My mother watches us before looking back at my father, who's still completely ignoring Max.

What. The. Fuck.

Have they always been this rude, and I've just been too blind to see it? I'm annoyed and frustrated and would prefer to be anywhere but here. But if I leave now, I know I'll be left wondering why the hell they were so adamant about dinner.

"So Father, what's this dinner about?"

"We just wanted you to meet the new intern at our firm.

She's absolutely perfect for the job. Blew everyone else out of the water. I can't wait for you to meet her! She goes to your school, so I wouldn't be surprised if you already knew her. She's just darling," my mother drones on, an actual smile on her face.

They've really set up this dinner just for me to meet some intern from their firm. I guess that's on me for thinking they might actually be taking an interest in their daughter and her life, but it seems they have someone else to dote on.

"Oh, that's . . . wonderful. Is she here?" I ask, looking around the restaurant.

"She had to use the restroom. She should be back any moment," my father says gruffly.

The waitress brings out five glasses of wine and a few appetizers. My parents must have ordered before we arrived. I could care less about the food, though. I'm no longer hungry. I came here tonight with some stupid hope that my parents actually cared. That they were reaching out to make amends. That I would be able to tell them about my internship and make them proud.

But instead, it's just another one of their little games where they try and take control of everything. I'm so over it. Right as I'm about to say something, I feel the tension build in my shoulders, an annoying sensation taking over my body. Then, I hear her speak.

"Mr. and Mrs. Wright, I'm so sorry I kept you waiting. There was such a long line for the ladies' room," Carina says, her words coated with venom as she smiles sweetly at my parents.

What is she doing here?

"Cassie, I didn't know you would be here tonight," she says, her eyes filled with mischief as she turns towards Max. "Hi, Max. It's so good to see you."

Cassie

I hate her. I hate this woman with every fiber of my being. I hate that she's here with my parents. I hate that she's even speaking to Max, and honestly, I hate having her in my presence. She's a leech who sucks out the energy of everyone she interacts with.

"Well, these are my parents, and they invited me to dinner with my boyfriend. The real question is, what are you doing here?"

I don't miss how her eyes turn dark when I say my boyfriend, telling me she's still not over him. Max grips my hand tighter—whether for him or me, I'm not sure. He's just as uncomfortable with this situation as I am.

"She's our guest, Cassie. Don't be rude," my mother quips.

"This is my new intern, Carina. Her father and I have worked together in the past. He told me she was looking for an internship, and we thought it would be the perfect fit."

"Oh, that's just great," I say sarcastically. "That still doesn't explain why she's here when you asked me and my boyfriend to come to dinner," I snap.

"She's been working so closely with us after we learned you took a different internship. She's been a godsend. She mentioned she would love to meet you, so we figured the more, the merrier. She also told us she had a history with Max, and it seemed pretty . . . intense. Although he wasn't always the nicest to her, it seemed they truly had a connection," my father rattles off, but I don't hear him. All I can hear is that my parents literally don't care about my feelings, my emotions, anything. They're just trying to sabotage my relationship.

"So, this is how it's going to be now?" I start, my voice trembling ever so slightly. They never take an interest in my hopes, my dreams, or my achievements, but now they're letting Carina join them for family dinners, talking about how wonderful she is, all while she's the same girl who has been out to get me for months.

It's official. I hate them. They may be my parents, but I hate them. They want me to be a pawn, an obedient little girl that they can use and abuse however they see fit, and if I don't oblige, they're done with me. I've been so afraid to open up and trust people because of everything my parents have done to me over the years, and all that's ever gotten me is being alone.

Well, I'm done with them.

I'm done playing their game. And the man sitting next to me, holding my hand, gives me both strength and comfort. He says I'm his princess, and that's a role I'll gladly play.

Standing up, I look down at Max. His eyes are filled with unease, but he understands and stands as well. "Well, this was lovely," I say, grabbing my wine glass and finishing it. "Thanks for the wine, but we have places to be. Literally anywhere but here."

Carina just sits there, a smirk plastered on her face telling me she knew exactly what she was doing when she agreed to this dinner. I just wonder how much my parents actually know.

"Cassie Wright, sit down," my father bellows.

"That's about enough," Max says from behind me, shocking everyone at the table, especially my father. "Don't speak to her like she's a child. She's smart, capable, beautiful, brilliant, and so many other things that you two are too dense to notice. You have your heads so far up your asses that you're incapable of seeing what's right in front of you. But I do, and I will not allow you to speak to her like she's anything less than incredible."

"She's my daughter. Cassie, think about the choice you are making. If you walk out of here with him, you know the repercussions."

"I do understand the repercussions, Father. But I'm done. Take your money away, take everything. I don't care anymore. Max, baby, let's go.

Without looking back, Max and I walk out of the restaurant, ignoring everyone's shocked faces as we depart. We don't talk the entire time we wait for valet, but once we get inside the privacy of the car, when it's just the two of us, I feel the emotions slam into me without mercy.

"Cassie, I—" Max starts, worry coating his words.

"No, Max. Please. Not tonight. Not right now. I just . . . just take me home, please," I cry, unable to control the crushing feeling of loss any longer.

Chapter Sixteen

Max

Why do lobsters hate to share?

PRINCESS

Because they haven't found their lobster
yet?

ME

Cassie, we aren't talking about Friends
right now. It's joke time, we can discuss
"their break" later.

PRINCESS

Fine…why? P.S. They were totally on a
break.

ME

Because they're shellfish. :)

Like Ross when he cheated. Selfish. Team
Rachel.

"You ready for your first season with the big boys?" Miles asks from across the table.

I met up with Rex and the rest of the guys after I went to the gym this afternoon. I was thankful for the invite; it's been weirdly tense in the apartment with Cassie. It's not like she's been rude or snippy, she's just . . . disconnected. I know it's because she has a lot going on and is still reeling from the conversation with her parents. Trust me, I get how challenging it can be to finally tell your parents to fuck off. I know she's going through a million different emotions. To this day, I know my mother still thinks the door is open for a relationship with me, and I've been too nervous to slam it shut.

It's just been hard. Ever since that night we argued, I've wanted to talk to her about what she said, about everything that happened, but I can tell she's not ready. I'm not surprised. It was a lot.

"I'm as ready as I'll ever be. The real question is, are you ready to get your ass kicked in December?" I ask as I sip my beer, trying to hide my smirk.

"A lot of shit talk coming from a rookie," Cade shoots back.

"I mean, are you surprised? When you've got a killer slap shot and left hook, you're to talk a little shit," I quip arrogantly.

"Kid, you get a shot past me, then you can talk shit. Until then, it's all just noise," Cade says, a twinkle of excitement in his eyes at the challenge. "Hell, you get a shot past me, and I'll talk shit about me with you."

Cade is intriguing, he's an enigma. He's nothing like I expected when I first met him, and honestly, he continues to fucking surprise me. When I first met him, I thought he was an asshole. But once you get to know him, he's a really cool guy. Plus, I have mad respect for him. He's an incredible goalie, the best in the league. He's way more hands-on than goalies usually are when needed. His boys do a great job keeping him protected, but he's been known to drop his gloves a time or two when a situation calls for it.

"Deal, man. I love a fucking challenge," I say, raising my glass to seal the deal. "In reality, though, I'm stoked–especially to be with this pain in the ass." I nod towards Rex, who's at the end of the table bullshitting with Trevor.

"Oh, I'm the pain in the ass?" Rex says with a smile before nodding back at Trevor.

"Yeah, you got yourself a great fucking coach. He'll whip your ass into shape in no time." Harris laughs as he slides into his seat with a tray of drinks from the bar.

"Hey, my ass is just fine, thank you very much."

"Oh? Did your roomie tell you your ass is fine? You two were a little handsy the other night," Harris says, an annoying smirk plastered across his face.

Geez, is it this fucking obvious, or does my sister just have a big mouth? I doubt Rex would've said anything.

"Oh, shut up," I grumble, but it sounds more like a whine. At some point, I need to decide if I'm going to remain a coward and avoid the conversation. I mean it's been easy so far with her avoiding me since dinner with her parents. But I know that I'm going to have to face her. Never trying with her, never putting myself out there, would be so much worse than being turned down. At least then, I'd know for sure what would have happened if I had tried, fought for her. Would she have chosen me?

Would she now?

"Earth to Max. Anyone home?" Harris says, his hand waving in front of my face.

Shaking my head, I snap out of my daydream. It seems that my brain attaches to any thought and situation surrounding Cassie, and it's like I'm not even aware of anything that exists around me. It's even worse when she's actually in the room.

"Yeah, I'm here. Sorry, just . . . just lost in thought," I tell him. I'm thankful it's just him and I having this conversation. The rest of the guys have now switched to hockey talk. But I can't focus on that. All I can focus on is the spicy little spitfire that has me wrapped around her finger. Again.

"I can see that. You keep drifting. I can see it in your eyes. I know that look all too well," Harris says from next to me. "Trust me on that one."

I look over at Harris, who's gripping his beer like it's trying to escape from him, his jaw clenched as if he's lost in a memory of his own.

"Is that so? What's her name?" I ask, taking some of the heat off myself. If he wants to get information out of me, he's going to have to give up some of his own.

"Avery. Avery Walton," Harris says, a sad look in his eyes that I'm not quite sure what to do with. It's even more than that, though. His face is blank, eyes far away, and, at this moment, I don't think I've ever connected with someone more. I realize he and I are a lot alike, almost exactly the same. Both pining for a woman and covering it up by losing ourselves in a playboy image that is just that. An image.

"Yeah, it happens. I'm usually better at forcing myself not to think about it. It's been easier that way. I've lived this way a long time, and I'm gonna give it to you straight; it sucks. I can tell you're going through it right now—don't even try to deny it. I've seen you two together. It's clear as day."

"Yeah, Sawyer called me out on it a couple of weeks ago."

"Oh, shit!" Harris laughs. "We figured it would take you guys longer to realize you weren't actually faking anything. Or fooling anyone for that matter. But if Sawyer knows, then what's the hold up?"

"Wait . . . what? You guys have been talking about this?" I ask incredulously. He just smirks. "And why do you seem so excited?"

"I have sisters, dude, they're always talking about their romance books and why people aren't together. I guess that's why I'm a hopeless romantic," Harris says with a wink. "Besides, it's fun trying to figure out what your guys' trope would be."

"Our what? Did you just fucking say trope? What the fuck is a trope?"

"You know . . . it's like a theme. My sisters drone on about it anytime they're together. They read a bunch of smut, and apparently, certain tropes are superior. Like– sister's best friend...that's a big one. Or so I've heard."

I gape at him. Is he speaking English?

"Dude, don't look at me like that. I have sisters. Three of them. When I tell you that girls are way dirtier than guys, believe me. I've had to listen to them and my mother talk about these dirty-ass books they read while my dad and I try to drown it out with sports. That's not important, though. Stop trying to change the subject."

"Uh, I guess it's probably part of the hold-up for Cass. She doesn't exactly know that Sawyer knows. Plus, Sawyer doesn't know everything about the situation. She just, uh, she knows the stuff I was fine telling my sister about," I tell him before downing my beer.

Thankfully, our waitress comes over with a new pitcher,

but before she can turn away, Harris stops her, "Can we grab a couple of shots of bourbon? Hell, just bring a bottle for the table."

"Of course. I'll be right back with that. Any preferences?"

"Nope, surprise me, sweetheart." Harris winks as she blushes and walks to the bar. "Start from the beginning. And, Max, I don't want the Sawyer version, I want the real story."

We spend the next twenty minutes drinking bourbon while I recount mine and Cassie's history. Starting from the beginning, I tell him the whole story, even the parts Sawyer and Cassie just found out about my family. Something about them knowing gives me the courage to speak it aloud again.

"This all makes so much more sense. I always figured you two had a history, but I never knew for sure. Plus, we allllll saw that kiss the other night," Harris says with a sly smile. "That was not acting, and definitely not a first kiss."

He's right. It wasn't our first kiss, more of a reintroduction. Two parts of a whole finally coming back together. There was no awkwardness, she fit perfectly with me, following my lead so flawlessly.

"Yeah, I guess we do have history. But it gets complicated. Remember when Rex and I were talking about that video of me?" I ask. The guys all heard about the video because I was freaking out that the team would get pissed and drop me, or it would ruin my reputation before I even started. The guys were all awesome, though. They helped me realize it could very well be an idle threat, but that I'd deal with it if something happened.

"Yeah . . ."

"So, here's the whole story. Six months ago, Cassie was

playing strip beer pong at the house I lived in with a few of the guys. We weren't there together, but I got pissed at my roommate because he wouldn't give her her clothes back and kept trying to bring them to his room. Well, I walked away from Carina, who's been practically harassing me to get me to date or sleep with her."

"So, what happened? Did you two just talk?"

"Well, I mean, yeah, we talked. We drank. I also kinda went down on her on the patio by the fire. Shirtless. So, uh, yeah, there's that."

"Fuckin' right you did," Harris says with a laugh before winking. "Real men love to be on their knees."

I just shake my head. He ain't wrong, though. I'd gladly stay on my knees forever for that girl.

"Oh, shit. Wait, does that mean the video is real?"

"Yep. Either that or whoever took the video knew what to do to make it look real. But it's not only my career that I'm worried about. If people figure out that it's Cassie, her parents will lose their fucking minds."

"Well, I get that. It's not easy making choices that hurt, especially when you're trying to protect someone you love."

My eyes shoot up at the word love, but I don't disagree. I can't. Because I know damn well it's true. But hearing it out loud makes it feel more . . . real. I choose not to dive into that right now, though.

"Have you thought that maybe it's Carina behind the video?"

My eyebrows lift, the wheels start turning in my mind. Holy shit, he might be right.

"I mean, yeah, it could be her. She was definitely mad enough to do something stupid. But if that's the case, then it kind of works in our favor. Our hope was that if people thought we were dating, they would see the video as a violation of our privacy, like revenge porn. So, if it's from some pissed-off girl who's mad because I didn't want to fuck her, that'd work out even better. It'd be her invading a private moment—granted, it was in public—instead of just some drunk sexcapade caught on video at a party. I received another part of the video the other day. It was a little more . . . explicit and definitely shows that it's me in the video. The worst part? I haven't been able to tell Cassie yet because she hasn't been talking to me since the night with her parents."

"Another video? Fucking hell. Still from an unknown number?"

"Yep," I grumble.

"You've gotta tell her, man," Harris says, his voice oddly serious. "You've talked to the PR team already, right?"

"Yeah, they think it's a good idea that we're 'dating.' Amanda thinks it'll help make it go away faster if the video gets released."

"But are you actually faking it? That would imply you didn't want to be with the girl."

"Between her and I, we've said this is all fake. Just to help us both out. But between you and me? She's well aware of where I stand, and she knows I want her, want to see what this could be. But at the end of the day, the ball's in her court."

"Hope you've got patience. That one seems like a stubborn one unless you know how to break her in." He winks.

"God damn it." Is all I can muster, and Harris just laughs, standing up from our spot. "Come on, that's enough therapy for the night. We can meet again next week. Now let's go play pool and get drunk."

I smile and stand, knowing he's right. I walk with him to the empty table next to our friends, who are all ready to watch me kick his ass like usual. Harris has already detonated so many fucking mind bombs that I'm going to be spending weeks pulling them out, so he deserves this ass-kicking, that's for sure.

It isn't until I overhear Rex telling Miles that Sawyer is home with Rory having some bonding time that I really know Harris is right. Cassie told me she was going out, and I assumed it was with Sawyer. Fuck, I need to go to her and stop this whole fucking charade.

Fuck. Is she on a date? Not only will this look horrible for us, but if some Motherfucker touches her, I'll go to jail.

Grabbing my phone, I immediately find her name and shoot her a text.

ME

Where are you?

We need to talk.

PRINCESS

I'm out.

ME

Like, on a fucking date?

PRINCESS

Does it matter?

ME

Of course, it fucking matters.

Answer my fucking question.

Are. You. Out. On. A. Fucking. Date.

???

PRINCESS

The person you are trying to reach is currently unavailable. Please try again later.

Max

Picking up my phone, I try to call her, but she sends it directly to voicemail. Damn brat. I immediately dial my sister's number, maybe they are together, and Rex is just fucking with me. She wouldn't be stupid enough to actually go out on a date . . . would she? Not only are we supposed to be 'dating' in the eyes of the world, but she's fucking mine, and it's about God damn time she fucking realized it.

Chapter Seventeen

Max

The bar she's at is . . . nice. Nice enough that I'm officially pissed off that she's here with another guy. The lights are all dim, and people seem to be paired off, giving the entire bar an intimate vibe. The only saving grace to this situation is that Cassie fucking detests places like this, and the forced smile she's rocking all but confirms that. She's a lot like me when it comes to going out. She'd much prefer to find somewhere with cheap beer and greasy bar food where she can relax and be herself rather than hanging out in some bougie upscale bar.

On the bright side, though, the bar isn't too far from our apartment, which is convenient as fuck because that's where she and I will be heading. Together. Soon.

These last couple of weeks have been fucking difficult. Between her getting drunk, spilling all her secrets and standing up for me to her parents. All it's done is prove to me that something is definitely still there. Something we've been holding in for years, so there's no fucking way I'm letting her go out on a date. We've spent years apart and there's no fucking chance I'm letting this stupid game go on for even another minute. I've done my best to hate her, tried to push her out of my life and heart, but I've failed.

Truthfully? I'm absolutely miserable without her. I always have been. I'm a shell of the person I once was when she was in my life. Which is probably why I've been so horrible to her for these last few years. It was easier to blame her for not choosing me than to deal with my emotions. But when she finally told me her side of the story and the real reason she hated me, I honestly can't describe what it did to me. I felt broken, like my heart had been ripped out of my chest. Well, what was fucking left of it.

Don't get me wrong, I see my side, but I also see hers. We were young and dumb, definitely too dumb to communicate correctly. Which is how we've ended up here. With me, sitting at a bar, while Cassie and some guy named Spencer sit together at a table. I've seen the guy somewhere, and it just makes me want to punch him even more.

Cassie noticed me the second they walked in, her eyes finding mine like a magnet and locking in. Her eyes narrowed on mine before she turned back to Spencer as he led them to a table in the bar. He wasn't overly touchy, but I wanted to rip his hands off every time they did touch. When they finally sat down, and she reached across the table to grab his hand with a smirk, I knew she was playing a game.

Is she fucking goading me?

She knows I'm here, knows I'm watching, and she's purposely making me watch her touch another man. She's absolutely the most fucking infuriating woman I've ever met, but goddamn, I crave her. I want to walk over there, grab her by her ponytail and drag her into the bathroom where I can spank her ass red for teasing me before finally shoving my cock so deep inside of her that she'll forget any man before me.

Watching these two is actually painful. He has a kind look about him, that I don't quite trust. Does he think she's his to take? To kiss? To devour? I don't know. And it's driving me fucking crazy. I've had to force myself to stay put and wait to make my move when all I want is to walk over to their table, knock him out, and carry her over my shoulder like a hunter with his prey. Every time she laughs at something he says, I nearly do it.

When she says something that makes him laugh and reach forward to grab her hand, I immediately see red.

Stop touching her, Motherfucker. She's not yours to touch.

Thankfully for all of us, Cassie excuses herself from the table and walks towards the restroom.

Smart woman. I couldn't have handled watching the two of them any longer.

I tried to stay away tonight, let her go out, and have the time she needs. The time she asked for. I told myself it didn't matter. I told Harris that it needed to come from her, that she needed to be the one to make the first move. But that lasted all of an hour before I realized it was a bald-faced lie.

I kept thinking about her out on a date, another man making her laugh, touching her, making her come. Needless to say, I lost it. I ended up leaving the guys at the bar and heading straight to this bar. Sawyer, of course, had to tell me where she was, which I thought would go against girl code or some bullshit. But she's been surprisingly supportive.

If Cassie wants a date, it's going to be with me. No one else. It has to be me. The woman drives me crazy. She's constantly pissing me off, and a giant pain in my ass. But that's just it. She's *my* pain in the ass. She's my everything.

I think she always has been, and we've just spent years pretending it wasn't true. But not anymore. This stupid game is over. Tonight, when we go home, we'll go together.

As soon as she gets far enough away from her table to not make it obvious, I follow her. Watching her walk away from me is both infuriating and hot as fuck. She's wearing a tiny black skirt, barely long enough to cover her perfectly round ass, and her long, sexy legs are on display, strapped into hot pink heels.

God, I could fuck her so hard in those heels, bend her over one of these tables and fuck her until she's writhing in pleasure, screaming my name, and my name only. I'd fuck her so hard she'd know her pussy belongs to me and only me.

When she slips into the bathroom, I step into the darkened hallway across from the ladies room. There's a small little alcove hidden off to the side, where I can see the door, but it's too dark for anyone to see me.

Waiting for her to come out is torturous, but the second that door opens, all bets are off.

I pounce. Gripping her wrist with one hand, I yank her back into my chest while my free hand covers her mouth, muffling her surprised scream. I bring my mouth down by her ear and fight the urge to bite her. "Quiet, Princess. Don't make this any more difficult than it needs to be."

I peer down, watching her eyes narrow, anger flashing through, mixed with the sparkles of desire. She may be furious, and if looks could kill, her anger-filled eyes would do the trick. But her feisty side just turns me on even more; it's hot as fuck. It'd be nice to let her come out and play, bring that side out just enough to have some fun.

Fuck, all of these images are sending the blood directly to my cock, which is now pressed firmly into her back. When she pushes back against me, I know there's no chance she didn't feel it, but she doesn't move away. In fact, she pushes against me again, this time intentionally.

She's so obedient, her body pliable under my touch, even if her attempt at a glare tells a different story. That's one of the things I've always loved about Cassie—her actions tell more of a story than her words ever have, and she wants this. She wants this so badly that she has to fight me, argue with me, and prove that, at the end of the day, she's still a little brat.

A brat sent into my life to challenge me, frustrate me, push me, and make me question everything.

Pulling her back into the alcove I was waiting in, I turn us so my body shields her, hiding her from any company we might have. Her eyes are still fiery; only now, I can tell she's enjoying this. As my hand slides down from her mouth, I grip her throat, urging her on more.

"Listen to me and listen well. You're going to walk back out there, and you're going to tell your little date you're leaving. Alone. I don't care what you have to do, fake an illness, a death in the family, I don't give a fuck. Hell, you could tell him the truth that you're leaving with me to go back to our place to get fucked. I'm the only one allowed to put their hands on you. It's your call. Either way, do it now."

Anger flashes through her eyes at my demand, immediately making me crave her even more. She doesn't like being told what to do, even in situations like this. And given that her anger turns me on, it really works in my favor.

"No," she snaps defiantly. Her eyes fierce, disobedience bubbling out into her voice.

I immediately grip her hips, spinning her around until

her back is pressed up against my front, her ass pushing against my already hardened cock, showing her just how much I want her. Slipping my hand between her thighs, I slide it up until I feel the lace of her panties. My fingers tease the edge just long enough to have her squirming in my arms. In one quick movement, I grip the lace, ripping it clean off of her body. I cover her mouth just in time to muffle her scream.

"How about now, Princess? Ready to go tell your date? Or do you really want to fight me on this when I'm seconds away from losing control and bending you over right here, right now? Those are your options. I can claim you where anyone—your date included—can fucking watch. They'll hear you moan, hear your screams as you come apart all over my cock, proving to the entire world who exactly you fucking belong to. Is that what you want?"

Her mouth opens and closes like she doesn't know what to say, her eyes blazing with lust. The little movements her legs make as she rubs her thighs together, attempting to get the friction she desperately needs, tells me she wants this just as badly as I do.

I grip her jaw with just enough force to hold her attention but not enough to cause pain. Well, not too much pain, just enough that she knows I'm in charge right now. But what's pleasure without a little pain?

Her big plump lips are teasing me; the gloss she has on makes me want to devour her whole. I want to kiss her until she's senseless, only aware of the pleasure I'm giving her and not one goddamn other thing in this world. But I won't. As much as I want to slam my lips down against hers, I won't give her that until she finally admits it's me she wants. She doesn't want to fake date me anymore. She wants this, she wants me, and I'm done helping her pretend.

Chapter Seventeen

"Turn around. Put your hands on the wall and keep your fucking mouth closed. If you make any noise, I promise I'm not letting you come." As she turns without question, my fingers slip beneath her skirt, brushing against her pussy, and coating myself in her wetness.

"You're such a good girl for me," I growl, my teeth slowly sliding down her neck, sucking and biting as I push my fingers further. "Such a good fucking girl. I can't stand you being on a date with another man, a man who isn't me. I can't stomach the thought of him touching you. It makes me want to punish you," I tell her, my fingers slowly sliding in and out of her tight wet cunt. "I want to redden this perfect little ass. Spank you until you're begging for my cock. But right now? Right now, you're going to prove just how sorry you are for making me watch you with another man."

"But I'm n—"

I slam my hand over her mouth, refusing to hear her spew nonsense, knowing it will only piss me off further. "I'd be very fucking careful about what comes out of that mouth next. I'm already being very generous and not fucking you in this hallway. But if you keep testing me and pushing my buttons, I'll do it. I'll do it right here, right now, in this bar, for your date and the rest of these fucking idiots to see. Do you fucking understand me?" I snarl, only stopping when I realize the hand covering her lips has now slid down to grip her throat, the pressure firm and tight, perfect to feel her nod in understanding.

Thank fuck she's not arguing. I'm not sure how much more I can take. As much as I'm trying not to be, I'm fucking furious that she's here with someone else. After everything—the other night, dinner with her parents—this just fucking infuriates me. I tried to give her the space she needed, but if that space lands her with another man . . .

Fuck the space.

She's mine.

"Now, be my good little whore and get down on your knees. The only sound I want to hear from you is you gagging on my cock."

There's a little twinkle in her eyes as she drops to her knees, her hands tentatively gripping the waist of my jeans as I unbutton them, sliding them down just enough to release my cock for her. The last time Cassie saw me like this, naked and exposed, we were seventeen, and if the look in her eye tells me anything, things have definitely changed.

But she's not deterred. In fact, she seems excited as she reaches out, her hand gripping my cock as her tongue swirls around the tip, slowly licking the bead of precum as she waits for my reaction. She teases me, her tongue swirling around the tip, up the shaft, before making its way back. Her hand remains gripped on my cock while the other holds my balls. Her grip is firm, unwavering, giving me the pressure and the pain I so desperately crave.

With her lips spread, surrounding my cock, she slides me all the way to the back. I have to think about every hockey play and math fact I can just to keep myself from blowing down her throat without getting to savor this.

She continues to stroke my cock, using her hand like it's an extension of her mouth. Her tongue slides along my length, making it all wet and slobbery.

Exactly the way I like it.

I'd be lying if I said I hadn't dreamed about having Cassie in this position for fucking years. But now that it's happening, I plan to never let it stop.

My hips start thrusting forward of their own accord, my cock sliding in and out of her mouth, each time pushing a little further down her throat. Her eyes start to water as I slide in just past the resistance, my thumb collecting her tears as she deepthroats my cock, completely at my mercy.

Her hands hold on to my hips, steadying herself as I continue driving down her throat, with one hand gripping her hair to hold her in place as she starts to pull back slightly.

"Don't you dare fucking stop, Princess," I groan right as her mouth slides off my cock, the saliva clinging from her lips to the tip of my cock. Her eyes are wet from tears as I've given her little to no reprieve. I don't care, though. This isn't meant to be fun for her. This is me showing her who she belongs to. If that means I have to shamelessly fuck her mouth in the back of a bar, so be it. Gripping her jaw, I gaze down at her; something about seeing her on her knees, disheveled and looking like a beautiful, hot mess when I've barely even touched her is sexy as hell.

"Open up. You don't get to fucking stop until I say so. Now be a good girl and finish the job. I'm going to pump my cum down this pretty little throat, and you'll swallow it all. Every. Last. Drop. Then, you're going to take your sexy little ass back there and join your date while I sit back and finish my drink."

She just sits there, watching me, her eyes twinkling in the dim light as my hand caresses her jaw.

"And Cassie, just remember. If you let that mother-fucker touch you or kiss you, it'll be my cum he tastes on your lips. Do you fucking understand me?"

All she does is nod before opening her lips and sliding me all the way down her throat.

Fuuuuck.

It doesn't take long until I'm right back to the edge, only this time, she doesn't stop. She doesn't slow down. She continues to let me fuck her mouth as she swallows me all the way back, holding me still as one hand massages my balls until I finally come. Hard.

I feel myself nearly blackout as I thrust my hips in and out of her mouth, pulling out every last drop of my orgasm. Our eyes remain locked. I'm surprised because I expect her to look angry or violated, but instead, she looks . . . happy. We stay like this, my hand caressing her jaw, her tongue sliding along my cock until every drop of my cum is cleaned up.

"Oh, Princess. You're in for a long fucking night," I growl. "Now get your perky ass back out there and end your date. Now. There's been a change of plans."

"What do you mean?" Cassie asks quietly.

"It's time to go home."

Chapter Eighteen

Cassie

Max is mad. Angrier than I've ever seen him before. And this time, it's directed at me. I've seen him angry, pissed off, and in plenty of bad moods, so I know just how fucked up his attention can be. But this is the first time he's been this angry at me. This is a darker, a different kind of anger than I've ever seen from him, and I have no idea what to do.

You'd think that after getting a blow job in the back hallway of a bar, he'd be in a cheerful fucking mood, shouting his happiness from the rooftop. But no. Of course he isn't.

I'm not sure how he found out about Spencer and I going out, but my guess is that Sawyer told him. Which means that sneaky little witch probably made him believe it was a date, even though that's the furthest thing from the truth. Spencer and I became fast friends since starting our internship together, but it's nothing romantic. In fact, Spencer and I are out tonight scoping out places for him to take his boyfriend for their anniversary.

Luckily for me, he knows all about Max, so as soon as I

mentioned that he's here, Spencer practically kicked me out to go home with him. He just made me promise to share all the juicy details next time we see each other.

Fucking deal.

When I got back to Max after talking with Spencer, he didn't speak, he just grabbed my hand and started pulling me down the street towards our apartment. I hope.

"Why are you here?"

"I came to get you," Max grumbles, eyes facing forward as he continues dragging me with him.

"But, why?"

Max turns to me, fire in his eyes as he brings us to a stop. "Because I'm done fucking pretending, Cassie. I'm done pretending you're not meant to be mine, and I'm really fucking done pretending I'm not already yours."

"Max, I'm not yours. You're not mine. We are nothing. We never were," I say, breaking my own heart in the process. Five years ago, I would have screamed from the rooftop if he'd said those words to me, but now it's just a depressing reminder of what we could have been.

"Do you hear yourself? Are you fucking listening to me?" he shouts, surprising me with his tone. "How can you pretend that we don't matter?"

"How can you say that we do? You literally ghosted me less than twenty-four hours after fucking me, only to go out and fuck half the school. That obviously proves we were nothing."

"Stop repeating yourself, Cassie. Okay, yeah, I slept with a few girls back in high school. But that was my fucked-up attempt of getting you out at my head," Max growls.

He runs his hands through his dark brown hair, pulling on the ends, a nervous habit he's always had.

"Should I have done it? Of course not. But it's been six years. I can't really go back and fix the things I've fucked up. I should have explained it, explained everything that happened that night, but I was lost. I was scared, and I felt completely unlovable. So, when I saw you with him, I just lost it. But I can't take that back. All I can do is explain that to this day, you're still the only one that matters to me."

"I'm sure, Max," I say, turning to walk away. When I get to our building, I make a beeline for the elevator before slamming the *up* button. Unfortunately, Max is hot on my heels. "I'm sure I mattered just as much as the girls before me but not quite as much as the girls after me."

I'm barely inside the elevator before Max spins me around, pinning me against the wall. Leaning over me, he presses our number before his arms cage me in, his dark eyes demanding my attention. "I need you to listen, and I need you to listen fucking well, do you understand?" he says as he reaches one hand up, gripping my jaw, holding me in place. "Answer me, Princess, or I'll move to less socially appropriate ways to make sure I keep your attention."

I try to tune him out, try to ignore the way his hand feels on my jaw, the way his touch causes sparks to fly inside my body. It makes me wonder if he feels it too. His eyes trail down my body, and when he pauses on my lips, I nearly combust at the thought of his lips on mine again.

I'm so fucking confused it hurts. I want to believe him, but how can I trust him after all these years?

"Use your words, Princess," Max commands before a sly grin crosses his face. "Unless you'd like to see my less socially acceptable ways."

"Fine, just spit it out so we can be done with this conversation," I blurt as the elevator dings. We walk out and into the apartment. The second he's locked the door, he's back in my space.

"Get it straight in your mind, Cassie. You were my first. Everyone after you didn't matter. It all starts and ends with you," he says, his voice wavering just a touch. "I'm not sure how you got it in your head that you were just another notch for me, but that's bullshit."

Is he really trying to tell me that I was his first? That at seventeen, while all the girls were chasing the high school hockey star, he waited to give himself to me? There's no fucking way. Besides, I've been with a virgin before, and it was nothing like that time with Max. The guy I was with I pretty much needed to get him MapQuest directions to my clit.

"Don't lie to me, Max. There's no point."

"Exactly, so why the hell would I lie about it? You were all my firsts. Every last one of them. My first kiss, my first fuck, my first love, and my first heartbreak. You've got them all, Princess."

"No . . ." I whisper, my brain trying but failing to process what he's saying. I've always known Max as the keeper of my firsts because he took *Every. Single. One.* To me, that means that no matter where our relationship ended up, he would always be special to me. He was always the one holding my heart. But I never considered the fact that maybe, just maybe, he'd trusted me with his heart all those years ago too.

"Wait, you don't trust me?" Max asks, hurt coating his words.

"It's not that. I just...I don't know how this all got so fucked up. I mean, I do trust you . . . I just can't trust you with my heart, Max." Max is one of the best guys I've ever known, even with his downfalls. I was lucky enough to get to know him before his life became jaded. Back in high school, the kind, sweet, caring Max that only I truly got to see. But after everything that happened, I'm just too scared to trust him with my heart again. If he were to break it again, I wouldn't survive. But trust him with my body? Yeah, that bitch can take it.

"I trust you with my body, but Max . . . I can't. I won't survive another broken heart," I stammer out, my eyes welling with tears as he reels back like I just slapped him, his eyes filling with hurt.

Fuck, I almost wish I could take it back, and force myself to trust him. But I don't know how.

"I'm going to change your mind, Princess. This I promise you. I'm going to remind you of what we were . . . what we could still be if you just let me in. It was never nothing. It's still not nothing. It's not gone, Cassie. It's just buried under years of lies and bullshit. But we can find our way back. Even if I have to crawl and dig my way there, I'll get us there, Princess. I promise. You weren't the only one who had their heart broken."

My brain feels like it's short-circuiting. I'm not sure what has changed. He went from acting like a feral animal at the bar to now telling me he thinks we should be together.

What the hell did I miss?

"I—"

"No need to respond. It's not up for discussion," he says, caging me in with his arms as he licks his lips, looking at me like he's ready to devour me. "Go into your room and get undressed. I want you naked on your bed when I come in," Max commands.

First off, why does he think he gets to tell me what to do? Why does he expect I'll obey him? Second . . . why am I already complying?

Cassie

"Or what?" I ask, unable to help myself. Who knows, I might just like the punishment. Maybe he'll take me over his knee, spank my ass until it's red. That's like a bucket list type of experience, and I'll be damned if I don't get to cross it off.

He just smirks, like he's hearing my thoughts too. "Oh, Princess, you and I are going to get along very well. Now go. You have two minutes. Don't make me wait." Spinning me towards my room, he swats my ass before heading off in the other direction of the kitchen. Without another thought, I'm in my bedroom, immediately stripping my clothes off and climbing onto my bed to wait. The anticipation is high, and I'm nervous as fuck, but I'd be lying if I said this wasn't turning me on like nobody's business.

Once I hear his footsteps coming down the hallway, the nerves take over, adding to the high I'm already feeling. I freeze, lying on the bed, with my eyes closed while I wait for what he's going to do next. When the door opens, I feel like I'm frozen in place, unable to move as he makes his way over to me.

"Look at you. Such a good girl. You follow my directions so well. It's almost like you were made to do it, for me," his deep voice bellows in the quiet room.

My whole body is buzzing from his praise, his deep voice stirring up all sorts of naughty desires in my body. When his fingers graze the inside of my ankle, I nearly break. As his fingers slide against my skin, it feels electric. All coherent thoughts have flown out the window as his fingers continue to trail up along the inside of my thigh, only to slide right past where I desperately crave him. When he leans in and blows against my clit, I nearly scream from the sensation.

"Max, I swear to god, if you keep teasing me, I'm going

226

to grab my damn vibrator and take care of myself right here."

"While that's a sight I would love to see, we'll pencil it in for another time. If you even try that, I'll tie your hands behind your back and tease you until you're begging me to let you come. I'm the only one in charge of your pleasure right now. Not you, not a damn toy, and sure as fuck not another man. Do you understand me?"

I nod as he stands up, his eyes watching me as he takes a step back. The energy is charged, electric, and filled with the tension building between us, but I can't peel my gaze away from his eyes. They're nervous, unsure, almost like he's scared to fuck anything up. He could breathe on my clit wrong, and I'd still probably explode from how wound up I am after everything that's happened tonight.

When his fingers start playing with the buttons on his shirt, I practically salivate as I wait for him to fully unwrap himself in front of me. He makes a show of it, slowly undressing, his shirt falling to the ground, leaving his perfectly sculpted abs on display.

He watches me stare at him, a smirk playing on his lips, and I'm sure he can see the desire in my eyes. My mind is filled with dirty thoughts that I'm just dying to act out. As his hands slide down and begin to undo the buckle on his belt, I have to stop myself from helping him get them off quicker.

But he doesn't take his pants off, at least, not at first. Instead, he slides his belt from his pants, his eyes never leaving mine as he lays the belt down next to me. Returning to his pants, he slides them down, leaving him completely bare in front of me.

Holy fuck, he's hot.

"So Princess, wanna play?" he asks, his deep, baritone voice feels like tiny vibrations against my skin.

"Play what?"

"I want to show you how well I know your body. How I can pull pleasure out of you that you've only dreamed of. But you'll have to trust me."

"I don't know what you mean . . ." I say nervously, unsure what he has planned for me. The scary thing is, though, when it comes to my body, I do trust him. Completely. It's my heart that's unsure.

"Then let me show you."

"Okay," I say, hoping he can't tell just how vulnerable I feel right now.

"Slide down to the end of the bed with your head hanging off," he adds as he walks further into the room.

I do as I'm told, sliding to the very end of the bed, my head perfectly angled off the edge. My tongue slides out to lick my lips, practically begging for him to bring his cock closer. I want to taste him again. My clit throbs just at the thought of having him in my mouth again. My mouth is watering, the bead of precum on the tip of his cock teasing me, begging me to lick it off, but he's in control right now.

"Good girl," Max purrs as he stares down at me, one hand reaching for his belt while the other caresses my cheek. His eyes are dark, blown out with lust as he eyes me curiously. He slides his belt beneath my neck and pulls it snug. I should be nervous, scared even, having his belt hooked around my neck, his cock in his hand, hard and ready.

But I'm not. I'm turned on, and honestly, I'm excited.

He stands there, one hand slowly stroking his cock while the other tugs on the belt again, just enough to make it secure. With fire in his eyes, he takes a step closer until the tip of his cock brushes along my lips, teasing me as he rubs the precum dripping from his length across my lips. He's enjoying the torture, the teasing, the control–and so am I.

"Ready to play, Princess?" Max asks with a smile before his face turns hungry.

I nod, my mouth open, tongue out, ready for anything and everything.

"Do you trust me, Princess?"

Chapter Nineteen

Max

F uck me, when I showed up at that bar tonight, I didn't expect it to end like this. I figured I'd have to drag her ass out of there kicking and screaming before eventually getting the silent treatment back at the apartment. But now, I'm only getting the silent treatment because my belt is wrapped around her throat, and my dick is out.

Looking down, I see she's smirking, her eyes a silent dare, seeing just how far I'll take this. But that's not what this is. I don't want to take this too far. I only want to prove to her that she can trust me, even if it's only with her body right now.

Stepping forward, I brush my cock against her lips, and her eyes widen as she groans. Her lips are soft, supple, and warm, her tongue flicking out just enough to be a damn tease. It's just enough to make me snap.

I need her. Now.

I slowly slide my cock further into her warm mouth, the feeling so good, I nearly come on the spot. Pulling back, I take deep breaths as I slowly start pushing in and out of her mouth. She attempts to follow me, steal some of the control, her needy hands gripping my legs.

"Greedy, greedy girl," I tisk, sliding in even further until I nearly hit the back of her throat, saliva filling her mouth as I grip her hair, holding her in place. Her hands slide up, gripping the base of my cock. Swatting them away, I laugh.

"No hands, Princess."

With her mouth full, she nods eagerly, dropping her hands to her sides as I slide out, giving her a moment to breathe before immediately sliding back in.

There's a fire in her eyes that I haven't seen before. She's no longer angry, and she's definitely not plotting my demise anymore. She's fucking loving this just as much as I am, and as she leans up, sliding me in even further, stealing some of my control, but I don't stop her because fuck it feels good. When she swirls her tongue around the tip of my cock, my hand pulls, tightening the belt, eliciting the sexiest moan I've ever heard from her pretty mouth.

Jesus Christ, this woman knows how to suck a cock.

I feel the pressure building at the base of my spine, my orgasm creeping. She continues sliding her mouth up and down my cock as I tighten the belt.

"Fuck, baby, you're going to make me come." Her eyes widen with excitement as she brings one hand up again, cupping my balls. "Use your other hand, Princess. I want you to play with yourself. I want us to come together, okay?"

She nods eagerly as her fingers move to her clit, pressing in firm circles, causing her to wiggle beneath me on the bed.

"You're such a pretty little whore for me, Princess. I love watching you pleasure yourself while sucking my cock." My hips start thrusting in and out of her mouth, fucking her face hard. I tighten the belt around her neck as she dips a finger into her wetness.

Chapter Nineteen

It doesn't take long before the tingling at the base of my spine explodes, my whole body on fire as her body shakes, trembling with her orgasm as I come down her throat. I thrust in a few more times, emptying completely down her throat as she continues to moan around my cock.

When I'm finished, I slide my cock out, looking down at this gorgeous girl beneath me. Her makeup is smeared, her cheeks stained with tears and mascara, but she's smiling wide, and it's the prettiest sight I've ever seen. Fuck, this woman has me by the balls, and I don't think she even realizes it.

Leaning back, I lift her up into my arms and gently press kisses along her neck to her cheeks. She's boneless against me and has to lean into my body for support. I wipe a drop of cum off her lips and press it into her mouth with my thumb, my cock twitching as she sucks on it, swirling her tongue, licking it clean.

"Fuck, baby, you're absolutely perfect," I mumble against her lips before I devour her.

I kiss her with every ounce of passion, wanting her to know just how much she affects me. Tasting myself on her tongue is such an erotic sensation; it spurs me on, urging me to deepen the kiss and ravish her with everything I have left. It doesn't matter that I just came, as the blood is already rushing back to my cock, ready for more.

Leaning down, I lay her on the bed. Climbing above her, I rest my elbows on either side of her face as I bring my lips back down to her, devouring her pretty mouth as our tongues tangle in the most perfect dance.

"Max, I need more. Fuck me, please," Cassie's voice trembles as she lifts her hips, rubbing her wetness along my cock, urging me on with just how badly she needs this.

Gripping my cock in one hand, I stare into her eyes as I

233

continue sliding my cock through her wetness until I position my cock at her entrance, just the tip sliding in as she tries to raise her hips enough to steal more of me.

"Patience, greedy girl. You'll get my cock soon. I promise," I growl. Taking a deep breath, I push in. She's so wet that I slide all the way inside her in one go.

"Your cunt was made for me, Princess. You're absolutely perfect. Look down at us. See just how perfectly we fit together," I growl. "It's like we were made for this."

Our eyes are still locked as I begin to slide in and out of her body, moving in tandem. There's no thinking, just feeling, our bodies reacting to each other perfectly like it's a dance they were always meant to do.

Bringing one hand down, I rub small circles along her clit, driving her wild beneath me as her nails scratch down my back, urging me on.

Harder.

Faster.

More.

Then she's screaming beneath me.

Pausing my assault on her clit, I lift one leg over my shoulder, changing our position to get even deeper, hitting a spot most men couldn't find with a map. The way she begins to tremble, screaming from pleasure, I know damn well I'm hitting it with every thrust. Her G-spot is like a magnet for my cock as I drive her closer and closer to another orgasm. I've never been able to come twice in such a small period of time, but as she whimpers beneath me, her tight cunt clenching my cock, I know I'm a goner.

I speed up, hitting all the right spots as I rub firm circles around her clit. I thrust in and out until we're both falling apart. I collapse on top of her. Rolling us both over, I position her to lay on my chest, our breathing so heavy as we both lay trying to catch our breath.

I couldn't tell you how long we laid like that, but the moment I try to talk and tell her just how perfect tonight was, how much it meant to me, I hear a soft snore escape her lips.

So instead, I lie there, holding her, until we both are fast asleep.

———

WHEN I WAKE UP, THE FIRST THING I FEEL IS MY COCK pressed into something hard. When I open my eyes and see Cassie lying against my body, all the memories from last night come rushing back. I freeze, afraid that if I move, I'll pop this bubble we're in, and everything will go to shit.

"Good morning," she mumbles as her body presses against mine. She freezes when she realizes just what her ass is pressed into.

"Last night was perfect," I mumble into Cassie's hair, her ass still pressed firmly against my cock. I save this image and this feeling to add to my spank bank because fuck, it's so hot.

I want to slide my hand between her legs and coat my fingers in her wetness, but before I can make my move, she's pulling away from my touch. She stands up and looks at me, her face distorted with a pained expression.

"Look, Max. Last night, it was incredible. But let's not try to make this something it's not," Cassie says as she steps back toward the door. She's thrown on one of my sweatshirts and nothing else. She's cute as fuck. "This was a fun time, a good fuck for the both of us, but we can't be anything more than that. It's not what we're meant to be. Maybe this was good. Maybe we got each other out of our systems. I know you think that it's more. I know you want more. But that's not us, Max. That's not our story. We aren't some wrong place, wrong time, right person bullshit. We're real, but we're really fucked up."

I take a step closer, loving the way her eyes widen in fear. She tries to hide it, but I notice a quick flash of desire as well. I could watch the emotions battle in her eyes forever, the two contradictory emotions fighting for control.

I want to bathe in the fire of her eyes and watch the world burn through her view.

"You really think that's what this was? A way for me to fuck you out of my system? Fuck, Cass, if that were the case, I'd have done it years ago. You've been in my heart and on my mind every single fucking day for the last six years! Always a reminder of what I couldn't have," I growl as I take another step closer.

"Then why have you always been so hateful toward me? Why have you been so mean and uncaring these last six years? It felt like the boy I once knew no longer existed."

"That's where you're mistaken, Princess. The boy you knew has always existed. He was just buried deep under the pain of losing you. The pain of you choosing someone else. I figured if I wasn't good enough for you, then I wasn't worth anything. I hid, created a facade, and hid behind smoke and mirrors to make you—and myself—believe I didn't want you."

She takes a deep breath, her eyes on mine as she drops her chin. "I just don't know what to believe anymore."

Reaching forward, I gently lift her chin, forcing her gaze back to mine. I want to see her sadness. I want to feel it, so I always remember what I never want her to feel again. I want to take that load off her shoulders and carry it for her.

I'm going to give her the honesty she craves. "Then let's start again. Let's rewrite our story and create something new. I miss you, and I want to give this a shot."

She still looks hesitant but nods anyway.

"I'm leaving for our preseason games, tomorrow. I'll be gone for five days. It's killing me to leave when I've finally gotten you, but I want you to promise you won't run from me. I want you to promise that every night we'll talk. You can ask me anything."

"Max, I—" Cassie starts, but I cover her mouth with my hand.

"Nope, listen to me. I want you to be able to look at me and honestly tell me that you trust me. And I think the only way to do that is by being brutally honest with each other. So, we have to talk. We have to ask the hard questions to get to a place where we can remember the good and hold on to it. Look, I know we said we were fake dating and living together for our image, but maybe, just maybe, it's our chance. A chance to right our wrongs and try."

"I—okay. But Max, if you break my heart again, I hope you know I won't survive."

"If I break your heart again, I won't survive either, Princess."

Chapter Twenty

Cassie

MAX

What's your favorite flavor of jolly rancher?

ME

Watermelon. I love anything watermelon, I love how sweet it is.

What's yours?

MAX

Lemon.

I like things a little tart, keeps life interesting.

Must be why I like you.

ME

I knew there was something wrong with you.

"Y ou ready to head out?" I hear Rex shout from the living room, where he and Sawyer are sitting curled up on the couch while they wait for Max to finish getting ready.

"Yeah, just about. I'm throwing the last of my stuff in this bag, then I'm ready to go," he shouts from his room down the hall. "Just trying to find the right skates."

"You and those damn skates," Sawyer mumbles from the couch.

"They're my lucky skates, Sawyer. I've never played a game without them, and I'm sure as fuck not going to start now."

I've been hanging out in the kitchen under the guise of making a drink, but honestly, I'm hiding. I've been hiding ever since Rex and Sawyer got here, terrified they might pick up on the vibe. I feel like I have a neon sign above my head that says, *"I sucked your brother's dick in the hallway of a bar before he brought me home and fucked me like his life depended on it. Oh, and I liked it."*

I don't fucking know, all I know is I'm stressed, and when I'm stressed, I avoid. So now, I'm acting like a child hiding in the kitchen all because we slept together, and I'm too much of a baby to face his sister—my best friend— because that bitch can read my face better than anyone.

Max hasn't made it easy, either. He keeps coming into the kitchen and grabbing random shit like vitamins and his protein powder, taking every opportunity he can to brush against me or lean against my back while he reaches for things. Smirking at my reactions.

God, I hate that this man knows just how much he affects me.

The guys are heading to the airport for an away game,

Chapter Twenty

so naturally, Sawyer and I are having a girls' night.

It sounded like a good idea the other day when she asked me, but now I'm freaking out. Sawyer should work for the FBI with how good she is at figuring things out. She can read my face and my body language and is excellent at reading between the lines. So I know damn well she's going to figure everything out.

I've been off since last night. Max played my body and my mind better than I could have dreamed of. He pulled the words from my heart, the screams from my mouth, and the orgasms from my body, relentlessly playing my body like he was an expert. It was unnerving, it made me feel vulnerable, but he held me all night, showing me he was there.

Now, I'm supposed to spend all night with my best friend, right after I just got fucked seven ways to Sunday by her brother. That's the part I've been avoiding. I've always wanted to talk to Sawyer about Max, but I never really knew what to say or how to even start that conversation. Like, *"Hey, best friend, I like your brother, and I really like his dick."* Yeah, I don't anticipate that conversation going over too well.

So I have to somehow survive tonight without saying something stupid like that. Gwen was supposed to come, which would have taken the spotlight off of me a little, but I guess she's been slammed between work and her internship, so she couldn't make it. Gwen interns at the children's hospital. She's going to school to be a pediatric oncologist.

As much as I am nervous about tonight, I'm glad Sawyer is staying. I hate being in the apartment alone. For as much as I love crime shows, I'm a wuss when it comes to being home alone. Plus, I'm going to miss Max being here, even if I should be avoiding him after last night and finding some way to get my vagina on a leash.

Maybe I should invest in a chastity belt or a contraption to keep my vagina on lockdown when I'm around him. She seems to have a mind of her own, and right now, she's telling me to hop on and take that man for a ride. I'm not supposed to crave him. I shouldn't desire someone that I'm struggling to trust. I mean, yeah, he's fucking hot, and he has a great dick, but he's still my best friend's dickhead brother who broke my heart.

It isn't until the guys start moving towards the door that I finally head back into the living room in search of the comfy couch and trashy TV.

"You ladies have fun while we're gone," Max says, looking at Sawyer, but out of the corner of my eye, I catch him stealing a quick glance at me, his boyish grin on full display, making my insides all tingly. When I feel my cheeks heat up, I realize it's probably obvious as hell what his presence does to me.

"Oh, we will," Sawyer says, taking a drink of the margarita I brought out for her. "It'll be low-key. I plan on getting caught up with the housewives."

"I think she means *Criminal Minds*. You promised you'd watch two episodes with me," I say with a pout.

"Yeah, yeah, I didn't forget," Sawyer says with a dramatic eye roll. "Just make sure it's not one of the home invasion episodes. Just what I need is for Rory and me to be alone tomorrow and be freaking out at every noise. Yeah, no thanks."

Rex just shakes his head, his little smirk telling me that he thinks everything Sawyer says and does is cute as fuck. I love seeing how much he adores her. If I'm being honest, their relationship is what made me agree to this whole fake dating thing. I want what they have; I'm just scared.

"Alright, ladies. Be safe. Don't do anything stupid. And,

Sawyer?" Rex shoots her a smirk that makes her immediately blush. "I expect lots of dirty pictures to get me through the next couple of days."

"Gross, man," Max says as he punches Rex's arm.

"Not my fault she's hot and all mine. You should hear the dirty thoughts going through my mind all day."

"Yeah, no thanks. You keep those thoughts to yourself so that innocent, unsuspecting brothers don't have to listen to you talk about wanting to defile their sister," Max says as he grabs his suitcase, heading towards the door, leaving Rex and Sawyer behind to say goodbye. "I'll meet you at the car," he shouts to Max.

Rex and Sawyer say a quick goodbye, and then he's on his way to meet Max, leaving us alone with an empty apartment, frozen pizzas, and a pitcher of margaritas.

They haven't been gone for five minutes before I feel my phone vibrate.

MAX

I'll miss you, princess.

I feel butterflies erupt in my stomach at how sweet he can be sometimes. I shoot off a quick response about how I'll miss him too, before putting my phone away. Blushing while texting will be a sure fire way to get Sawyer to give me the third degree.

Three hours later, we've polished off a pitcher of margaritas, ate frozen pizzas, and danced in the living room to whatever Spotify station we could find. My brain feels like mush from all the tequila, and it feels so nice to relax.

That all goes to shit when Sawyer turns to look at me, a devious smile on her face as she stares at me, watching me intently.

She looks like a cat trying to get a toy filled with catnip.

Cassie

"Cassie, just spill already. I've gotten you plenty tipsy. I just want all the details . . . wait, scratch that. That's a lie. I want most of the details, but I don't want to hear about you and my brother fucking. Gross. I want to hear the story, but I'd prefer not to go home and bleach my brain," Sawyer starts rambling.

My jaw drops.

I knew Sawyer was perceptive, but for her to know about everything without us talking about it is fucking weird.

"Wha . . . what are you talking about?"

"Don't play coy, Cassie. It's not a cute look on you. Besides, we both know I can read you like a book, so don't even try to play me."

"I–I, uh . . ." I stammer, not sure how the hell to explain this to her, especially when I'm the world's worst liar, and she knows all my tricks. The only weird thing is I've always expected her to be pissed if she ever found out, but right now, she's the opposite. She's laughing, and it's then that I realize I have no fucking idea what's happening.

"Girl, it's so obvious somethings going on, so don't even try. Besides, my brother is an even worse liar than you are, so I already know how he feels about you." She shrugs nonchalantly like this conversation is no big deal. Taking a drink of her margarita, she sets it down, pinning me with a stare, that as much as I want out of, I'm too afraid to break. She scares me sometimes. "As gross as it is, you two have loads of tension just rolling off you. Every time he looks at you, I feel like one of you is going to burst into flames. It doesn't help that you avoided me right before they left, you wouldn't even look at him, and he just kept smirking."

My jaw drops. I don't know if it's because I'm dumbfounded that she's caught on to everything so quickly or if

244

it's the fact that she's not screaming at me out of anger. When tears start streaming down my face, her smile falls, and she immediately wraps me in a hug. A hug I don't feel I deserve after all the lies she's been told.

"Whoa, whoa. Are you okay?" Sawyer asks, hugging me tighter.

"No, I'm not okay! Everything is a mess, and I don't even know what to do or think anymore. It's all just so fucked up," I blubber between my tears.

"Tell me what's going on. Do I need to kick my brother's ass? Because I probably can't, but I'm sure Rex would do something if I asked him nicely enough. Maybe he'll make him skate till he pukes or something."

I'm crying because I know the second I tell her this story and everything that's happened, our relationship will forever be changed. I hate that more than anything. But she's just smiling at me, so kind, like the best friend I've always known her to be. I know I owe it to her to tell her the whole story, even the parts she doesn't want to hear. So, after a deep breath, I tell her everything.

By the time I'm done telling her the story, we're both crying. I expect her to be upset, mad at me. Which I would get, it's hard when your best friend and brother keep something from you. But she's not. She's sad for me.

"I can't believe you kept this to yourself all these years! You know I would've been there for you–for both of you–if you'd told me."

"Sawyer, you had enough going on in your life, and I felt like I'd betrayed you. I felt like I'd ruined our relationship by crossing that line with him," I tell her truthfully.

"When I met Max for lunch a couple of weeks ago, he told me some of this, but I mainly focused on everything he said about our family," Sawyer says as she wipes tears from her eyes. "It's even worse knowing you both went through so much separately. There's so much pain and heartbreak between you guys, and I couldn't be there for either of you because I didn't know. Don't get me wrong, I always knew Max had a thing for you. But I guess I never knew just how serious it was or that it had continued once we all grew up."

I don't deserve Sawyer. I don't deserve a friend like her, a friend that feels my pain and who wishes she could change things for me.

She's validating every one of my feelings and is proving to me what a best friend should be like. She's irreplaceable.

"I don't think we realized how serious it was either. We were so young, only seventeen when everything went down. We didn't handle it the best, obviously. After everything, we cut each other out of our lives instead of being mature enough to actually have a damn conversation about it. But I didn't know what to do. I didn't talk to anyone about this because you were my person, and I was afraid to have that conversation. If I could go back, I'd do things differently."

"Would you still have slept with him, or would you have done that differently?"

She doesn't beat around the bush when it comes to conversations like this, especially with me. It feels a little like an interrogation, like if I say one wrong thing, she'll be mad.

"If I'm being honest, I wouldn't have changed that. But I would have changed how I reacted the next day. When you left for college, my parents were even more controlling. Max was all I truly had. I used to sneak out almost every night to go hang out with him. We would sit on the roof, and he'd play guitar while I listened. That step was natural for us, and I think if we'd been open and honest the following day, we might've actually figured it out and given ourselves a chance to see where our relationship could go," I say, taking a deep breath as I let everything I've said sink in before I go on.

"Has anything happened since then? God, I bet it's so weird living together. Just another reason you should have told me about this, you bitch. I wouldn't have pushed the idea of you two living together," Sawyer says like it's no big deal.

"Wait, you're still not mad at me after everything I've told you?"

"Mad? Fuck no. Sure, I wish I'd been able to be there for both of you back then, but I get it. Honestly, there was so much going on back then that I probably wouldn't have been in the right mindset to be there for you guys. Or I would've just gotten pissed because let's be honest, I kinda went through a blame everyone else phase, and that wouldn't have been good for anyone involved." She laughs. "You're my best friend, and he's my brother. I think I'm a perfect example that you can't help who you fall in love with. But, Cassie?"

"Yeah?" I ask hesitantly.

"I will get mad if you keep avoiding my question. Has anything happened since then? Or is all of this awkward-ness and tension just built up from the past?"

"I . . . uh, no, it's not all from the past," I practically whisper. "We got a little carried away after you told him I was out on a date."

"I knew he'd lose his fucking mind." Sawyer fist pumps the air with excitement. "Look, I don't want all the gory details. Just tell me how you two left everything."

"I told him I didn't trust him, but, uh, he promised me that he'd earn it. He wants to try. He wants to be together, but I'm scared, Sawyer. I'm so fucking scared. If we were

ruined all those years ago because of a stupid miscommunication, how can I trust that it's not going to happen again?
But I want to believe him. I want to try because even after
all these years, it's still him. It's only ever been him."

"Cassie, I'm going to give you my advice. It's been six
years, and you're still hung up on the man. You've barely
dated, you've never been in a relationship, and have had like
three hookups. You're obviously still crazy about him,
whether you're ready to admit it or not. So, take it slow. You
don't have to rush into marriage and babies and all that
nonsense, but spend time together. Just give it a chance.
Give him a chance. He's a great guy, and I know he cares
about you so much."

"Ugh. I think you're right. I know you're right. I just
don't know how to change our dynamic."

"Sit back, Cassie. Hear me out," she says, a sly smile
sneaking across her face.

By the time I head to my room, I'm practically
dragging myself to bed. I'm exhausted from last night and
completely drained from how emotional tonight got, but I'm
also happy. It feels like a relief to have the whole story out in
the open and no longer feel like I'm hiding everything from
my best friend.

I'm able to make it through my shower without breaking
down, but when I step back into my room and see a familiar
sweatshirt on my bed, I almost lose it. I'd recognize that
sweatshirt anywhere. I used to steal it from Max all the time
when we would sit on the roof. When I grab it, a hand-
written note falls to the ground. Max's chicken scratch
written all over it.

248

Princess,

You may not remember this sweatshirt, but I'll never forget all those nights you wore it, leaving it smelling just like you. I used to wear it anytime I missed you, but I thought with me leaving, you might take a turn wearing it. Sorry it's so worn out. I missed you . . . a lot.

I'll miss you.

<3 Max

I immediately drop the towel, pulling on the sweatshirt as tears threaten to fall from my eyes. Grabbing my phone, I snap a picture, my wet hair hanging down with his sweatshirt barely hitting mid-thigh, giving him a view of just enough skin to make him crazy. I take a few more photos until I find one I like and send it to him before I can second guess myself. Butterflies take over my stomach as I want impatiently for his response.

ME

I hate you.

MAX

I miss you too, beautiful girl.

With that, I crawl into bed, curling in on myself, and cry. I cry for everything that could've been, everything that was, and everything that still could be if I could just let myself fall.

Chapter Twenty-One

Max

PRINCESS

What's one thing you regret from your childhood?

ME

Deep questions today. Um…probably that I didn't do more besides hockey. I love it, but it became my life so early on.

You?

PRINCESS

That my parents never let me build a fort.

Stupid, I know.

ME

Not stupid, princess. Never stupid.

Max

W e've finished the first couple of games on this road trip, and it's been quite the fucking experience. We were able to bring home two wins, but the Carolina Cougars ended up beating us in OT during our second game. The loss sucked, but we were able to learn about our team and make some adjustments that hopefully will help us the next time we play them.

In our first game, we won four to three, with Alex scoring two goals and myself and Caleb each scoring another one. It was incredible. I'll never forget Alex skating up to me after my first goal, easily just as excited as I was when that puck went in the net. There's just something about scoring a goal in your first NHL game that just makes you feel unstoppable. Losing the second game sucked, but we were able to win our third game three to one against last year's Stanley Cup champions, which has everyone fired up.

No one thought we'd come out as strong as we have, especially with a new coach, but we're proving to everyone that we have what it takes.

The only thing that would've made the experience better was if Cassie and my sister had been in the stands watching. Rex was excited for me, though, and that alone felt good. Even if his smile lasted only a second, it was long enough to see the pride in his eyes.

But I'd still give anything to have Cassie in those stands wearing a jersey with my name on the back.

Fuck, that would be hot.

I laid in bed last night for far too long, my hand stroking my cock to the thought of her wearing my jersey and nothing else as I fucked her from behind, seeing my name and number on her back.

Chapter Twenty-One

Jesus, I can't keep thinking like this, but I can't get her out of my head. We've talked every day since I left. Thankfully, she kept her promise and didn't run the second I was gone. I'm not going to lie, the first day away was . . . awkward. Almost like she didn't know how to talk to me. Surprisingly though, she got over it quickly and has been texting me any chance she gets. We even got to Facetime the other night.

We didn't talk about anything too deep, but the longer we talked, the more I could feel our conversation shifting to a more natural, comfortable place. It felt like she was finally opening up to me. We talked about our parents, and she told me about her goals with the internships and how her dad has been giving her a hard time about the choices she's making. But let's be real, he isn't going to like anything she does if it's not what he's chosen, so fuck him. He can take his opinion and shove it directly up his ass.

We also talked about small stuff like our favorite restaurants, our favorite places to go swimming and even things we wished we'd gotten to do as a child. I always regret that I never got to go to Disneyland. Something about that place seems like it would be amazing to experience as a kid. Her regret is that she never got to make a fort growing up. Like the ones where you take pillows, blankets, and chairs and make a big, messy fort to hide in.

Sawyer and I used to make those all the time as kids. It was like our little hideaway from the drama our parents usually brought. Knowing that Cassie never got to experience such a trivial little thing hit me hard.

One of these days, I want to give her all of those things.

I want to give her everything.

Max

WHEN WE FINALLY BOARD THE PLANE TO HEAD HOME, it's late, and all I want to do is sleep the flight away so when I wake up, I can crawl in my bed. My phone keeps blowing up in my pocket, though, ruining any chance of me sleeping, but when I see it's from her, I can't help but smile.

PRINCESS

Good game tonight.

ME

You watched?

PRINCESS

Nope, just a good guess.

Yes, we watched your game, you big dummy.

She sends a picture of her and Sawyer wearing Ice Hawks jerseys, smiling at the camera.

She looks so fucking cute wearing it that I nearly miss the fact that the number 36 is on it. Alex's jersey number.

ME

I may be a big dummy, but at least I'm not wearing a jersey that's NOT my boyfriend's. Take it off.

I'm imagining all the shit the team would give me if they knew my girlfriend was wearing another man's jersey. Alex is a damn good player, but his head would get even bigger if he found out, and we can't have that. He's a cocky motherfucker as it is.

PRINCESS

It was all we could find. At least it's the right team. Sawyer thought it'd be funny to get Cyclones jerseys, but I didn't think you and Rex would find the humor in that. But I can't take it off, I'm at a bar, don't you think that'd be inappropriate?

I mean, unless you're fine with other guys seeing me topless?

I'll take your silence as a yes.

Taking the jersey off now.

This little brat. I pick up the phone and call her. There's not a chance in hell I'm letting my girlfriend go topless in a random bar. I hate the fucking jersey, but I'd prefer her clothed when she's around other men.

"Hello?" Cassie says when she answers the phone.

"Find a jacket and take it off," I growl, getting straight to the point.

"Hello to you too," Cassie jokes.

"Take. Off. The. Jersey."

"Calm down, Daddy.," Cassie laughs like she doesn't believe I'm serious. If we're being honest, I wouldn't even believe I'm being serious, but something switched inside of me seeing her wearing another man's jersey. I hate it. I can't stand the sight of her wearing another man's name and number on her back. The only thing that belongs on her back is me.

"I swear to God, Cassie. Don't fuck with me on this. Take it the fuck off. And don't call me Daddy unless you're ready to get spanked," I snarl in response. Who would have thought I'd be acting so possessive over a chick? But it's not just a chick. It's Cassie.

"Ugh. Fine. But the best I can do is to put a sweatshirt

on."

"That'll do. Just as long as that jersey is gone."

"You're a barbarian," Cassie snaps back, but there's no bite to her words. Instead, it actually sounds like an endearment.

"Only with you, Princess."

"I'm hanging up now," she purrs into the phone. Her seductive tone makes me want to keep her talking, but I know she's busy. "Text me later?" she questions.

"Okay, Princess. Be safe."

"Okay, Daddy."

———

AT EIGHT A.M. ON SATURDAY MORNING, I FINALLY make it back to our apartment. It's early, so I do my best to sneak in, expecting Cassie to still be asleep. Instead, I'm welcomed home by the smell of cinnamon banana bread, and holy hell, it smells delicious.

I don't see her anywhere, but I can hear the music playing in the kitchen, so I know she's somewhere close. After throwing all my bags in my room, I hunt for Cassie. Ever since our conversation the night after we slept together, I can't get over the fact that maybe, just maybe, we're on the same page. I know she's scared. And I get it. But I also know how I feel about her. I can't explain it, but this girl is it for me.

Even with her crazy antics like stress eating graham crackers and peanut butter, or the fact that she's made me do bright purple face masks every weekend I've been home. I don't think she even realizes half the things she does that shows me how much she cares about me. She switched the brand of ranch she buys because she knows I'm a *Hidden*

Valley guy. She always makes a big pot of coffee while I'm at the gym so when I come back, there are two cups waiting for me. And all of these things started happening before our conversation.

When I finally get to the kitchen, I stop dead in my tracks, a huge smile immediately taking over my face. Cassie is dancing around in a t-shirt, singing into her coffee cup like she's auditioning for American Idol. It's cute as fuck.

I lean back in the doorway, just waiting and watching the show. It takes me back to simpler times when this was a more common occurrence. A flashback hits me, bringing me back to a teenage Cassie dancing in my parent's kitchen, just like she is now. The only difference is, this time, I know what she's hiding under that baggy t-shirt, and, fucking hell, I want it. I want it all.

I push myself off the wall and make my way into the kitchen for some coffee and to tell her good morning, but before I even make it two steps, I've startled her. It happens in a blur, but one moment she's standing there in the kitchen, singing her heart out into a fake coffee cup microphone, and the next, she's screaming and throwing her mug on the ground like it's an explosive about to detonate.

"Fucking hell, Max. Don't sneak up on people!" Cassie grumbles, her hand pressed to her heart and her eyes wide. She looks around at the mess of coffee and flour before attempting to step over it. But she missteps and ends up stepping on her broken cup, blood immediately dripping onto our floor. "Motherfucker!"

Walking over to her, I'm trying not to laugh at the site of her hopping on one foot. I'm not trying to be mean, but she looks so cute. Gripping her hips, I lift her up, her body so tiny in my hands, as I place her on the counter. "Sit. Don't move."

"But I—" she starts.

"Don't fucking move, Cassie, you're bleeding everywhere, and you're barefoot," I say as I turn to grab the broom and start cleaning up the mess.

"Fine, Daddy."

"Cassie Elizabeth. If you call me Daddy one more time, I will bend you over my knee and spank your ass raw until you're begging for me to stop. Then I'm going to fuck you, hard, while I stare at my handiwork of a well-deserved punishment."

I see her gulp, but the tiny little smirk on her lips tells me she doesn't hate that idea.

After the floor is clean, I grab a first aid kit before heading back to Cassie, who's currently trying to clean her cut with a paper towel. I move her foot to rest on the edge of the counter, and her legs part, leaving me space to stand between them. When I look down at her foot, I catch a glimpse of her legs. Legs that lead all the way up to her t-shirt, with only a tiny scrap of pink lace covering her pussy. Fuck, it's so tempting to drop to my knees and worship her. Worship her body until she's screaming my name.

She must notice me staring at the edge of her t-shirt because a faint blush starts to spread down her neck. But she doesn't shy away, she just pulls the edge of her shirt down a bit before looking away, obviously embarrassed. "Sorry," she whispers, avoiding my gaze.

It's then that I notice what shirt she's wearing. It's my T-shirt—a hockey T-shirt—with my name and number on the back. She must've gone into my room to get it.

Looking at her face, I smile. Then, I'm crashing my lips onto hers. I don't push it, though. I don't want to push her. This feels like a step in the right direction, and lord knows, I don't want to scare her off.

Chapter Twenty-One

Pulling back, I smile. "Sorry, I just really like seeing my name on you."

Cassie blushes even more, but her smile widens.

"I kind of really like wearing it," she says, biting her lip as she fights an even bigger smile.

Jesus fuck. I need to pull my shit together. I'm a fucking NHL player who's hit on all the fucking time, yet standing in front of Cassie wearing just my shirt and skimpy panties, is enough to make me feel like I'm back in middle school. I can't spend my life having these thoughts every single second I'm around her, especially not when I'm supposed to be helping her.

Looking down at her foot, I try to busy myself with taking care of her, but it's a challenge. My brain keeps telling me that I should take her, claim her, drop to my knees, and devour her, ruining her for anyone that dares to come after. But I force myself to focus on the cut. It's not huge. It won't require stitches, thankfully. I hate the hospital.

"So, why are you up this early on a Saturday?" I ask, trying to distract her.

"I thought I'd make you a treat for when you got home. I know you loved this recipe as kids, and I just figured it'd be a nice way to say I'm sorry for everything."

"What are you sorry for?"

"For not fighting for you. I can't get mad at you for not fighting for me when I didn't fight for you either."

"I'm still here, Princess."

She just nods.

"I . . . I just don't know how to do this. I don't know where to start, but..." she takes a deep breath. "I think I want to try."

Did I hear her correctly?

"Are you saying what I think you're saying?"

"I'm saying I want to see what we could be. I want to take it slow. I guess I just want to keep doing what we're doing. I want to explore this," she says sheepishly. "But as much as I want to talk about this, I'm dripping blood all over your shoes."

I chuckle and get back to work. Luckily, she didn't get any of the glass stuck in her foot, but I can tell it's uncomfortable based on the pained look in her eyes. Without thinking, I reach forward and gently brush her hair away from her face. I hold her cheek, caressing it as I relish in the sensation of being able to touch her again.

She doesn't move. In fact, I'm not even sure either one of us is breathing right now, too afraid to ruin this moment. My eyes fall to her lips, and I start to lean forward, craving her touch. Just when I'm about to press my lips to hers, she beats me to it and kisses me softly.

It's a quick kiss but probably the best one we've ever had.

It felt like a promise. A promise to try.

"Let's go watch TV, my foot throbs like a bitch," she says before attempting to hop down from the counter but I'm in her way.

"Easy there,Pprincess. Don't go hurting yourself even more than you already have." I smirk, grabbing her tiny waist and lifting her. Her legs wrap around my waist to steady herself. She pushes back on my shoulders, staring down at my face, but I'm already walking her into the living room, where we spend the rest of the day snuggled on the couch watching endless episodes of *Criminal Minds*.

I've finally got my girl.

Chapter Twenty-Two

Cassie

ME

What did the toaster say to the bread?

MAX <3

It's gonna get hot in here?

Me

I want you inside me.

MAX<3

Is it hot in here or is it just me? *pants*

You can't do that to me, princess, I just got to practice.

ME

Hurry back. :)

I t's been a week.

Well, ten days, if we're being exact.

It's been ten days since Max came back from his trip, and everything changed. I knew everything would be different when I talked to him; I couldn't let him go. I couldn't move on without at least trying to figure out if we could be something more. Something real.

It's all I've been able to think about since that night. It's the only thing on my mind for the last ten days. It's controlling my thoughts, my emotions, and everything in between. I can't even focus when I'm at work. It's hard because the season has really kicked off, and my schedule has been jampacked. I've been split between focusing on tasks that have to be done and meeting and getting to know the players better so that I can help everyone the best I can. Yet, I've spent every spare second I have thinking about Max.

I know things started to shift between us way before that night. It was probably back when we had our first kiss at the bar. I was just too oblivious and naive to realize it. But now that it's over, and I don't hate him anymore, I'm realizing I don't think I ever did.

Everything is amplified and so intense between us that I crave him. Desire him constantly. It's not even just because he's a fucking snack. Of course, that does help. It doesn't take a rocket scientist to determine just how fucking good-looking the man is. It doesn't matter if he's on or off the ice; he's fucking hot with his rugged and strong body, his muscles begging for my tongue to come explore.

But that's not even what I think about. It's the little moments with him that I think about constantly. The little moments that have started to mean so much more. The breakfast he picks up for me after his morning run, the way he took care of me last week when I hurt myself. It's all adding up, and it's so overwhelming.

Having him back in my life, I know what has felt so off these last few years. He's the reason I've been so lost. He's the reason I felt alone. He's what's been missing. When he left, he took a piece of me with him.

Now I know that he's always been my missing piece.

I've spent years avoiding any sort of feelings towards him in an effort to protect my heart and my emotions, but now? Now, I'm slowly opening up to him despite being scared. Scared of letting myself have fun and be happy, knowing that it could all blow up in my face and I could lose him again. I know now that I can't be scared for the rest of my life. I can't give up because I'm afraid of the unknown. If you had said I'd be dating Max for real a few months ago, I would have said you're crazy. But now . . . I'm excited.

That's the thing about Max, though. I enjoy doing just about everything with him, even sitting around doing absolutely nothing. Normally, I go stir-crazy if I'm not up and doing a bunch of things, but last weekend, when he took care of me, was probably one of the best weekends I've ever had, and we did a whole lot of nothing. Although, it became exponentially more enjoyable after he took his shirt off during our snuggle sesh. There's something about that man in a pair of sweats, his hair a mess, and his abs on full display that makes lying around suck a whole lot less.

Max was a good sport, and we ended up having a full-on spa night where he told me to lather him up and make him pretty. Which, of course, I did. He looked fucking adorable with a bright purple face mask on. He was so pretty I had to send Sawyer all the pictures. He wouldn't let me paint his nails, though. Apparently, only Rory is allowed to give him a manicure. He deemed it their "special time" and refused to budge even when I begged. If that doesn't make your ovaries explode, I don't think anything will.

But now, I'm here at the arena on my day off because Sawyer is a tricky little thing and somehow convinced me to pick up lunch for the guys during their break. We haven't really told our friends we aren't faking this anymore, that we're giving this an actual shot, but Sawyer...she's not just anyone, so of course she knows. Although, I have a sneaking suspicion that Max and I were the last to realize it wasn't fake anymore. Okay, that's not true. Maybe it was just me.

As much as coming to work on your day off isn't fun, it's a welcome distraction from the fact that Sawyer and I are about to go shopping for the Lockwood's gala. Thankfully, Mama Lockwood hooked us up and had dresses delivered for us to choose from. Given that the gala is coming up fast, it's probably for the best. And it'll get Max off my back. He keeps bugging me about what my dress looks like. He says he wants to get a tux that matches. It's pretty sweet when you think about it.

I'm sitting with Max while he finishes his food, waiting for Sawyer to come out of Rex's office, where they're doing God only knows what.

"What do you ladies have planned for this afternoon?" Max asks before shoving more fries into his mouth.

"Oh, just pure torture," I groan. Leaning back on my arms, I stretch my legs out and look up at Max, perched on the picnic table outside the arena. "Rex's Mom sent over a bunch of dresses for us to choose from, so I'll be spending getting dressed up by your sister and Gwen, who both love this shit."

"Sounds terrible," Max says with a smirk. "I'm surprised

that Gwen loves shopping just as much as my sister. She doesn't strike me as a girly girl."

"She's not, but she loves a good excuse to dress up. She spends most of her time in hospital scrubs, so I think she just likes being able to feel glamorous every once in a while."

Gwen is a badass, and not many realize just how fucking cool she is. She's quiet about her education and career goals, but damn, she's got some big ones. She graduated with her bachelor's by the time she was twenty, and now at twenty-five, she's in her first year of residency after already completing four years of medical school. She currently works at the pediatric hospital in the oncology unit, and from what she's told us, it's where she wants to land a job one day. She's a badass little rocker chick, always dressed in black, but when she goes to the hospital, she's the one rocking bright scrubs with *Disney* princesses, or superheroes all over them.

"Makes sense. Everyone deserves to feel that way every once in a while," Max says as he throws the rest of his trash in the bag. He keeps talking, but all I can focus on is the ketchup sitting on top of his lip that he missed when cleaning up.

"Even you? Do you like to feel glamorous, Mr. Daniels?" I smirk, grabbing a napkin to wipe his face. As I reach for him, he quickly grabs my wrist, yanking me forward, laughing as he brings us both down to the ground.

"What are you doing, you buffoon?" I laugh, pushing up on his chest to sit up. I'm straddling him now with a leg on either side of him. Even with ketchup smeared across his face, his boyish smile makes him look so handsome.

"You looked like you were up to no good, so I struck

first," Max says, his hands sliding up until they're resting on my hips, his thumb rubbing circles on my hip bone.

"I was *not* up to no good! Your face is a mess."

"What if I like when my face is messy? Especially when you're on top of me," he says, a devilish grin on his face as he winks at me. "In fact, I think we both like when my face is a little messy."

Before I can even respond, Sawyer is walking down the hall with Rex, both of them watching us intently, smiling. Motherfucker. It may be innocent, but I guarantee it doesn't look that way, and Sawyer will damn well make sure to get whatever she can out of me.

Can I just stay here while she goes and picks out our dresses?

"Keep it clean, kids," Rex says when they finally make it to us. "No baby-making in the arena."

Sawyer gives him a sly look, making the big grump actually blush. I love seeing my friend find her happy ending, but I especially love seeing the big, bad Coach Lockwood blush from embarrassment because of her. It makes me giddy knowing he's just as in love with her as she is with him.

Pushing off of Max, I go to stand, but he keeps his hands on me, holding me firmly in place. I try again, but when I feel his cock harden beneath me, I can't help but giggle as I look over at Sawyer, who's still watching us intently. Thankfully, Max is good at diffusing situations, but he can also make them even more fucking awkward, depending on which way you look at it.

"That's rich, Coach, coming from you. I mean, what could you possibly have to talk to my sister about in your office for what? Twenty minutes?" Max retorts, making Rex blush even while Sawyer just laughs. She doesn't give a single fuck.

I fall forward onto Max's chest, laughing until he gives me a quick hug and kisses me on my forehead as we stand up, laughing at Rex's expense.

"Oh, fuck off, both of you. Only I get to laugh at him," Sawyer adds as she continues to giggle. "Cassie, ready to go shopping?!"

"As ready as I'll ever be. Let's get Gwen and get the torture session started; you promised me tacos after."

"See ya later, boys."

"So, how's everything been going since Max got back? You two looked . . . friendly," Sawyer says, an evil smirk on her face as she pretends to look through the different dresses lined up in her living room.

She's not wrong. That was definitely friendlier than I'm used to acting with Max, especially in public. But it felt good. It felt right. And honestly? I was just fucking happy to be with him.

It's like as soon as I told him we could try and see where this goes, every single one of my walls just disappeared without warning. They were my safety, my backup. They helped me ensure we were taking things slow and would eventually find our way there.

But now? I'm ready to be at the finish line. I want to climb him like a tree and ride his face until I'm screaming his name, letting everyone know who I belong to. Who he belongs to.

"Earth to Cassie," Sawyer teases, waving her hand in front of my face when she catches me zoning out.

"What?" I ask, noticing both her and Gwen staring at me.

"I asked how everything's been going. That PDA outside of the arena was way different than how you two normally are, even with your "'fake dating'," Sawyer uses air quotes dramatically, earning her an equally dramatic eye roll.

"Oh, spill the tea," Gwen says, plopping down on the couch next to me. She's already picked out her dress, which isn't surprising. That girl could rock a paper bag and make it look hot as fuck.

"Wait, why am I the one being interrogated when you and Rex spent nearly half an hour "talking" in his office? What were you doing? That's the more imperative question."

"Girl, we both know damn well what they were doing. That is not what we need to talk about right now."

Sawyer just shrugs, knowing there's no use in pretending otherwise. I don't even think Rex and her try to be sneaky around us anymore. They don't give a shit who knows what they're doing.

"Come on, spill," Sawyer deadpans, obviously over my attempt at derailing this conversation.

"I mean, we've talked. We, uh…I guess we're just seeing what happens. We both like each other, but I'm scared."

"Love is always scary," Sawyer says with a smile as she hands me a pile of dresses to try on.

"Who said anything about love?" I ask, anxiety immediately hitting me at the mention of the word.

"You didn't have to," Gwen chimes in. *Fuck.* With the way this conversation is going, I'll need another mimosa. Or six. "It's written all over both of your faces anytime you're around each other. It's like you both follow each other around the room, always keeping tabs on the other, even when you're with other people. It's so cute, it's disgusting."

"It's obvious you both loved exploring these emotions under the guise that you're faking it. But it's nice to see that you both finally caught up to the rest of us and realized it wasn't fake anymore. I noticed it after their last game a couple of weeks ago. You two just seemed so happy. So in love," Sawyer says with hearts in her eyes. I'm not sure why it surprises me; Sawyer always wants to make people happy. I guess I just never expected her to root for her best friend and her brother, but here we are, and she's easily our number-one fan.

"Ugh, you guys. I still feel like I have one toe on the line. I'm scared to be 100% in because there's always that chance that he could break my heart again. I was honest with him and told him I didn't think I would survive it if he did," I tell them truthfully. There's no point in lying to them anymore, they would have figured it out at some point, but in this case, they seemed to know before me.

"Hell, even grumbly Cade noticed. I believe his exact words were, 'When did those two start shooting hearts and rainbows out of their assholes anytime they're around each other?'" Gwen chuckles.

"Max is confusing, infuriating, and somehow still the sweetest man, all combined into one hot as fuck body. Anytime I'm around him, I practically forget which way is up because I'm so focused on him. But it's not only that. He's just . . . different. He makes me feel safe. He makes me feel like I'm capable of anything, and I've never had that before. But what if I'm not enough to keep him?" I ask, not holding back anymore. This is my biggest fear. I felt like I wasn't enough for him back then. What if the same thing happens?

As I pull on the first dress, I'm immediately in love. It's an emerald green dress that matches my eyes, with a slit up the side that I'm pretty sure cuts out any chance of me wearing panties. Not that Max would complain.

Turning to face the mirror, Gwen gets up and zips it for me right as Sawyer shouts, "Yes."

"I love it. It looks perfect on you. That color with your hair and your eyes. I love it so much," Sawyer says, finally slumping down on the couch like her work is done. "But I'm not driving to the event with you and Max if you're wearing that dress. You're gonna end up pregnant if he sees you wearing this. My brother will be absolutely feral for you. It's definitely the one."

"Ugh, do you really think so? Not that I want to try more on, but are you sure this is the one? Do you think he'll like it?

"Yes. Definitely. Trust me. When it comes to my brother, he won't be able to keep his hands off you," Sawyer says with a smile before fake gagging over her mimosa. "Okay, but hear me out. I know you're scared, but as much as I don't want to think about you guys hiding all this shit from me for years, you obviously hid it for a reason, and my gut tells me it's because it mattered to you. I'm talking soul-crushing, heart-melting, once-in-a-lifetime kinda mattered. My brother doesn't hold on to anyone. Well, except me, but I'm the only family left. I see the way he looks at you, I hear the way he talks about you, and I'll be the first to say it. My brother is so in love with you that it makes me physically ill."

"Sure that's not the alcohol?"

"Fuck off," Sawyer says with a laugh. "I have to enjoy it while I can. And before you even joke, NO, I am not pregnant. Not yet, at least."

"Fucking excuse me?" Gwen and I both say in unison as I grab my mimosa and sit back on the couch for Sawyer's turn in the hot seat.

"I'm not pregnant, but I wouldn't be mad if that changed sometime in the near future. Rex has this idea that he wants us to get married before I get pregnant, but damn, the more time I spend with Rory, the more I want to give her a sibling to grow up with. I love that little girl more than life and I can't wait to watch her be a big sister."

"You two are so cute I'm going to puke," Gwen deadpans.

"I'm so happy for you, Sawyer. You two seem like the perfect team," I tell her with a smile.

"You and Max could be too. You just need to figure your shit out. Because I can promise you one thing, he's going to make you his, and you need to be ready for when he does."

Fuck, I hope she's right because the more I think about me and Max together, the more I want it to be real.

Chapter Twenty-Three

Max

I still can't believe you chose to bring her over your own Mother for the event tonight. You're bringing a puck bunny over your mother, the person who helped you become the star you are today.

ME

I'm not.

I'm choosing to bring the woman who helped me become the man I am today, which is more important than my hockey performance. Refer to Cassie as anything offensive again, and I promise it'll be the last time we ever talk. Have a nice day.

PRINCESS

Can't wait to see you, handsome.

Max

ME

> You, too, princess. I can't wait to see that dress on you.

> See if it looks better on you now, or on my floor later ;)

"So, when do we need to head out to get the girls?" I shout down the hall to Rex. He came over this morning to get ready after Sawyer and Cassie kicked him out so they could get ready together. "Aren't we supposed to be there a little early?"

It's nice having him here because if he wasn't, I probably would spend all my time pacing, just waiting to see her. Tonight feels like a redo of the school dance Cassie and I never got to go to together. It feels big. Important. So, naturally, I'm anxious as fuck. I'm a twenty-three-year-old guy, a rookie in the NHL, yet I'm instantly transported back to high school, acting like I did when I had a crush on her.

It doesn't help that the only thing she told me about her dress is that it's emerald green, and she can't wear a bra or panties with it. So every time I think about her in the dress, I'm instantly rock hard imagining her bare beneath the thin fabric.

"Not unti six. They did the set-up yesterday, so my mom just wants us there before the doors open at six-thirty. We can leave here in like half an hour and go grab them, Sawyer told me they were already ready, so they're just having a glass of champagne while they wait."

"That's gonna take so long," I grumble, planting myself up on a barstool to scroll on my phone. I'm doing everything I can to distract myself because, god damn it, I can't wait to

274

see this gorgeous woman and spend the night out together, no longer faking a damn thing.

"You sound like Rory," Rex says, walking into the living room when he's finally ready. "Why are you throwing a tantrum? What's got you so wound up about a gala?"

"I am not throwing a temper tantrum. It's not even the gala that has me stressed. It's just everything, I guess."

"What do you mean?" Rex asks, grabbing us each a glass of bourbon before taking his spot on the couch across from me.

Thankful for the drink, I immediately take a sip, relishing in the burn as it slides down my throat. "It's Cassie. This girl has me fucked up, and I don't know what to do about it. I'm just super nervous about tonight. The last time we were going to something special together, everything went to shit."

"Ah, it makes sense now," Rex says, smirking over his glass as he sits back, letting those five simple words ruminate in my brain, bounce around, and cause havoc. What makes sense? What does he know that I don't? He filled that sentence with so much innuendo and mystery that I can't quite understand what he's trying to say.

"What makes sense?"

"The way you're acting. You're in love with her," Rex says nonchalantly. Like it's so obvious.

"I—" I start, but can't finish.

I want to tell him he's wrong. That I do really like the girl. I always have, but love? That's too much. That's too big for us. We only just found each other again and are finally exploring what this is. But the feelings I have for Cassie are bigger than just liking her, they always have been, and it's not like they've gone away. If anything, they've grown and intensified as the years have passed.

From loving her, to losing her, to longing for her. I've been through it all.

And now?

I'm back to loving her.

Having her.

And hopefully, keeping her.

"I, uh, yeah. I guess you're right. I am in love with her. I think I always have been."

"So now that you've realized that, why are you so nervous about tonight?"

"Because what if something goes wrong?"

"Then it goes wrong. It doesn't mean anything has to change between you guys. We're adults now. If something goes wrong, we handle it. But you stick together through it, regardless of the noise around you."

"I'm scared. What if we can't make it out together?"

"Welcome to being in love. It's a wild fucking ride, but god damn, it's worth it," Rex says with a smile. "Now, let's go get our girls and get this night started."

WHEN SHE WALKS OUT OF THE BUILDING, MY HEART starts racing. I feel like I can't breathe, can't think, can't do anything except watch her. She offers me a soft smile when she notices me, her black, sparkly stilettos clicking on the sidewalk as she glides over to me. She's dressed in a beautiful deep emerald green dress with a cut out on one side, showcasing her long, tanned legs that I crave. I'm nearly desperate to act out my fantasy, hooking one of her legs over my hip, and slipping deep inside of her. Fucking her against the wall. Hell, I'll fuck her against the car on this busy sidewalk, fully clothed, if I have to. Her pussy is bare in this sexy dress, and I'd bet anything she's dripping already.

Fuck. Now is not the time or place to be daydreaming about fucking her, as she's walking to me with my sister, for fuck's sake. But I can't help it. The second I see her, my cock has a mind of its own and craves every last bit of her.

"You look beautiful, Princess. So fucking beautiful," I tell her, grabbing her hand to pull her closer to me, immediately pressing my lips to hers. We don't make a scene of it. It's a quick kiss, just enough that I can hear her soft whimper as I bring my lips to her ear and whisper, "Tell me, beautiful girl, are you wet for me? If I slip my fingers up this dress, am I going to find your tight little cunt dripping for me?"

She trembles in my hold, my words affecting her just the way I'd hoped, but as she murmurs yes in response, I nearly lose it and bring her back up to the apartment. I know she said she wanted to take this slow and not rush into everything as we give this a real shot. But fuck, seeing her in this dress, it's hard not to.

It's even more challenging when her eyes light up from my words. Her body trembles from my touch, and a slight blush travels up her neck to the spot behind her ear that I already know is so sensitive. When I press a kiss there, I hear her quick intake of breath as her hands grip me harder.

"Gross, guys. Come on. We've gotta get to the gala before Rex's mom castrates the guys. You two will have plenty of time to be all touchy-feely and gross later," Sawyer says dramatically, shooting a playful wink to Cass before gagging at me.

Cassie laughs, ignoring her, as she pulls back from me with a satisfied smile. "You look very dapper yourself, Mr. Daniels."

Her calling me by my last name almost gives me butter-flies. I hope to make it hers one day.

"I like when you call me that."

"Is that so?" Cassie asks with a wink. "I'll have to remember that later."

"I thought we were taking this slow, Princess. Don't be a tease."

"Things change, Max baby. We're just along for the ride," Cassie says, a true smile on her face as she squeezes my hand.

"Let's go, children." Sawyer says with a smile before shoving us both into the car.

MAMA LOCKWOOD OUTDID HERSELF TONIGHT. THE ballroom is decked out in creams, whites, and sage greens, with candles and lights everywhere. It looks like a fairy tale. Cassie's eyes light up like a kid in a candy store as she looks around, marveling at everything—the decora-tions, the food, the lighting, and everyone dressed to the nines.

Servers are walking around with trays of champagne, so I snatch two glasses and pass one to Cassie, who takes it with a smile. She's so at ease here, so happy, and it makes all my nerves go away knowing we will have a nice evening together.

"It's so pretty," she says with wonder in her eyes as she looks all around.

"It is, but you're even prettier."

The blush returns to her cheeks, slowly traveling down her neck until finally stopping just above her collarbone. A gorgeous faint pink has dusted over her skin, and I want to trail my tongue along it, follow its path. I love the way she gets all worked up.

"You're ridiculous," she says with an awkward laugh and a shy smile as I pull her closer. Setting our champagne off to the side, I wrap her in my arms, my hands resting just above her hips, holding her in place.

"Take the compliment, Princess. It's about time you got used to them. There are so many things I love about you already, and this is just the beginning," I tell her with a smile, pressing a kiss to the tip of her nose. When I pull back, her eyes are glistening with unshed tears as she looks at me with a soft smile. "You're incredible, Cassie, and I'm going to tell you each and every day until you finally believe just how fucking incredible you are," I whisper, getting closer and closer to her mouth with every word.

She tries to pull away, but I don't let her. Huffing out a sigh, she finally stops and looks up at me. "What if I never believe you?"

"Then I'll spend every day for the rest of our lives trying."

She stares up at me, a look of marvel in her eyes as we stand in the middle of the ballroom. It feels like we're the only people in this crowded room. Without a word, she smirks before lifting up on her toes and planting a chaste kiss on my lips, her strawberry lip gloss so sweet, I nearly pull her in again to devour her mouth for more of that sweet taste.

"There you guys are. We've been looking for you," Gwen says, popping our quiet little bubble without even realizing it. We turn to see her smiling, as she, Cade, and Harris all come walking over.

"We haven't moved too much. I've kind of been in awe over this place. It's absolutely gorgeous."

"Yeah, Mama Lockwood is the best. She throws the best parties, but this one always takes the cake. She goes all out every time. She single-handedly made this event the most sought-after invite in the city," Cade grumbles, his usual overbearing cheerfulness seeping into his voice. "Plus, open bar, which is actually what we came to find. Let's go."

We follow Cade, who weaves through the crowd like he's much smaller than his 6'3" self, as we head straight for the bar. Cade likes to have some drinks here and there, but I don't think I've ever seen him actually drunk. He usually gets a solid buzz and then coasts the rest of the night, while anyone else that tries to go drink-for-drink with him ends up sick or passed out under a table. Either he has the tolerance of a damn giant, or he just hides it really fucking well.

"Y'all grab a table over by the front. Rex and Sawyer are meeting us here in just a minute to dance. I'll go grab a round of drinks," Cade adds before turning to head toward the bar. He seems extra bossy today.

Gwen is staring at him as he walks away, shaking her head before looking back at us. "I'm going to go help Mr. Grumps. See if he needs to eat or something. Hanger could explain his dickish self this evening. Maybe I'll slip some of these little appetizers into his pocket. They can be little surprises to keep him nice."

Gwen smiles before scurrying off in the same direction Cade just went while the rest of us go find a table right as Rex and Sawyer walk over. Everyone is here tonight in support of Rex's Mom and her foundation for the children, so it's like one big hang-out session, just fancier.

Miles and Trevor are both here tonight too, but last I saw Miles, he was running around helping Rex's sister, Stella, with some of the setup for the dessert table, while Trevor was with his parents, meeting one of his father's old friends. Standing here, we all fall into comfortable conversation. Cade and Gwen each carry a tray of drinks over while Cade finishes chewing whatever Gwen had shoved down his throat. He does look happier.

Sawyer wastes no time, though, and immediately drags a disgruntled Rex onto the dance floor. She looks happy, while he rolls his eyes as he starts to dance, doing anything she wants from him. I'm happy my sister found someone who loves her the way Rex does.

"I'm so fucking happy we're on break right now. I'm not sure what it is about this year, but it's been especially fucking exhausting. I mean, I know it's been a lot more traveling back and forth than usual, so it's at least nice knowing we don't have to catch a flight anywhere for the next two weeks," Harris grumbles as he slides up next to me, letting Gwen and Cassie continue on about the decorations.

"It really is. We haven't done as much traveling as you guys so far, but it's nice being able to relax and spend some more time at home for the next few weeks."

"You mean, home with your girl? In bed?"

I smirk. What he's saying sounds like the perfect fucking way to spend these next two weeks and make up for lost time. It's just funny that Harris immediately called me out on it, proving yet again that these fuckers are far too in tune with everyone around them. These guys know me pretty well by now, even if we haven't been friends all that long. I'm not sure what it is, but they're a very fucking perceptive bunch and usually don't hesitate to call each other out on shit that we'd probably rather just ignore.

It's annoying as fuck, but also nice not to have to hide it any longer.

I'm tired of hiding, it's exhausting, and I'm ready to live.

"I mean, that'll be an added benefit. But it'll just be nice to spend some time with her, it'll give us a chance to really figure everything out. This whole thing is odd between us because it feels like the only thing we're changing is the way we see each other. I mean, yeah, we weren't dating for real, but it never felt fake. We never had to force anything. I guess we just needed to stop lying to ourselves. We still act the same because, somehow, we had already fallen into this comfortable relationship. Cassie just wasn't quite ready to admit it was real."

"Good. It took you two long enough," Harris says with a chuckle before looking around the room. "I'm surprised Rex's mom isn't starting her speech yet. It looks like she's still busy making her rounds and talking to everyone."

"Does she usually—" I start to ask, but he's no longer looking at me. Instead, his face is white, like he's seen a ghost and is immediately on the move.

"I'll be back. I just need a few. I . . . I need some fresh air," he mumbles as he spins and walks away before I even have time to ask if he's okay.

"What's his deal?" Rex asks, returning from dancing with Sawyer, who's now pulled Gwen out to the dance floor.

"I don't know. All of a sudden, he just kind of went blank. Said something about needing air and then walked away. It's Harris. If he wanted to talk about it, he would."

Looking around, I can't help that my gaze keeps landing on Cassie. She's more than gorgeous. She's perfect. She's literally my princess. My fairy tale. My happy ending.

"Weird. Hey, before the girls come back, I wanted to talk to you. I heard from my cousin just a bit ago, and she was able to find out who the phone number belongs to. It, uh, it was listed under two names," Rex tells me quietly.

"Really? Who?" I ask. I reached out to Rex when I got

the second picture. I wanted to know what he thought I should do. He mentioned that his cousin owned an internet security company and that his wife was an excellent hacker. We thought this was the best way to figure out for sure who it was.

"We were right about Carina. Her vindictive bullshit was definitely behind this. But the other one wasn't Fez . . . it was your mom."

"Are you kidding me?" I mumble. "What a fucking bitch." As happy as I am that I know who was behind everything, I'm still pissed she's that much of a twat that she was willing to release such a personal video.

"Well, speak of the devil, there she is," Rex says, staring at someone over my shoulder. I turn and see my mother walking around, arm and arm with Carina's father. "How the fuck did she get in here?"

Motherfucker.

"So those two were in on it together?" I ask. I'm shocked, but I'm not. I'm not stupid enough to think she actually cares about me. She only cares about getting the attention she wants.

"Yeah, her name was on it as well. Vanessa was able to look into it a bit. I guess the two have been in communication for a while. She wasn't able to pull the whole conversation, but it seems like they were trying to break you and Cassie up while trying to force you back to talking to your mom. She was desperate to get more control over your life and thought if there was a scandal, you'd need family support. I guess they figured if you lost Cassie in the process, maybe Carina could 'pick up the broken pieces of your heart.' Don't give me that look, it's verbatim what one of her messages said. She's a little crazy if you ask me," Rex says, his eyes still on my mother, who's unfortunately making her way over to us. "This should be good. I texted my mom. She'll have security escort her out if she pulls anything."

"Let's see what she has to say. It'll be her last words before I fucking bury her," I seethe, my fists clenching in frustration. Out of the corner of my eye, I look for Cassie and Sawyer. I want them as far away from this as possible. My mother has done enough to both of them, and they don't deserve any more of her vile bullshit.

"Hello, Max." Her fake pleasantry is so thick in the air, I feel like I'm choking. "It's so delightful to see you. It's been far too long. Where's your date tonight?" she adds, looking around in distaste.

"I wish I shared the sentiment, but unfortunately, I don't. As for where my girlfriend is, that's none of your business," I snap back, refusing to save face just because of who she's with. "Hello, Mr. Alastar. It's nice to finally meet you. I've heard such great things about you."

"Likewise, Mr. Daniels. Your mother has been bragging about you all night. And Mr. Lockwood, it's always a pleasure," he says, turning to Rex and shaking his hand.

"As always, the pleasure is mine, Mr. Alastar. Unless it's gameday, of course," Rex says with a wink, earning a smile from Mr. Alastar and a scowl from my mother, who interrupts the conversation.

"Mr. Alastar mentioned how disappointed he was to not see you in the draft. He actually mentioned that he was interested in discussing your future, right Thomas?" she says smugly like she's doing something I should be thankful for.

Does she really think I am interested in her doing anything for me? Favor or not? First of all, I'm fucking thrilled to be on the Ice Hawks. Yeah, I grew up watching the Cyclones, and I always dreamed that's where I'd end up, but things change. Dreams change. In the end, I couldn't be happier to be where I am. Secondly, I literally want nothing to do with this woman. No help, no favors, and preferably, no communication. At all.

Ever.

"He already has a contract," Rex interjects, annoyance coating his words, but somehow, he remains polite.

"Yes, but Mr. Alastar can be very convincing," she says, practically purring in his ear. To his credit, he looks uncomfortable as he watches me, but doesn't say anything as he looks past her. "Just find me later, Max. We can discuss it all together."

With that, she grabs his hand, and they continue on, mingling with people and drinking champagne like they didn't just come over here and drop a fucking bomb on us.

"What. The. Fuck. Was. That?" I growl. "She's always been nuts, but this? The woman is batshit crazy."

"Yeah, man, I didn't think it'd be that bad. I've heard your stories, and I already disliked the woman. But now? I fucking hate her. But, Max, I have to ask. You wouldn't actually consider listening to her, right? About the contract? That's not why you didn't confront her, right?"

"Fuck no. I'm happy where I'm at. The Cyclones were the dream, but this? This is much better than my dream," I tell Rex truthfully. "As for talking to her? I didn't want to mess up the event your mother has worked so hard at, so I figured I'd let the police handle it. I'll need a lawyer first anyways."

"Good, I would've hated pissing Sawyer off when I had to kick your ass," Rex says, a smirk playing on his lips.

"Aw, you would've missed me," I smirk, but look down

at my phone when I feel it vibrate. Rex checks his phone too.

Opening up the notification, I'm shocked into silence. They sent it. They sent out the entire fucking video. Only this time, it wasn't just to me.

This time they sent it in a group message to over a dozen people. This is confirmed when Rex turns to look at me, holding his phone to show that he received it too.

Shaking my head, I scan the room for Cassie. I need to find her. I want to tell her about this before someone else does. But first, I need to start my plan because, by the end of the night, I want them gone.

"Call your cousin," I growl at Rex. "Tell her now. I need a lawyer. I'm going to fucking destroy these two."

He just nods before turning to head onto the balcony, his phone already in hand.

Fuck, and I thought tonight was just going to be fun, but when I look up and see Mr. Alastar, I know what I have to do. I finally see Cassie in the crowd but just smile as I turn and walk toward him.

I want to take care of the situation first. I don't want either of those vile women getting near Cassie again, and handling it alone is the easiest way to ensure that.

Hopefully Sawyer keeps dancing.

Chapter Twenty Four

Cassie

It's hard to pay attention to anything anyone is saying right now because my attention keeps snapping back to Max as he and Rex talk, both looking far too stressed right now. Sawyer wanted to introduce me to Rex's dad, but being the busy man he is, he couldn't stay too long before being summoned to help his wife. It didn't take long to realize that he's easily the sweetest man I've ever met. Just watching him gush over his wife and her event and how he spoke about Rex, he's adorable. I see where Rex gets it from. When these men love, they love hard.

"Can we grab a drink? I know they'll stop serving during the introduction speech, and I definitely don't want an empty glass then. Toasting with an empty glass is practically a crime," Sawyer says as she searches for the nearest bar.

"Yeah, of course. But first, the bathroom. If I drink any more right now, my bladder will burst," I tell her seriously.

"Okay, drama queen, let's go."

Making our way over to the bathroom, we get stopped a

few times to talk, but thankfully it's quick. I wasn't joking when I said my bladder was going to explode, and right now, I feel like my saliva is enough to push me over the edge. Luckily, there's no line, so I'm washing my hands and doing a quick touch-up on my makeup in no time.

"Well, looky here, it's Max's little whore," Carina quips from behind me, coming out of one of the last stalls.

"You say that like it's an insult when in reality, it just means I get fucked seven ways to Sunday. But I understand your confusion; you never got to experience his cock and the magic tricks it does inside a woman's body," I snap back, over her bullshit already. I suspected she would end up at the event tonight because of who her father is, but I was really hoping I could avoid having to interact with her.

"How is being a whore a good thing?"

"Well, I'd prefer to be his whore than everyone's whore. But that's just my preference. You keep doing you, boo," I say, turning my back to her right as Sawyer comes out of the stall. I touch up my lipstick as Carina seethes next to me.

"You . . . I hate you. You've ruined everything. But that's changing tonight. It's all changing, and Max will realize you're nothing. That you don't fit into his life."

"Wait, let me get this straight," Sawyer interjects. "You think Max is going to leave Cassie, the woman he's been in love with since he was seventeen, for you—the girl who spreads her legs for anyone wearing a jersey and has no sense of self-respect or respect for others? Yeah, keep dreaming, sweetheart."

"And you are?" Carina snaps, her eyes narrowing at Sawyer.

"His sister, you twat."

"She never said he had a sister," Carina mumbles under

her breath before turning back to me. "You just wait. He will be mine."

With that, she walks out, letting the bathroom door slam behind her.

"Well, she's a fucking treat," Sawyer grumbles as we make our way back out into the ballroom. "Has she always been that crazy?"

"Yep, don't you just want to cunt-punt her?" I joke, scouring the room to find Max. I want to tell him about Carina, and after all of that, I really just want to be near him.

Feeling my phone vibrate, I grab it out of my clutch, and my heart stops the moment I see the message from an unknown number.

"Motherfucker," I grumble, turning my phone to show Sawyer. "Remember that video that Max was in?" I groan as I turn down my volume before opening the message.

"Yeah, I try not to, but unfortunately, I remember." Sawyer eyes me warily.

"Well, surprise, it's even worse than you thought. It was him and I, and if this message is what I think it is, it was just sent to over a dozen people."

"Oh, fuck. Yeah, I can't even be mad. I understand why you wouldn't tell me right away," Sawyer says, her thinking face on as she looks at the list of people it was just sent to. "I see Rex and Max's numbers, and I'm pretty sure this is our mother's number, but besides that, I don't recognize any of these people. Who have you pissed off enough that they want to release a sex tape of you?"

"I don't know."

"Could it be Carina? Do you think she's crazy enough to pull this?"

"Do I think she's crazy enough? Yeah. But I'm not quite sure she's smart enough."

"I'd agree, but it still could be her. Don't you think it's weird that you just had a verbal spar with her, and then not even five minutes later, this gets released?"

"Fuck! That bitch," I nearly shout. Looking around, I try to find where she ended up, but I find Max instead. He looks frustrated as he stares down at this phone intently. When he looks up, he finds me immediately, and damn, he looks stressed.

He must've seen the video.

Before I can go to him, he disappears with Mr. Alastar, and my stomach drops. Was Carina telling the truth? The fear of her words hit me like a freight train.

It seems I can't catch a break tonight, though, as my parents choose now to show their faces. They're walking over, my father practically seething as he holds up his phone like it's going to make me feel bad, but I can't seem to find it in me to care.

All I can think about is that my father looks like one of those old cartoon characters with steam coming out of their ears. I'm worried if he doesn't open his mouth, he's going to explode.

It should upset me that I don't care about my parent's opinion of me, but it doesn't. Any of it. They've shown their true colors, and I've realized I have so many other people on my side that it doesn't actually matter anymore. They didn't care when I was struggling, and they don't care now that I'm successful; they only care when they feel I've disgraced them.

This will be fun.

"Why did I just receive a video of your boyfriend with

another woman?" My father spits out, his face so red it's almost the same shade of purple as a ripe plum.

"Well, Father, it seems someone is unaware that it's inappropriate to videotape someone's private moment. And apparently, they took it upon themselves to share it with the world, something else they had no right to do. But by all means, worry about your reputation and not someone's personal life being violated. Such a righteous, supportive lawyer you are," I snap, thankful for Sawyer, who's still standing by my side, her silent support giving me the courage I need to do this.

"This is not a personal moment. This is your boyfriend with some girl, and lord knows what kind of upbringing this girl had to be willing to do such a thing with a man like Max. Her parents should be ashamed of themselves. But Max–he's disgracing our name now that you're dating him. It ends now. You're leaving him, and you're coming with us. We're going home until we can figure out how to fix this."

"No," I spit out, refusing to let him bully me into what they want.

"Cassandra Elizabeth, don't fucking argue with me right now. Let's go," he practically snarls, spittle flying everywhere.

"I. Said. No. I'm aware that's not a word you are able to comprehend, but I'm not going anywhere unless it's to go find my boyfriend," I snap back, ignoring his use of my full name. It's only reserved for when he's pissed because he knows how much I hate it, but right now? I'm more pissed than he is.

"You're a disgrace to our last name," my father bellows, no longer caring that he's causing a scene as people around us have started to stare and whisper.

"Good thing she'll have a new one soon," Max says,

walking up from behind me, offering a quick wink before putting an arm around my shoulder and pulling me close.

I smile up at him, forcing myself not to squeal in excitement over his comment. The thought of being his, of sharing his last name, is a dream come true.

My father is fuming, his cheeks turning a deeper shade of purple, as he prepares to start screaming again. But before he can, Rex's mother decides to come out and join us.

"I decided the welcome speech should wait until only people who are welcome were in attendance," she says, shooting a glare towards my parents. "Mr. and Mrs. Wright, you've unfortunately, overstayed your welcome. This is a charity event, one of love, compassion, and integrity. It seems you've proved that you don't have any of the traits we stand for. Now leave, before I have you escorted out."

"Are you seri—"

"As a heart attack. You come for my family, or anyone close to us, and this is what you get. Now, I don't like repeating myself. Get. Out. Of. My. Event," she says, her husband now at her side, holding her shoulder like he's keeping her from attacking.

My mother at least has the decency to look embarrassed, although I'm sure it's only because my father is causing a scene. Rex's mom takes a step closer to them, getting ready to lead them out of the event.

Unable to help myself, I take one final dig, "By the way, Father. It wasn't some random puck bunny in the video. It was me, so next time you look in the mirror, remind yourself of how ashamed of your parenting you are. I know I am." I turn to look at Max, who's smiling down. "But, Father, get it right. I'm not a puck bunny. I'm his princess."

I smile as Max leads me to the dance floor, far away

from the drama, as Mama Lockwood helps escort my parents out of the gala and, quite frankly, my life.

"Max, I'm so sorry about them. They aren't good people, and I was looking for you when they came up to me. I saw the video, but I think I know who's behind it," I whisper, wrapping my arms around him tightly, the feeling of his body grounding me.

"It was Carina, beautiful girl."

"How did you figure that out?"

"I had Rex's cousin do a little digging. It was her. She also had a little help from my lovely mother," Max says, disgust coating his words. I know he's probably feeling betrayed on the highest level.

"Are you fucking serious?" I stammer, not sure how a parent could do that to their own child. "I mean, I'm glad we know, I just . . . I can't believe they'd actually stoop that low. Are you okay? Is the team? What do we do now? Do I need to call Amanda?" I ramble.

"Yeah, all the staff knows, even the owner, so it's not a complete dumpster fire. It actually helps that it was the two of them because now they've become the center of attention. It doesn't look good when someone tries to damage your reputation for revenge. As for what we do now? I'm working on it. I'll let you know when we get it taken care of. I just need you to trust me."

He looks concerned. Like he's expecting me to be upset with him, but honestly, I'm relieved. It's finally over.

"I can do that." I smile, looking up at him as we dance. "Is it weird that I'm relieved my parents left? That we were able to have some finality to our relationship? It was a long time coming; we all know that. It seems the older I get, the less room I have for people who don't serve a purpose in my life. Everyone should bring something positive into our lives, but they only took from me, bringing only negativity with them. They want me to be their pawn, but I want to live my own life. Which is what I'll do until they can find a way to be happy for me being myself."

He smiles down at me before pressing a long, slow, passionate kiss to my lips as we sway to a soft song. For the first time in a long time, I know I'm exactly where I'm supposed to be.

Pulling back when the song ends, Max smiles as he walks me to our table. "I'm going to run outside for a second. I need to make a phone call. I'll be back shortly."

With a quick kiss, he walks away, leaving me with Sawyer, who's waiting for Rex to return. When I sit down, she passes me a glass of champagne and smiles.

"You good?"

"Perfect."

"Where'd my brother go?"

"A phone ca—" I start to say but am immediately cut off.

"Actually, he's having that talk I mentioned earlier with my father. He actually just requested I come join them. It's probably to celebrate Max playing for the Cyclones instead of being stuck with the Ice Hawks."

"Watch your mouth when you're talking, Carina. I'm not above punching you in public," Sawyer snaps, and surprisingly Carina takes a step back.

I didn't think she was smart enough to know fear.

"Carina, I don't trust a single thing that comes out of your mouth, and neither does Max. We both know . . ." I trail off when I notice Max walking with Carina's father. Both of them are smiling as they shake hands.

Holy shit.

Is she telling me the truth? I know he told me to trust

him, but this feels like a knife in the back. Would he really do this? Would he abandon Rex and his team? And worst of all, is he willing to make these decisions without talking to me? I feel like everything these twats have done to sabotage my life has actually worked.

I feel like I'm going to be sick.

I vaguely hear Sawyer giving her a verbal lashing, but I turn around, refusing to speak to her anymore. I walk away to get some fresh air. When I get to the balcony, I'm surprised to see Mama Lockwood with a bottle of champagne, sitting and watching the busyness of New York.

"I had a feeling I might run into you out here. You've had quite the busy night, sweetheart," she says, a smile on her face I feel I don't deserve. "Why don't you sit down and have a glass of champagne with me? I think we both could use a moment of peace."

Sitting down, I grab the glass she offers, emotions hitting me as this woman who barely knows me has shown me more kindness than I've ever experienced from my own other. Even after I just ruined her event.

"I'm so sorry about all of this. Had I known it would go down like this, I wouldn't have come with Max."

She just waves her hand, dismissing me like it's nothing. "Your folks caused that, not you. You are not responsible for their actions. You'd think adults would be more respectful than that and that they'd support their daughter, but they showed they're incapable of that, so they're no longer welcome at any of my events."

"I, uh . . . I don't really know what to say," I tell her, tears welling in my eyes from her kindness.

"Well, you can start by telling me why you're out here with me and not inside with that handsome man of yours," she says, her eyes twinkling with mischief and curiosity as she sips her champagne.

"Max? Last I saw, he was shaking hands with Mr. Alastar, probably signing his life away or something. After my little talk with Carina, the whole thing is making me feel pretty uneasy. I just don't know what to think right now."

"What do you mean? Sawyer told me all about your little situation. I mean, it's not really a situation, more like you just mislabeled your relationship, but sweetie, we've all been there. It doesn't take a genius to realize there's not a damn thing between you and Max that's fake. Carina knows that too, which is why she's being such a fucking drama queen. But I wouldn't worry about her. Max only has eyes for you. I might've overheard some of his conversation with Mr. Alastar, and Carina won't be a problem much longer."

"What do you mean?"

"Oh, sweet girl, just trust that man of yours. I can promise you he's not up to anything. Unless protecting you counts. He was trying to be respectful of Carina's father by letting him know about his daughter's involvement with the video while also doing his best to shield you and Sawyer from the backlash. It's been a bit messy, to say the least. Carina's father immediately cut ties with Max's mother and told Max it was time for him to let his daughter face the consequences. Apparently, she's pulled stuff like this in the past, and he couldn't believe she was willing to go down this path again. He thinks it's time she gets a wake-up call."

"So, he's not leaving me? Carina made it seem like he was leaving the team and me."

"No, Cassie. He's protecting you. The police have already escorted his mother out. Last I heard, they were handling Carina next. They were hoping not to make a big scene, although if I'm being honest, a little excitement never hurts on an evening like this," she says with a wink. "Go find him, though. It's not my story to tell."

She's right. I need to make sure he's still with me.

I need to go find Max.

Chapter Twenty-Five

Max

Do you ever do something with the best intentions, but the second your plan is in motion, you realize you might've fucked up? Yeah, that's my life right now. I thought I was doing the right thing by protecting Cassie, but now I wonder if I hurt her in the process. Sawyer texted me and told me Carina was spouting her normal b.s. and trying to convince Cassie that I'm leaving her.

Not that there's any truth to it, but I can only imagine how it looked to Cassie when she saw Mr. Alastar and I walking together and shaking hands like we just made a deal.

We did make a deal, but not about hockey.

He'd just worked out a deal with Reece, Rex's cousin, who also happens to be a lawyer. Carina will face charges, and there will also be a restraining order, but we didn't want Mr. Alastar's name drug through the mud at the same time. Discretion is important, especially when the entire world is so opinionated and judgmental.

He told Carina to come to an office down the hall, and

she came in smiling like she just won the lottery. That is until I pulled up the video and told her we knew it was her and that the police were on their way. She started sobbing, and immediately threw my mother right under the bus. Said that it was her idea for Carina to get close to me. Once Carina had the video, though, it all blew up and went too far. She looked so shocked that her daddy wasn't stepping in to save her. At this point, he's just as done with her shit as I am.

But now that they're both gone, I've been running around the ballroom trying to find Cassie. I keep getting this dark feeling that she left. Does she think I'd ever choose anyone over her?

It isn't until I see her walking in from the balcony that I feel like I can breathe again.

She's still here.

I rush over to her, making my way through the dance floor, ignoring the couple grinding on each other and the servers passing out glasses of champagne. I don't care about any of it. The only thing I care about is her.

Fuck going slow. If tonight has taught me anything, it's that Cassie is my world, my everything, and I'll do absolutely everything I can to protect her. When she sees me, she looks nervous.

"It's over," I tell her, immediately regretting my choice of words as I watch her face fall and her eyes fill with unshed tears as she clenches her jaw.

"What . . . what do you mean? What's over?"

"Fuck, Cassie, I'm sorry, I didn't think my words through. I've been talking with Mr. Alastar," I tell her, pulling her in closer and resting my hands on her hips to help calm her, "We were discussing Carina, the video, and my mother. He took care of them. I just wanted to protect you from them, from everything."

"It's over?"

"I mean, as over as it can be. There will be backlash from the video, of course. Stupid people always have to make jokes and have too much of an opinion. But I think once people see us together, they'll stop caring entirely."

"What do you mean see us?"

"Cassie, we're so much more than this. The second people see us together, with nothing holding us back, they'll know we're more. We're not something that can be broken by some manipulative witches."

"So . . . you're not leaving me?"

"What? Of course, I'm not leaving you. What would make you think that?"

"Carina . . . I mean, I knew it was dumb, that I shouldn't believe her, but she said you were leaving the team, then I saw you guys together, shaking hands and smiling, and I just... I thought you were done with me too, but Rex's mom talked to me and convinced me to come find you."

"Princess, I'm not leaving you. I'm never leaving you again. You're mine. Do you understand that? Mine. I love you, Cassie."

The smile on her face hits me hard, and butterflies practically take off in my stomach. I can't believe this beautiful woman is looking at me with such adoration. Such love.

I feel like the luckiest man alive.

"Max, I—"

"You don't have to say it, Princess. I know you said you needed time. That you wanted to take it slow, I respect that. I just wanted you to be sure of how I feel about you."

"Max, with all due respect. Fuck taking it slow. I love you too."

301

She hasn't even finished her sentence before I'm crashing my lips to hers, pulling her in close as she moans into my mouth.

Our tongues tangle, our hands pulling on each other as we lose ourselves in one another, finally giving in. Finally saying those three words. Those three words I've never truly understood the meaning of until now.

I love Cassie. I have since we were kids, and she would sit and listen to me play guitar for hours, knowing I didn't want to be alone. I've loved her through the good and the bad, and I'll continue to do so for as long as I'm alive.

"Get a room, you crazy kids," Trevor says with a laugh as Rex lets out a loud whistle with Sawyer pulled into his side.

They're all just as smiley as I feel right now.

Cassie laughs, hiding her face in my chest as I smile back. I don't even care that they just called us out. She's here, she's mine, and I want the world to know it. Slapping my chest, she looks up at me with a naughty gleam in her eye that sends blood directly to my cock. But her next words are what do me in.

"Take me home, Mr. Daniels."

"As you wish, my little puck princess."

THE NEXT MORNING, I'M UP BEFORE THE SUN.

Well, if we're being honest, I don't think we even slept.

When we got back to the apartment last night, we immediately went to bed, but there was exactly zero sleep to be had. We spent all night learning each other's bodies again. Over and over until Cassie was so spent from orgasming so much that she practically melted into the bed.

I'm not surprised, though. We did a little bit of everything, going until our bodies were completely depleted. We went slow, fast, hard, and everything in between, and somehow, every time felt even more perfect than the last.

That's how everything is with Cassie. It just gets better over time.

"You're breathing on me," Cassie mumbles, her smile evident in her voice.

"And you're in my bed again, Princess," I tell her, curling my body around hers as she pushes her ass against my hard cock.

Hey, it's not my fault. It's morning, and well, she's naked and sexy as fuck.

"I like it here. It's warm, comfy, and you're here," Cassie says as she rolls over, turning to face me, nose to nose. "Besides, Max, if we're doing this, we're doing it right. Meaning, I don't want this to be just your bed anymore. I want it to be ours."

I beam. I feel it even before the smile hits her face. Her words make me feel so happy, so loved, so confident that we're right where we're supposed to be. "Of course, Princess. I told you last night, I'm all yours, forever and always."

Her lips brush against mine as she throws one leg over me, climbing on top until she's straddling me, my hard cock rubbing against her clit as she rocks her hips back and forth.

Her movements are so slow, so gentle that it drives me wild as she moans every time I hit her clit.

"Have I told you lately that I love you, Max?"

"Not quite enough. Ride me and tell me how much you love me. Make me believe it while you suffocate my cock," I growl, gripping her hips as I lift her. Her hand reaches down to position my cock at her entrance.

When she wets her lips and braces her hands on my chest, I drop her hips, thrusting up at the same time. Entering her in one hard go.

"Oh, Max," she moans as she circles her hips, grinding her clit against my pelvis as she adjusts to my size.

It doesn't matter that we spent all night fucking; little to no foreplay makes it difficult for her to adjust easily to my size. She's a tiny little thing, and I'm thick enough that it takes some effort. Knowing that she's willing and ready to take it all so soon is almost enough to have me blowing inside of her without even getting started.

It doesn't take long until she's lifting her body, sliding up and down my cock as she moans in pleasure, her eyes never leaving mine and her nails clawing into my chest. "You're so fucking beautiful, Princess. The flush on your chest, the sweat on your neck, it's so fucking sexy. Knowing I'm causing each and every one of these reactions is fucking intoxicating." I don't stop as I lift my hips, holding her up as I piston in and out of her, my thumb finding her clit and rubbing soft circles, driving her wild.

"Don't stop, Max. Fuck. I'm so close," Cassie says, right as her tight little cunt squeezes around my cock, suffocating me, practically pulling my orgasm from me, but I won't. I can't come until she does.

"Cassie, fuck," I pant, barely getting the words out as I focus on stopping my orgasm while drawing hers closer and closer. "I need you to come, Princess. I need you to come right now. Give it to me."

She falls apart.

I lean up and kiss her, drowning her screams with my kisses as I empty inside her. Thrusting in and out, I don't stop until we've both collapsed, having drawn out every last ounce of our pleasure.

"If you keep fucking me like this, Max, we're never going to leave this bed. I'll be a pile of mush, spent from being your little whore," Cassie says, excitement in her eyes at being used by me.

"Funny you should say that, because that's my plan for these next two weeks."

"What, to fuck me like I'm your little whore?"

"No, to fuck you like you're mine.

Because she is.

She always has been. Only now . . .

Now she knows it too.

Epilogue

Cassie, Two Weeks Later

Did you know that at the north pole, the sun only rises and sets one time per year? Only once.

MAX<3

I did know that.

ME

Did you know that snowy owls can fly fast enough to knock over a grown human.

He could knock you over.

MAX<3

I could take him.

What's with the random facts about...
animals? and cold?

ME

The north pole.

It's because it's cold as fuck. I'm pretty sure New York is the new north pole so I was doing research to prepare myself.

MAX<3

Dramatic much, princess?

It's fucking cold. Like full-blown frigid temps with snow. And ice.

I'm not sure who the fuck pissed off Elsa, but for the love of Sky Daddy, say you're sorry.

It'd be all fine and dandy if I were dressed for the weather, or in my home with a fire on. But now, I'm currently in a black leather miniskirt and an Ice Hawks jersey.

It's their first home game since having two weeks off, and I think I'm more excited for the game than Max. When he told me a while ago how much his teammates loved when their girls were in the stands, wearing their jerseys, I knew right then I wanted to get one. I wanted to surprise him because the last time he and I talked, I was supposed to be working with the Cyclones tonight and wouldn't be able to come.

After texting with Amanda, I was able to switch games with one of the other interns, and instead of telling Max, I told Sawyer and we made a plan.

I just wasn't aware that the plan included me being outside, in the middle of winter, wearing far too little clothing. But this is what I get for including Sawyer. She's a sneaky little thing who likes to take things one step further, but it's all in fun. When she was at our apartment, she switched out Max's skates without him knowing, so he'd have to text her to bring the correct ones. Which is why I'm now standing outside in the cold. I feel like some creeper, outside of the arena, freezing my panty-less ass off while I hold onto Max's skates.

Fixing my skirt, I check the time, thankfully seeing it's already 5:28 pm, he should be here any minute. The man is always on time, and just like clockwork, my phone vibrates with my gameday text from Max.

MAX <3

Have fun at work tonight. I miss you already. Send me a pic ;)

ME

No. ;)

MAX<3

What do you mean 'No'? I don't understand the word. ;)

I just grin, as I stare down at my phone before pocketing it, knowing he'll be coming up the path any moment now.

3...

2...

1...

Stepping out, I grab his arm as he passes, only catching him off guard for a moment before a devilishly handsome smirk takes over his face, his eyes darkening as I pull him back to my hiding spot a few feet off the path.

I feel like a predator, dragging her prey, kicking and screaming, away before devouring it. Except, my prey isn't fighting me. No, he's coming willingly.

"Oooh, I like this better...it's nice and cozy back here. But what're we doing, Princess?" Max whispers as I push him against the building, his bag dropping at his side as he looks me up and down, his eyes darkening when he takes in my exposed legs, growing feral when he notices the jersey. "More importantly, what are you wearing? Turn around, lemme look at you," he growls, spinning me away from him to see the back.

#17.

Daniels.

His jersey.

"Fuck, Princess. I didn't think it could get any better, or that you could get any hotter, but goddamn. Seeing you in my jersey, with my last name on your back. It does something to me."

"I can tell." I joke, pushing my ass against his groin, against his already hardening cock, earning a growl as he swats my ass.

Sliding his hands up, he grips my hips before turning me to face him, his mouth just inches away, as he holds me still.

His face is close. His eyes are dark, almost black, light barely reflecting in them as he stares down at my mouth, his tongue rubbing along his lower lip. I feel like I can't breathe, Max turning the tables on me. Stealing the power without even trying, my plans are immediately thrown out the window. All I want to do right now is make this sweet, incredible, sexy, man as happy as he makes me. If he wants to call the shots, then he can go for it, I'll be along for the ride.

"Don't tease me, Princess. Right now, I'm not sure what I want to do more," Max grumbles. "I'm not sure if I want to lift up this tiny thing you call a skirt, grip you by your ponytail and fuck you against the wall right here. My last name on your back, my first on your lips as you scream my name," Max growls.

His lips brush against my ear as he slides his hands down my body until he reaches the edge of my skirt. His fingertips brush against my skin, so gently I can barely feel it as they slide up my legs. He has an adorably boyish grin on his face, which is a complete contradiction to the dirty things he's doing to me.

"On the other hand, Princess, I *really* like the way this jersey looks on you...I like it so much, I kinda think we should go make it your last name too."

"How about a little of both? We'll do the first part now," I tell him with a smile as I grind my ass against his erection, earning me a delicious growl from Max as one hand grips my throat, the other my hip as he holds me in place. "I have no doubt I'll have your last name one day, so what's the rush?"

Max nips my ear, his teeth dragging along my neck, my heart racing, practically dying to hear his words. It's not even what he's saying so much as it's what he's implying. We have plenty of time for all that. No, it's the desperation in his words, seeing the possessiveness in him of wanting to claim me, but not knowing which way he wants to claim me first. I feel that constantly, and fuck, if I don't love seeing that same feeling reflect back in his eyes.

"The rush is, I've fucking dreamed about you having my last name since we were teenagers. As cheesy as that is, I've only ever wanted you. So if we know it's going to happen, why can't we just do it?"

"Let me enjoy having what I've dreamed about since we were teenagers, first, at least for a little while."

"And what's that?" Max asks, still grinding his erection against me.

"The infamous Max Daniels, as *my* boyfriend," I say, looking back at him over my shoulder.

One moment he's holding me in place, the next, he's undone his belt and is gripping his cock as he lines up at my entrance. Without a warning, he slides in all the way to the hilt in one quick, rough, motion.

"Max," I groan, the sensation of being filled so quickly so intense I can't help it.

"Fuckkkkk," Max growls as his hands grasp the bottom of my skirt, controlling my movements as he slides in and out at a slow, torturous pace. "I like you like this. At my control...my name on your back...my name on your lips. My girlfriend."

He starts moving his hips quicker, each thrust harder as he slides on hand in front of me pressing soft circles against my clit as he brings us both closer and closer to finishing.

"Jesus, Cassie. I love you, like this. I just fucking love you," he says, thrusting each time he says something. "Fuck. You're mine. Do you hear me?"

I can't speak, I hold onto the building in front of me, every thrust bringing me closer to the orgasm that's violently building inside of me, dangerously close to exploding. My whole body feels like I've touched a livewire, everywhere he's touching me catching fire.

It's perfect...until he stops.

"Say it, Princess. Tell me you're mine. I need to hear you say the words, then, I'll let you come," Max growls, nipping my ear as his fingers stop circling my clit, his thrusts stopping completely as he just waits.

My orgasm is in limbo, both there and not at the same time, as he patiently waits for my words. Without any hesitation, I tell him what he wants to hear.

"I'm yours, Max. Only yours."

That's all it takes. With a few rough thrusts, his fingers circle my clit, as he presses firmly, one hand gripping my throat, as he pushes us both over the edge. He doesn't stop immediately, his hips thrusting in and out slowly as he pulls every last drop of our orgasms out until we're both drained.

"Well, that was unexpected." He chuckles, helping me stand up before fixing my skirt. "I thought you had to work tonight?"

"Yeah, I switched with Tara so I could have the night off. Thought I'd surprise you by coming to watch your game with Sawyer. Oh, and I brought your skates."

"Thank you. I can't believe I forgot them."

"You kind of didn't... Sawyer switched them, so I'd bring them to you."

"I bet she didn't expect it to end like this," Max says with a smile as he fixes his pants, tucking himself away, with a content sigh.

"I mean, it was her idea to wear the skirt." I wink.

"Gross." Max laughs as he grabs his bag. "I've gotta go help win a game tonight, I'll meet you inside after the game?"

"Only if you score me a goal."

"Deal, Princess."

And he did.

In fact, he scored twice.

Epilogue

Max

Random fact of the day incoming:

PRINCESS

I'm eagerly awaiting your message.

ME

Don't be a brat. We both know what happens when you're a brat.

Did you know that in 1925, the New York Giants were purchased for just $500?

PRINCESS

I did not. Aren't you supposed to know only hockey facts? Is this cheating?

ME

I'm a man of many talents, princess. ;)

D o I love hockey?

Dumb question, because *obviously*.

But nothing compares to the way I feel looking up to see Cassie and Sawyer in the stands. When I saw them cheering for me, both my girlfriend *and* my sister wearing *my* jersey, I felt unstoppable. It made scoring both goals even better when I looked up to see Cassie smiling proudly as she watched me.

I've always thought I was fine on my own, that I didn't need anyone on my team, but I realize now just how wrong I was. It wasn't that I didn't want anyone on my team, it was that the team I had was shitty. I needed to find a new team to be a part of.

I found that with Cassie. She helped me fix things with my sister, and she's been by my side through this entire ordeal, and somehow that brought us closer. If you'd told me five years ago that Cassie and I would be in love and happy, I'd have called you a liar.

But that's how it turned out.

After we won the game, I was in and out of the locker room as fast as possible, doing my best to avoid the press. All I could think about after that win was Cassie and how I wanted to see her again and celebrate with her. I've never had someone I wanted to celebrate accomplishments with before–well after high school, I didn't. Now that she's back, I feel excited to have someone to share these moments with.

I was joking around earlier when I talked about taking her to get married...kind of.

It's going to happen. We both know it's going to happen.

Come hell or high water, Cassie Elizabeth Wright will be my wife.

But, I get that she wants us to enjoy what we have for a while. We've already decided that once the lease is up we will find a new place, but this time we'll do it together. Something new for us.

I told her I'd move anywhere with her, just try to keep it close to the arena.

But now, as I sit here in the bar watching her chat with Alex and Knox, probably giving me shit about something, I realize that's a lie. I'd go anywhere this girl asked me, regardless of what happened with hockey.

She's everything.

Standing up, I look at Cassie who's currently playing quarters with Knox. "Come on, Princess."

"Where are we going?" she asks with a smile, already standing up.

Grabbing her hand I pull her in, ignoring the guy's jokes. "We're going home," I mumble into her hair. "I want you all to myself right now."

"Okay. Let's go, you know I'll go anywhere with you," Cassie says with a smile that tells me she means it.

God, I love this girl.

It took some convincing, but I was able to convince Cassie to stay in her room, with music on, for a whole twenty minutes without her peeking.

After she came to the arena today and surprised me, I knew I wanted to do something for her. Show her how I listen, too. So now, as I put the final blanket over our massive pillow fort, I hope this does the trick.

I knock once and before I can even knock a second time, she's opening the door, excitement all over her face.

317

"Can I see now?" Cassie asks eagerness in her voice.

"Yes, Princess. Come on," I say, grabbing her hand to lead her out. We barely make it into the living room before I hear her gasp.

"Max...you didn't," Cassie says, her eyes welling with tears as she takes in the sight before crawling inside.

I had her favorite pizza ordered, along with her favorite beer, and set it all up inside a pillow fort, built for just us.

"I haven't even shown you the best part," I tell her, crawling inside next to her and grabbing the remote to turn it on. I already have *Criminal Minds* cued up and the excited, wiggle-butt dance that she's currently doing as she eats her pizza, tells me I've hit the mark. This whole thing was worth it.

"This really is the best part. I knew you'd love this show."

"It's not so much the show, as it is—"

"Nope. No mushy b.s. right now, Max baby. You totally love this show," Cassie says with an attempt at a grumpy face, only I just laugh.

"Maybe a little...but I still love you more, Princess," I tell her truthfully.

"Whatever, it's still the best show," Cassie says, before abandoning her pizza and curling up next to me to watch.

"I love you, Princess," I tell her, kissing the top of her head.

"I love you, too, Max. I mean it. I'll be your little puck princess, forever."

And that's all I've ever wanted.

Also by Lexi James

Read Rex and Sawyer's story here: Power Play

Keep reading to take a peak.

"Your career is over."

Those words have played in my head on a constant loop since my injury six months ago, when my doctors and coaches told me I would never get on the ice again. At least not playing hockey for the NHL. I tried to ignore them, pretend none of it was real. I went through with the surgery, the physical therapy, and even tried a new trial therapy that's supposed to be promising for injuries like mine.

But if I'm being honest, I've known it was over for a while, and it fucking sucks. Hockey has always been the one thing I had that no one could take from me. It's been something I've worked for since I was a little kid and have poured my heart and soul into. I'm not even sure where to go from here or what I'm supposed to be doing. It's not like I have a backup plan. Hockey was it. It's always been it. Hell, in college, I majored in fucking communications for fucks sake. If that doesn't scream "Athlete that doesn't know what he's fucking doing," I don't know what does.

But in the blink of an eye, it's gone, all because of a stupid accident.

Now, I'm injured with no idea where to go from here. It's just me and a bottle of pain pills that will hopefully numb more than just my knee.

One year later

Laying in my bed, I stare at the ceiling, like I do every day. It's where I think the most, which is a double-edged sword. I should definitely be thinking about my next steps, or how to pull myself out of this black hole. More importantly, I should probably think about cleaning my apartment, at some point. Looking around, the stench of vodka from the random empty bottles and leftover takeout containers isn't exactly a good look for anyone.

But anytime it's quiet, I end up thinking about the accident and how I lost the one thing that means the most to me.

I'm a mess. Between the prescription pills, the alcohol, and fucking a different woman as often as I can, I'm not sure where I'm supposed to go from here. Something's gotta give.

My parents have tried to help me. They even moved down here a couple of months ago to try and support me, but there's nothing they can do when I'm so unwilling to see anything positive. I'm stuck wasting away in my apartment.

In my mind everything is already over, so what's the point in trying to fight my way back? Even if I get more use out of my knee, I'm thirty-three years old. It's not like I'm exactly in my prime, just waiting for the opportunity to join another team or to get back with my old one. I'm old news. Washed up. That's a hard fucking pill to swallow, and trust me, I've had plenty of practice.

When the doorbell rings at seven a.m., I assume it's my parents doing their usual check-in, or at least my mom. Ever since I got injured, my dad and I have had an interesting relationship. He's not mad about the injury, but he's ready for me to man up, pull my head out of my ass, and start making better choices.

Throwing on a pair of sweats, I walk to the door, passing more take-out containers and liquor bottles in my living room that I've yet to clean up. My mom's going to have a field day with this mess.

But when I open the door, it's not my mom waiting there.

I recognize the woman standing in front of me but can't seem to recall her name or where I know her from. But that's not even the worst part.

Also by Lexi James

The worst part is that she's standing here on my doorstep, tears streaming down her face, holding a bundle of blankets in the shape of a baby.

What. The. Fuck.

"Uh, hi. Can I help you," I muster out, unease slowly creeping in as I battle the fogginess of my brain. Why does she look so familiar?

Maybe I've seen her around before. It's not unlikely, our apartment complex is weird.

"Rex?" she whispers tentatively.

Fuck me. Who the fuck is this?

"Uh, yeah, that's me. Who are you?"

"Miranda. We met at The Last Stop, the bar in old town. It was, uh, awhile back."

She's obviously nervous. Why is she here if she's so nervous?

"You obviously don't remember me, which isn't exactly surprising. It was a weird night, for both of us. But I remember your name, and what you looked like, and you seemed like a nice enough guy," she says, mumbling to herself and confusing me further.

It's way too damn early for this.

"Miranda, right? It's fucking early and you're speaking too fast for my brain to process anything. What did you say you needed?"

She looks upset, but confident when she says her next words.

"I need you to take your baby."

I know I'm hungover, possibly still drunk, plus it is only seven a.m., but there's no way in fuck I just heard her correctly . . . right?

My baby?

"Uh, excuse me? I don't have a baby."

322

She has a strange look on her face, a mixture of sadness, embarrassment, and what seems like panic.

"So, uh, we met about nine months ago. You probably don't remember much. I mean, I was bartending, and you easily put down enough shots to forget the night, if not the week. But we ended up in the bathroom at closing time, and apparently, we didn't use protection because she's here."

She.

I have a daughter.

"Maureen . . . I . . ."

"It's Miranda."

"Sorry, I, uh, I think you have the wrong person. There's no way I'm a father, plus I *always* use protection."

It's true. I always use protection, no matter what. I mean, even when I was on the team and would hook up with puck bunnies at our games, I never forgot protection. But . . . what if I did? If my math is right, this would have been shortly after I realized my career with hockey was over.

"Okay, Rex. Well, she's here, and she's yours. This is her bag, it has everything you'll need. You're much more capable than I am, even if it does seem like you're struggling right now," she says, glancing around my apartment, tears filling her eyes. "Look, I just want her to have a shot at a good life, and that's not with me. I don't want to be a mom; I never have." I try to stop her by putting my hand up, but she easily ignores me, continuing on as if she's afraid to stop talking. "Along with all her things, in the bag is her birth certificate and the paternity test I had done. Don't ask, but I promise you it's true. You can repeat the test, and you'll get the same results. I, uh, I also signed over my rights. After this, she's yours and only yours."

The reality of the situation starts to hit me, and I realize that there's no way my apartment is a good place for a baby right now.

"Uh, can you give me a minute? Come on in, I just need to gather my thoughts."

"I can't stay long; I have a train to catch in an hour."

"Wait. You're leaving already?"

"Yeah. I . . . I can't stay. I thought I could do this, but I can't, and honestly, this is going to make me sound like the worst person ever, but I don't want to do it. I don't want to be a mom. But I'm not evil. I don't want her to have a bad life. You're her father, her only shot."

Is she serious right now? I can't even take care of myself, and yet this woman thinks I'm able to take care of a baby that I didn't even know existed.

"Can I make a phone call before you leave?"

"Yeah, no problem."

Walking past the mess of my living room, I go back into my room to find my phone. There's only one person for me to call, and I just pray she can get here quickly.

"Mom? I need you. Now. Please come over."

Also by Lexi James

Keep reading to take a glimpse into Adam and Vanessa's
story:
The Mistake (The Maxwell Family)

Prologue, Adam

She's gone.

She's already moved everything out of our place and
even put her engagement ring on the kitchen counter as if
this were a movie or something.

Four years. That's how long we've been in this relationship, and she just threw it all down the drain, and for what?
I don't even recognize who I am anymore.

Everything lately has been done for Holly; we're always
going out with her friends and only ever doing what she
wants to do. I even distanced myself from my family
because she didn't want us to spend so much time with
them. Worse, I gave up my dream of starting my own tech
company and shut down my cyber security business
because she thought it would take too long to be financially
successful and wanted me to have "a safe source of money,"
which is how I ended up working for my father and will
eventually help open a new branch in Chicago.

I've loved New York, but I'm always the happiest when
I'm near Chicago, whether it's the city or our family farmhouse. That's my happy place. Holly always wanted to visit
the farmhouse because she would hear Amelia, my sister,
talk about it. Somehow, I always found excuses to not
bring her.

In reality, I think I knew that I didn't want her to taint
the place that made me so happy.

But what was the point? Luckily, I work with my family, so I get to see them. But I changed so much of my life just to make her happy, and now I'm alone while she's off doing whatever she wants with her latest victim.

The worst part is the only thing I really wanted was someone to share my life with. Someone I could discuss successes and failures with and, at the end of the day, support each other and have each other's back.

I guess my mistake was thinking that person was Holly when all she really wanted was a puppet to get her where she wanted to go in life.

Seems I'm stuck with the bachelor life now, because I'll be damned if I ever make the slip-up and open my heart up to someone again.

Instead, I'll just get lost in someone for a night and move on.

Love was a mistake, and it's one I'm not willing to open myself up to again.

Chapter One, Vanessa

"I can't do this," I say into the phone as I'm rushing onto the subway. Luckily, there's a seat right by the door, and I sit down right as the doors close.

"Does this mean that they offered you the job?!?" Blaire squeals into the phone.

"Yes, everything got messed up though. We couldn't have an in-person interview because their plane was delayed, so it ended up just being over the phone. Plus, instead of having a little time to prepare, I told them I had already quit my other job, so they asked if I could report on Monday. I guess the cyber-attacks have been more frequent."

"I'm not understanding what the issue is then. It's great that you got the job!"

"Yes, I just wish I could have been able to do an interview. That way, I would feel like they hired me for me. Now I just feel like they hired me because of my references, which unfortunately had to include someone from my father's company, which makes me not want to take this job. I don't want to get a job because of him after what he did to me".

Although we don't speak about him much, Blaire knows that my father helped me get started in this industry and that he was also the reason I nearly left the industry. Things between my father and I are . . . complicated, to say the least.

"You don't really have a choice now, do you? This is your dream job, what you've been waiting for. Who cares if he somehow had a hand in you getting the position? He has nothing to do with it now, so now is the time to prove it to yourself," my best friend says into the phone.

I know that she's right. I mean, I have been dreaming of this job ever since I can remember, but a job at Maxwell Investments is a big deal, and I'll be working directly with the CEO of the company to help change their security over to their newer branch here in Chicago.

"I know, but that doesn't make this reality any less scary. I wish I had gotten to meet them in person. Why do I have this irrational fear that I'm going to walk in on Monday and it's all going to be a big joke and my father will be there laughing. I just feel like if that's why they are hiring me, then they should know the whole story, or maybe they do know the whole story and that's why they're hir—"

"Whoa, whoa, whoa! Stop. We are not going down that path. It's Friday night. You don't start until Monday morning. We can sit here and overanalyze everything until we're blue in the face, or we can go out and celebrate and get you laid," Blaire laughs.

"Blaire, just because your job has loved you from day one, does not mean it's going to be that easy for all of us. You love your job; you were born to be a model. Ugh. I'm going home and going to bed. I will not be discussing my sex life with you," I whisper, looking around, realizing I'm still on the subway.

Thankfully, no one is paying attention to me. The lady next to me has her nose in a book, and the guy next to her has his headphones in and is watching Rick and Morty loud enough for me to hear. Pretty sure neither of them have even noticed I'm here.

"Ness, sorry, but discussing your sex life would mean that you have a sex life. And, before you try to convince me that sex with yourself counts, it doesn't. Sorry, but we need to get someone else in charge of your orgasms for once."

"Oh my god. You are the worst," I whisper into my phone like that'll stop everyone from hearing her.

"We're going out and finding you a man. Not someone you'll have to talk to tomorrow, just someone who seems like they might be able to give you an orgasm or two. If nothing else, this will at least help take your mind off of everything with the new job for a little while."

She's right. On all accounts. And that's the worst part. I'm able to admit that it has been a little while for me. Three years to be exact. That's what happens when someone you're supposed to be able to trust takes advantage of you. It's easy to forget who you are, and sometimes you end up single and lost.

It's been even longer since I've been in an actual relationship, everything that happened has just made it so hard for me to trust anyone.

Days turned into weeks, months, and then they began turning into years. Trust is something that is hard to give back to anyone once it has been destroyed. Which is why it's been so long since I've had sex. I've only had two one-night stands ever, and they were hard for me. I've always wanted a connection with someone, and it felt unreal to think I could have a connection with someone that quick, even just for sex.

But maybe she's right . . . maybe it's time to go have some fun, even if it's just drinks. And if sex happens, great. Maybe even an orgasm? Even better.

"I'll agree to the drinks, as long as I can borrow your black Jimmy Choo's," I say with a sigh, knowing there really is no way I'm getting out of this tonight.

"Okay, I'll be at your house at eight. I'm picking out your dress as well. No arguing. See you soon!"

She hangs up.

I look down at my watch and see it's 6:45. I have just over an hour to get home, eat, shower, and be ready for her intense energy.

Bring on the tequila.

It's 7:45 when I hear my apartment buzzer go off. Blaire is here, early as usual. I look down at my robe as I walk over to let her up. At least I had time to shower and eat something, but I'm not ready.

"You're early," I grunt into the speaker as I buzz her in.

"Yes, but I brought the shoes and I can help you with your hair. Oh! And I have tequila," Blaire says.

"You should have led with the tequila," I grumble into the speaker as I she comes up the stairs. I walk over to the door and let her in.

She's smiling as she walks in with bags in hand, bumping into me as she tries to give me a hug. She's cheerful, but not the normal cheerful that I'm used to from her. She's surpassed normal. She's practically bouncing with energy.

"What's happened?" I ask, looking at Blaire as she continues to set her stuff down in my living room.

"What do you mean?" she asks, with a perplexed expression like she doesn't understand.

"You're happy. Like cheerful. And smiling. Why? What's happened?"

"It's nothing! I'm just excited to go out tonight. It's been a while since we've been out. I know just the place too!" Blaire says, way too excitedly, as she pours us each a shot of tequila.

"Why do I feel like I'm not going to like where this is going?"

"Oh. Well, remember that guy from last week? From the modeling job?"

"Yeah . . ." I say, still looking at her confused.

"Well, it took him a couple of days, which was making me nervous. But he finally reached out and wants to meet up with us tonight at Lucky's."

Blaire looks up at me with a smile, and I know there's no way I can be annoyed with her. It's just that she knows I hate going out in larger groups and having to socialize.

"I know I said tonight was all about the two of us going out and celebrating, and finally finding you a man, but I was just so excited I didn't know what to say to him when he asked!"

"So, wait, now I'm going to be the third wheel? No thank you, Blaire!" I shoot my tequila back and grab a lime from the bowl. "I'll stay home, you go out."

At least this way, I might actually get to stay in for the night. She doesn't need me for a date.

"Nope! It's perfect! He's going to be there with some of his friends who are in town for a bit. I'm sure they'll be fun! Besides, out of towners? What better way to have a one-night stand?" Blaire jokes. "Are you mad?"

"Blaire, I'm not mad. Just hadn't prepared myself for a group event. It'll be okay though, totally fine. Just give me a minute, and more tequila. I mean, at least I get to meet this guy you keep talking about. But I'm sure as hell not hooking up with one of his friends." I look at her, expecting her to argue with me, but she just smiles.

That's the look she gives when she's planning something she knows I'll hate.

Fuck.

Grabbing the tequila, I pour us each a shot. She starts talking as I take mine, so I grab hers and take it as well. If she expects me to go out tonight with what she has planned, I'll need the alcohol more than she does.

———

Two hours and two more shots later, our cab pulls up to the curb of Lucky's. As we hop out of the car into the chilly fall air, I'm happy we took all of those tequila shots before we got here. The gentle numbness my body is feeling and the warmth in my tummy is helping battle the coldness of a Chicago night in October.

With the dress Blaire brought over for me, the warmth is necessary.

She tried to convince me that just because something has sleeves, that means it's appropriate for this time of the year. But it's backless and it's short. Very, very short.

"I can't believe you got me to wear this tonight," I say, as I tug the dress down over my ass again.

"What's wrong with your dress?" Blaire asks.

"Besides the fact that it's missing half of it." I deadpan.

"Stop it, Ness, you look hot. Your legs look fucking amazing in that dress. And with those shoes. Damn. I'd bet every man in this line is imagining what your legs would look like wrapped around their neck."

"Oh my gosh," I say, as my face heats up.

Blaire has no filter, and as always, she chooses the most inappropriate times to say things. Looking up, I notice a group of guys being escorted in through the VIP door directly in front of us.

I can't help but stare at them. Each is wearing a perfectly fitted suit that highlights their builds nicely. Definitely not just pulled off the shelf.

The last one to enter the club turns back around just in time and winks at me with a knowing smirk. Normally I'd be embarrassed, but I can't help but stare at him as he smiles my way, his eyes the most stunning emerald green I have ever seen.

Blaire interrupts my staring just in time for him to turn around and walk inside.

"Oh, please, everyone here is thinking it. Besides, anyone that is here is drunk, or will be. No one will remember any of this tomorrow, so who cares?" Blaire says as we walk up to the bouncer at the VIP door. She gives him our names and he lets us in. I guess it pays to be friends with Blaire.

"Did you see that group of men outside the club?" I ask nonchalantly.

"No, I didn't get a good look at them. This is a pretty high-profile club, so it wouldn't surprise me if there were celebrities here tonight."

"He didn't seem like a celebrity, he seemed . . . in charge, dominant. I don't know, something about the way he looked at me just made me feel like that's who he is."

"I'm confused. Are we talking about a group of guys, or one?" Blaire asks as we head towards the bar.

"It was a whole group of guys, probably four? But the guy at the end, I think he heard what you said. As they were heading in, he turned back around and winked at me. But hot damn, he was something else. The way he looked at me, I nearly melted right there," I tell her as we squeeze our way up to the bar.

Once we get up there, she grabs the attention of the bartender and orders us two shots of tequila each, which we immediately slam back one after another.

"Was he hot? Let's go look for him. If something is making you notice, it's worth finding out. You haven't been interested in anyone in . . . hmm . . . years."

Quickly, she pays for the drinks and grabs my hand, leading me away from the bar.

"Nope! We are not searching for him. We came to get drinks and to meet your friend. Let's go over there. Maybe we'll run into them later on the dance floor or something."

Blaire pauses for a minute, obviously weighing the decision. She must realize I actually don't want to go looking for a man because she finally nods.

"Isaac has a table over in the corner; we can go there," Blaire says, smiling from ear to ear. It feels like she's genuinely happy to be out with me, which is nice. I've been a little different lately with everyone except for Blaire, but it has made me more introverted.

It's hard not to feel a little sad at the loss of who I was. I can't help but think about this as I follow Blair. She pulls me through the crowd of people, walking towards a group of four guys, one of whom I assume is Isaac.

"Hey! You guys made it!" He quickly jumps up, giving Blaire a longer than necessary hug, proving just how happy he is that she made it.

Thankfully, I have a little liquid courage in me, which makes it less painful to be at a club on a Friday night, meeting new people, and wearing a dress that is much shorter than I like.

Isaac looks over at me, giving me a quick hug before turning back to sit down with his friends, pulling Blaire to sit next him.

As Isaac starts to go through introductions, I sit down in the only chair available. I barely notice the names Isaac is saying until he gets to the last guy. Sitting directly in front of me, with bright, emerald-green eyes and a sly smirk, is the man from outside the club.

"Finally, this is Adam." I realize that Toby must have been talking that whole time, and has just now finished his introductions, but honestly, I can't remember a word he just said.

The man, who Isaac just introduced as Adam, is sitting across from me at the end of the table, holding his scotch in one hand while the other rests on his chin.

His cocky smirk from earlier has returned. This man screams confidence and power, and although it shouldn't, it excites me.

Since Blaire is sitting down at the other end with Isaac, I realize that I should probably try to make conversation.

"Hi, I'm Vanessa," I say, having a hard time making eye contact with the man. Looking around for our server, I'm relieved when I see her at the table next to us, slowly making her way over. A quick distraction will be nice.

"I know. Isaac did the introductions," he says, and when I look up, he's staring at me with that irritating smirk still on his face.

It's unnerving. It feels like he can read my mind and knows my deepest, darkest thoughts. We've only said like five words to each other, but it feels like he's already seen too much.

As the waitress passes by our table, I notice him grab her attention. Quickly stopping at our table, she ignores me completely, giving Adam all of her attention.

"What can I get for you?" she asks in an almost seductive way.

"The same thing I had last time, another scotch," he says with an unamused smile. "But I stopped you because my friend here would like to order," he tells her, pointing to me.

I'm not sure what to focus on. The way this man can disarm me with a simple smile, or how he's standing up for me with the waitress who clearly just wanted to flirt. I don't miss the way she brushes his arm accidentally as she turns to look at him again.

"Oh, I know, handsome. You just flagged me down, so I was seeing if there was something else you needed my help with." Leaning forward, I notice she whispers something in his ear.

Instead of being excited, or even liking what she said, he appears annoyed.

"That won't be necessary, Maria. Now, if you wouldn't mind, take a step back and continue doing your actual job.

You know, taking everyone's order. Don't forget to start with Vanessa here." Adam commands the words as he says them, gaining every one's attention at our table.

I have literally spoken two words to this man, yet I can't help but feel a wave of possessiveness after watching the server with him, as well as a slight excitement that he isn't feeding into it.

What's even more unnerving, though, is the way he hasn't stopped staring at me this entire time, almost like he's watching to see how I'll react.

"What are you having?" she asks me rudely. "A white claw? Cosmopolitan?"

"I'll have the same as him," I reply, never once taking my eyes off of him.

"Are you sure?" She looks at me in disbelief. "You want to drink Macallan?"

"Yes, I do. Now, do you only have the fifteen year that they ordered?"

"Fifteen year what?" she asks.

"Macallan. Do you only have the fifteen year? Or do you have the fifty?"

Adam just smiles, obviously enjoying this.

The waitress's face flushes red, embarrassed that she's the one who looks dumb now instead of me like she wanted.

"Nope. Just the one he has. Would you like to start a tab?" she asks, still snippy.

I go to reach for my clutch, but Adams voice stops me.

"She's with me, just add it to mine."

Everyone can hear her audibly scoff, but she surprises me by keeping her mouth shut. Finally moving on, she takes everyone's orders, keeping her eyes down on her notepad. After she's finished, she heads back up to the bar without a second glance.

It took a moment for everyone to start talking again, and during that time, everyone's eyes were on Adam, while his eyes never left mine.

Needing to break the ice, I reach across the table. Adam looks surprised, thinking I'm going to hold his hand or something.

"Gimme," I tell him as I reach for his drink. "If everyone is like that around you guys, I need more alcohol, like ten minutes ago."

Chuckling under his breath, he slides me his glass and just watches me with curiosity.

It's always funny what people assume about others. He's probably thinking the same thing as the waitress but isn't bold enough to say it.

Picking up his glass, I never take my eyes off of him as I take a sip.

I see the moment he realizes I actually enjoy it.

"You weren't joking around with her? You actually like scotch?"

I turn to look at whoever said that, and I realize I still don't know their names.

"No, I wasn't playing around. I was introduced to scotch when I was twenty, my grandfather loved the stuff. I guess it grew on me."

Adam doesn't say anything, he just leans back, listening to my every word.

"I'm sorry, I feel terrible. I didn't catch everyone's names when Isaac was doing introductions. I was a little overwhelmed."

I hear laughing, and his friends are looking at me with a knowing smile. Their smiles say a lot, and I know they're not trying to be rude at all. Instead, for some reason, their smiles seem welcoming.

Adam steps up to do introductions again, causing his friends to share a quick smile.

"Vanessa, these two are my brothers. This is Caleb."

"It's nice to meet you, Vanessa," he says, smiling while shaking my hand.

"And this, this is Connor. My youngest brother."

"Hi, Vanessa, it's been so wonderful getting to meet you. You've brought an interesting change to our evening," Connor says with a wink.

I look over at Adam to see him glaring at his brother, which just seems to make Connor laugh harder.

"I must be missing something," I say with a laugh, while looking around, hoping our server will magically appear with our drinks.

I look over and see Isaac has his arms around Blaire, and she has moved into his lap.

Hoping to ease the tension at the table, I decide it's time to go dance. I stand up, getting the attention of Blaire as I do.

"Let's go dance!" I tell her with a smile.

Just then, our server returns, quickly setting down our drinks and walking away. Smiling at Blaire, I hand her the drink she ordered, and we quickly shoot them back.

"Alright, come on! I love this song!" She jumps up, and I watch as Isaac gets up as well.

Isaac grabs ahold of Blaire's hand and starts to lead her away from the table and toward the dance floor. He turns around to look at where he left me, to see that Adam has yet to move from his seat. He gives me a quick smile and I wave them on.

"That's our cue," Connor says, smiling. Both he and Caleb stand up and head towards the bachelorette party out on the dance floor.

"Are you coming?" Caleb asks.

I look back at Adam to see that he's still sitting down, staring at me.

"Well . . ." I say, right as Adam swallows down the rest of his scotch. Unable to take my eyes off him, I watch as his throat contracts when he swallows. He sets down his glass and stands up, all the while one last drop of scotch goes sliding down his lip.

Unable to stop my thoughts, I watch the drop of scotch, wondering what it would be like to taste it, the scotch, or him. I'm not entirely sure. But as the drop slides down his lip, I get the urge to trace it with my tongue and follow it down his throat.

Adam stops the drop, catching it with his thumb, before grazing his thumb ever so gently along my bottom lips, freezing me in place. Leaning forward, he brushes his lips over my ear and whispers, "You're thinking too loud." He smiles.

"If you wanted a taste, all you had to do was ask," he continues to whisper in my ear, before grabbing my hand and leading me out to the dance floor, passing his brothers, who both look shocked.

Embarrassment floods me as I realize that he was able to read my thoughts so easily. I have never been so transparent before. I'm usually able to hide my emotions, but the memory of his thumb against my lips causes my whole body to send tingles straight to my core, turning my embarrassment into desire.

Acknowledgments

First off, I want to thank you! Without readers, this wouldn't be happening. I love this community more than anything and as a new indie author, I wouldn't be anywhere with you. I love connecting and interacting with you all so feel free to say hi or let me know what you think!

To Candice, thank you for talking me off a ledge a time or two. Your love of Max really helped push me through those tough times. ;) You are seriously incredible and this book wouldn't be what it is today without you! Neither would my promo though, either. Without you and all your graphics and support behind the scenes, my disorganized self would have combusted.

To my Alpha readers, Candice, Lauren, Shannon and Emily. You ladies are fucking incredible, thank you for going along for the ride. Your feedback helped make this book what it is today. I also love the unhinged comments, they give me life.

To my Beta Readers. Again, y'all are incredible. Kristen, Megan, Jenn, Andi, and Tori. Thank you for all your feedback and all your help bring Max and Cassie's story to life.

To Caroline, you rock as a reader and as a friend. Thank you for loving these stories and not only reading them in the earlier stages...but proofreading them after I've no doubt added in errors in those final days. I appreciate you!

To my editor, Matti. This would not have happened without you. Thank you for everything you do, you're incredible and this book would be nothing like it is without you. Thank you for dealing with my stressed-out self and always pushing me, you're a rockstar editor and friend.

To my family, thank you for supporting me even though you've been forbidden to ever read my books. You're always so excited about the details I share and I love that. If you've read this, that means you failed. ;)

To my husband, you held down the fort and never complained when my face was in my laptop for hours on end, or my brain was in another world, lost in my stories. You're my rockstar, my book boyfriend come to life, and I couldn't have done this without you. You believe in me enough for both of us.

About the Author

Lexi James lives in Washington state with her husband and their two little boys. If she's not at work, you can find her out adventuring with her family, exploring trails, or curled up on the couch with a spicy book. She began reading after the birth of her kids when she needed something 'just for her' and since then she's read every day.

She's a daydreamer who always has characters and their has stories running through her mind. With encouragement from her husband and family, she sat down to write a book, giving a voice to her imaginary friends.

Printed in Great Britain
by Amazon